Village Fate

A Country Tale of Cooks, Crooks and Chickens

Hookline Books are chosen for publication by book groups from around the UK.
The writers are students or graduates of MA writing courses.

Book groups said:

'Exuberant writing style! The climax had me roaring with laughter.'

'An amusing take on a serious subject ... an enjoyable read.'

'A light-hearted modern morality tale.'

D1388672

Village Fate

A Country Tale of Cooks, Crooks and Chickens

By
PJ Davy

Hookline Books

Bookline & Thinker Ltd

Published by Hookline Books, 2010

Bookline and Thinker Ltd.
Suite 231
405 King's Road
London SW10 0BB
Tel: 0845 116 1476
Email: editor@booklinethinker.com
www.booklinethinker.com

A CIP catalogue for this book is available from the British Library

This book is a work of fiction. Names, characters, places and
incidents are either a product of the author's imagination or are
used ficticiously.

ISBN: 9780956517746

Cover design by Donald McColl

Printed and bound by Lightning Source UK

For Melanie, my sister

CHAPTER ONE

The chicken came first, we know that now.

Then egg followed chicken followed egg followed chicken in an orderly way.

Reliable. Comforting. One of life's constants. Sure as eggs.

Your average hen will, given the chance, settle down when she has laid a dozen or so eggs in what she believes to be a safe place. She lowers her fluffy skirts and warms her clutch, taking only short breaks for water and a peck of corn for the next three weeks. Then it's up to the chicks. Somewhere in their ovoid universe a flag is dropped and they're off, pecking their way to freedom.

Then out they come – Maran and Warren and Sussex and Border; Speckeldy, Welsummer, Orpington, Rhode Island Red and Black Rock alike – bendy beak, two stringy legs, soggy feathers and slow, blinking eyes.

But some chickens are different.

Withy Hill Farm chickens were different.

Very different.

Happiness for Neville was a successful soufflé.

On this particular day he was entirely focused on an authentic *Cassoulet Provençal*. This was a fresh challenge for him, and as always when embarking on a new recipe, he felt the familiar tension in his abdomen which only well managed excitement can bring. One might think a *Cassoulet, Provençal* or otherwise, was, in the scheme of things, no big deal. It is, after all, bean and sausage stew. Even cooked for the first time, how hard can it be? You gather the ingredients, follow the directions in the recipe, and there it is. No complex kneading and proving involved; no paper thin pastry to handle, no eggs threatening to curdle – in fact, no volatile ingredients whatsoever. Sausage and beans. But Neville did not see it that way. Finding a recipe which met his own exacting standards had required extensive research. Having settled upon the definitive receipt, he selected the ingredients with equal care. The authentic French *saucisson* had necessitated a trip to Bournemouth. Fortunately, he already had in his possession the ideal vessel – a terracotta pot (with well fitting lid, naturally) purchased on a gastronomic holiday in France the previous year.

It being Friday, Neville had no difficulty slipping quietly away from his desk at the Council Planning Office shortly before four o'clock. The journey home on his well-maintained bicycle had taken a mere fifteen minutes, eager anticipation of an evening's cooking lending wings to his pedalling heels.

He found Cilla, his ginger cat, waiting for him on the doorstep, as was her habit. She shared his passion for cooking and sprinted up the stairs to take her position on a high stool, from where she had a clear view of proceedings. Neville parked his bike in the hallway and followed her up the narrow staircase. In the kitchen he wriggled out of his small backpack and unloaded the contents onto the table. His lunchtime shopping trip had yielded some exceptionally fine smoked garlic. Ignoring the blinking light of his answering machine, Neville flicked through his box of CDs marked *cooking music*, and chose an early Dave Brubeck.

'We're cooking tonight, Cilla,' he said. 'This is going to be something rather special.'

He removed his jacket and hung it over the back of a chair before rolling up his sleeves.

'Now, let's get these haricots drained and rinsed. The perfect *cassoulet* cannot be rushed, you know. Dinner will not be served much before nine tonight.'

Sometimes, while Neville waited for some crucial cooking process to take effect, he would take advantage of the fine view from the first floor window. The small flat, and the Post Office on which it sat, benefited from the village green to the front, and open countryside behind. A long-shadowed, late spring afternoon fringed the fields and tagged the trees with cool tails. The sweet smelling Dorset landscape was in its prime. It did not dazzle with drama, nor attempt the spectacular. It made no pretence at wilderness, nor did it lay claim to impressive size or height. Instead it quietly got on with what it knew best – gentle greenery; an impressionist's palette of meadows and hedgerows; fescues inclining their weightless heads in the baby's breath of a breeze; a high sky freshly painted bridesmaid blue; timeless oak; impressive chestnuts; rustling poplars; the burnished pinchbeck bark of the birch; over-ripe hawthorn blossom filling the unremarkable hour with notions of bubble-bath; every leafy corner overflowing, growing, plumping out and spilling; the spreading turf a plush flat matt mat inviting chequered picnic cloths and lovers' recumbent forms, private but daring in the longer grass.

The village of Nettlecombe Hatchet had fought against change and modernity and won. Vigilant residents were quick to spot the smallest unnecessary signpost, unsympathetically painted porch, or plainly parked caravan lingering too long in a driveway. A ruthless policy of ethnic cleansing was applied to house style and construction, driving out all but the very best reproduction Portland stone. Living in a seventeenth century cottage would gain you coveted invitations to Cynthia Danby's soirees. Thatch put you beyond reproach.

At 3 Brook Terrace, a tatty blue transit van came to a smelly halt. The driver threw open his door and started to roll a cigarette.

Fliss Horton and her daughter Rhian climbed out the other side. Physically they were out of the same mould, but from very different schools of decoration. The same cane-straight auburn hair - half plaited, half flowing in Fliss's case; sleek and sharp on Rhian. The same angular, rangy body although Fliss was swathed in tie-die and velvet, while Rhian was buckled into cutting-edge high street. Both even had the same ivory complexion - naked and natural on Fliss, heavily kholed on Rhian.

Their temperaments could not have been more different. Rhian was salt to Fliss's sweetness. Rhian was quicksilver; a stormy night; a fiery drink; a fanfare. Fliss was a rainbow; a log fire; a dove; a nocturne.

'Oh look,' said Fliss, 'the honeysuckle's out. Mmmm, smells delicious.'

Rhian gave her the sort of withering look that teenagers do so well. 'Hoo-bloody-ray,' she said, sitting down on the low wall in front of the little house.

'It'll be great to have a garden,' Fliss went on. 'This bit's just full of flowers, and the one at the back has plenty of space for sunbathing. Or barbeques. Or badminton.'

'Oh well, that must be why we moved here then.' The expression on Rhian's face could have turned milk. 'So that we can freeze to death trying to sunbathe, because we are in fact in Dorset, not Ibiza; have pathetic, taste-free barbeques, because you don't want us to eat meat; and prance about playing badminton, like we know how.'

Fliss's bright smile stiffened into a grimace.

'That's the spirit, Rhi, hate everything before you've even given it a chance.'

'Look, this move wasn't my idea.'

'As you never tire of reminding me.'

'I didn't want to leave London. I didn't want to leave my friends. I didn't want to move to the arse-end of the planet, so don't expect me to suddenly start liking it just because you do.' Rhian pushed past her mother, hauled open the rear doors of the van and started pulling at the overstuffed boxes. 'And if my CD player is damaged after being in this crap van, Mr Driver of The Year can fork out for a new one.'

Fliss opened her mouth to speak but the ringing of her mobile saved her from having to think of a suitable reply.

'Daniel?' As a reflex Fliss stepped out of her daughter's hearing range, quickly walking to the stile opposite the house where she leant against the small sign that pointed walkers in the direction of Withy Hill Farm.

'Hi, Babe.'

'Where are you? I thought we were meeting here at three – it's gone four now.'

'Sorry, Sweet Thing. I'm up to my ears in it here.'

'You're still at work?'

'I know, I know, I feel terrible. I really wanted to be there to help, you know I did, but ...'

Fliss drooped visibly.

'Oh Dan, I was counting on you.'

'Please don't make me feel any worse about it. Look, I'll get away as soon as I can, okay? I can still be down there for supper. We can crack open a bottle of wine together, hmm?'

Fliss allowed a hefty sigh to answer for her.

'Anyway,' Daniel went on, 'it's not as if you've got any actual furniture to lug about. It's just your stuff, isn't it? And you've got White Van Man to help you.'

Fliss looked at the lumpen figure still in the driver's seat, most of his bulk obscured by a crumpled copy of *The Sun* he was pretending to read.

'Blue,' she said.

'What's that, Babe?'

'The van is blue, not white. Actually, I didn't really want you here to cart boxes. I thought it might help, you know, with Rhian. Present a united front. Stop her bitching at me all day. And I thought it would be nice – first day at our new home. Well, home for me and Rhi, weekend retreat for you. I wanted us to do it together.'

'Sorry, Fliss, had some idiot talking to me – didn't catch a word of that. What were you saying?'

'Oh. Never mind,' she shook her head and straightened up. 'Look, I'd better get on with it. I'll see you later.'

'Love you, Sweet Thing.' Daniel disconnected.

Fliss took a deep breath and moved towards the van.

'Right,' she said brightly, clapping her hands to the accompaniment of her tambourine of bangles, 'first person to find the box with the kettle in it gets a Hobnob.'

Across the lane from Fliss's home, set back a little in its frothy garden, sat the low thatch of Honeysuckle Cottage, the cosy nest of Daddy, Mummy, and Baby Behr. As the slow afternoon began to touch the soft edge of evening, Rose Behr held her sleepy baby in her arms and rocked him gently. For her, the moment of his bedtime was an exquisite point in the day. To lull him to a quiet, restful sleep and see him tucked snugly into his safe, gingham-trimmed crib filled her with pride and satisfaction. She was able to gaze upon him as he slumbered, knowing she had successfully nurtured him through another day. She found it hard to pull away, to separate from him so that she could go downstairs, straighten the house, and get everything ready for when next he awoke.

She didn't have to worry about her husband, as he would already be making his way to Dixie's Bar in the High Street in Barnchester. On a Friday night Rose knew better than to expect him home for dinner.

She hardly thought any more about how things used to be between them. Of how keen he had been when they were first going out together. Of how determined he had been that they get married and move into the cottage her grandmother had left her. She knew that the extra weight she had acquired over the last five years did not suit her and that Ryan found not only her pregnant, but her post-pregnancy body to be repugnant. She had long known his romantic interests lay elsewhere and that at only 28 she had become in his eyes, and indeed her own, an uninspiring middle-aged housewife.

But she didn't care. Not any more. Not one little bit. For now she had Baby.

Baby Behr was four months old and a tiny, plump, pinkness of perfection. He had transformed his mother's life. Now she knew what it meant to be in love. She was consumed by love – her love for her baby. This love was joy, was bliss, was warmth, home, hope, happiness – everything that was good and true and right. She had never imagined such a thing existed. The feeling fuelled her soul. The baby gave her all the emotional nourishment she would ever need. Her life had become golden, glowing, and special in a way that had altered her inestimably and forever. Let Daddy Behr dally with dolly-birds in Dixie's; Mummy Behr would be all Baby needed, and his tiny, powerful presence would sustain her.

Or at least, this was what she told herself. This was what she had to make herself believe.

Back in Neville's kitchen, steam had opaqued the windows, and Cilla now slept patiently on her stool as the dinner bubbled towards perfection. Neville sat at the table enjoying a glass of French red wine. The insistent light of the answerphone caught his attention at last. Reluctantly he reached over and pressed the button.

The first message was from his sister, Sandra.

'Hello, Neville? It's me.'

For Neville, her knowledge that he had so few young female callers that he would correctly identify 'me' was both depressing and irksome.

'Hope you are well, not suffering too much with your hay fever. Brian and the twins are off swimming, so I thought I'd grab a moment for a natter. You must still be at work. Anyway, I wanted to invite you for lunch on Sunday. Wendy's coming over. You remember Wendy? From my Aerobics class? You met her at our New Year's do – tall girl, big smile, nice nails – remember? Anyway, say you'll come. I'm at a PTA meeting tonight, so ring tomorrow. Okay? Bye.'

Neville was fond of his sister, and knew she cared about him, but he disliked her clumsy attempts at matchmaking. She seemed unable to accept the fact that a man of 45 can be perfectly fine living on his own. Neville was not lonely. He was used to his bachelor existence. Since his fiancée decided against marrying him and moved to Australia five years ago, there had been no romantic interest in his life, and he was content to leave it that way. He had no desire to have his world turned upside-down again. On top of which, he liked his life the way it was. He was able to indulge his passion for cooking as much as he liked, without bothering anyone. He enjoyed the simplicity and orderliness of his existence. He also enjoyed peaceful, solitary Sundays, particularly if the alternative was a noisy few hours at his sister's house, chewing his way through unyielding beef. Still, he would probably go. If the fine weather continued at least he could enjoy the bike ride into Barnchester.

The second message was much more disturbing. It was from Cynthia Danby. The very sound of her voice made Neville nervous.

'*Neville, darling boy!*' she boomed from the machine.

'*Cynthia here. Just wanted to have a word with you about a little idea of mine for the Nettlecombe Hatchet summer fundraiser this year. It's something culinary. Right up your street. I thought cuisine, then I thought Neville. I know you're the man for the job. Do ring, so we can put our little heads together. I've such exciting plans. A bientôt, mon cher!*'

Neville took a large swig of wine. The last thing he felt like doing was ringing Cynthia Danby, but if he didn't she would probably turn up, and then he would have to deal with her in person. A thought terrible enough to kill anyone's appetite. But she wouldn't come at night. He could leave it till the morning. He really didn't want the woman in his evening any more than she already was. There was something about her that made him behave like a sickly rabbit about to be devoured by an oversized fox. Although they had lived in the same village for four years, he had mercifully escaped her notice until quite recently. He had attended a French cookery weekend at the Hardy House Country Hotel, and the benighted woman had been there too. For reasons Neville would never understand, she had developed an instant, and to his mind insane, crush on him. He had spent most of the course sidestepping her advances. Had it been anyone else, he might have been flattered, but being pursued by a widow approaching sixty, apparently constructed entirely of tweed, reeking of lavender, carrying a stone or two more than was healthy, and with a tendency to become verbally incontinent after two glasses of wine, was an ego booster he could have done without.

He erased the messages, wishing Cynthia was as easy to get rid of, and picked up the *Barnchester Echo*. He needed to have his mind on other things by the time dinner was ready, or he wouldn't feel like eating anything at all.

At 3 Brook Terrace, Fliss was also attempting to distract herself with the local paper. She turned the pages slowly, trying to summon up enthusiasm for the misdemeanours of unemployed youths, the recent wedding of Miss A to Mr B, the success of the *Echo*'s raffle in aid of retired postmen, and the delights on offer in the way of evening classes at the village hall. None of it really held her interest, but at least it prevented her from looking at the clock or the telephone.

Daniel had still not arrived. He was often late for their dates, but it was unlike him not to phone and reassure her that he was on his way, and not dead in a ditch somewhere.

Her mother had always had people dead in ditches at 20 minutes late, and that was before the days of mobile phones. To Fliss's certain knowledge, she had not once been right. Perhaps, had they lived in Norfolk, she would have stood a better chance. In any case, there weren't too many ditches between Docklands and Nettlecombe Hatchet. Daniel had probably got engrossed in something at work and lost track of time – that was all. Fliss tried to focus on the paper once more to glean information about the area she had so carefully chosen as the best place to bring up Rhian. She was already beginning to question the wisdom of this choice. It had seemed so right, so sensible, so necessary. London was full of terrors and temptations for a young girl, and Rhian was not easily controlled. Maybe if she had a father's influence things would have been different. But Fliss had felt her connection with her daughter slipping away as each day brought more complaints from her teachers, arguments with her friends, and minor dramas of all shapes and sizes. A move to the country seemed the only possible solution.

Fliss's thoughts were interrupted by the muffled ringing of the phone. She recovered it from beneath the sofa cushion, where it was hidden so she wouldn't keep looking at it, and tried to answer in an unconcerned but somewhat pissed-off voice

'Hello? Yes?'

'Fliss! Babe! A thousand apologies. Had my head in a mess of figures and completely lost track of time. What can I say?'

'Sorry, perhaps?'

'Of course. You're right. I am sorry, gorgeous. I'll make it up to you, promise.'

'Never mind,' Fliss fell well short of the tone she had aimed at, hitting the mark somewhere near feebly miffed.

'Hope you didn't go to too much trouble. You have eaten, haven't you? Tell me you didn't wait with supper.'

'I didn't wait with supper,' she lied. 'Anyway, it doesn't matter now, I'm just glad you're okay.'

'Oh God, you were worried. Now I feel terrible.'

'No, no. Don't be silly.'

'Really! You weren't sitting there imagining me dead in a pile-up on the M3?'

'Pile-up! No, absolutely not. I've been reading the paper. Didn't realise it was so late myself, actually. Wasn't worried a bit.'

'Oh.'

'So,' she tried to forget the whole thing and start again. 'Are you going to make it down tonight, or ...?'

'Can't see it, Babe. Traffic will be hell by now. I'll come down in the morning. That okay?'

'Of course. That'll be fine.'

As she switched off the phone, Fliss fought to quell doubt as it grew in a fertile plot in the back of her mind. She had no reason to think Daniel was lying to her; he often stayed late at the IT Consultancy where he worked. In the two years they had been seeing each other she had known him bring huge amounts of work home for the weekend. He had a demanding job, and he was conscientious and hard working. She had never seen him so much as notice other women when they were out together. Indeed, she knew him well enough to be pretty certain he didn't have the spare time to cheat on her, even if the thought chanced to enter his head. No, her fears were more to do with her past, and deep down she knew this. She had been let down once too often. She had trusted too readily and she had been hurt. Still she continued to think the best of people. It was just that sometimes she lacked the self-confidence needed to believe that she could be enough for any man – particularly a good-looking, successful, wealthy, popular one, who had the female population of London on his penthouse doorstep. And now she had moved so far away from him. Had he ever really meant to drive out and spend weekends with her, as they had discussed?

In the kitchen she opened the oven and peered unenthusiastically at the patiently waiting veggie casserole. With a sigh she shut the door again, turned off the cooker, and went to bed.

CHAPTER TWO

Saturday morning saw a quiet breakfast in the Behr household. Baby Behr happily gurgled in his reclining chair on one end of the kitchen table. Ryan silently read the *Echo*. Rose Behr busied herself grilling bacon. She was accustomed to the lack of conversation, particularly on a Saturday morning. She had to satisfy herself with the background music of baby's babblings. As Ryan folded the paper a discreet notice caught her eye.

Beautiful Baby Competition.

She leant closer, spatula in hand.

Is your baby the bonniest in the Barnchester area? £100 and the title of Barnchester Beautiful Babe await the winner. Send photos.

'Don't do that,' Ryan shook the paper. 'I hate it when you read over my shoulder. Wait till I've finished, can't you? You've got all bloody day to read the thing. That bacon ready yet?'

Rose loaded her husband's plate and set it before him.

'Are you going in to the office today?' she ventured to ask.

'Isn't it Saturday? Don't I always go in on Saturday mornings?'

'Well, most Saturday mornings ...'

'And this is just like most Saturday mornings, so, yes, I will be going into the office today.' He ate noisily for a minute, then added, 'I've got an important client to show round a five-bedroom in Trenthide at twelve, could go on to lunch. Expect me when you see me.'

Rose sat down opposite him and sipped her tea.

'You on another diet?' he asked, nodding at the absence of a plate.

She shook her head.

'Just not very hungry,' she said, leaning over to squeeze Baby's hand and smile at him.

Ryan mopped up egg with fried bread.

'For someone who is often "not very hungry" you never seem to lose any weight. How d'you suppose that works?'

Rose offered no explanation.

He finished his food, stood up, and removed his tie from the back of his chair.

'Right, I'm off,' he announced. He turned to Baby and grinned, as if noticing him for the first time that morning. 'Alright, mate? Daddy's off to earn loads of dosh.' He made the little seat bounce more and the baby gave a happy squeal. 'Mind your mother doesn't get up to anything when I'm out, okay? Good man.'

He left his wife unkissed and uncherished as usual, whistling on his way to his warmly stabled Subaru Impreza.

Rose waited until she heard the engine start, and then reached for the *Echo*. She read the details of the competition again, and smiled at her little boy. How could she not enter him? She went quickly to the sitting room and fetched the album, determined to find the very best photograph she could.

Nettlecombe Hatchet was bathed in a gentle spring light beneath a Constable sky. As Rose pushed Baby in his chariot down the garden path, prodigious butterflies performed an erratic fly-past. An early flowering honeysuckle perfumed their progress. Small birds flitted busily, and trilled from the blossom-filled branches of the old apple tree by the gate. Wheeling carefully onto the narrow pavement, Rose headed toward the Post Office, Baby's competition entry tucked safely under his quilt. It was only a short walk past the duck pond and around the green to the village stores and Post Office.

Rose pushed the button on the pelican crossing and waited a few seconds for the lights to change. As she stepped onto the road it was clear of traffic, but before she could reach the safety of the opposite pavement a large lorry steamed around the bend at the top of the village, saw the red light, and noisily airbraked to a halt. For Rose, time froze on an in-breath. The silence that followed the clamour of the truck's emergency stop was filled with what could have happened. Her heart thudding beneath her cardigan, Rose shakily guided the pram up the kerb. She regarded the driver coldly as he put the vehicle into gear and moved off at a more suitable speed. As it passed Rose saw *Withy Hill Farm Enterprises* proclaimed in large red letters above a gaudy chicken logo.

Baby Behr had slept peacefully through the whole event, and dreamed on undisturbed. Rose parked him in front of the shop window where she would have a clear view of him at all times, and went inside.

Behind the counter Sally Siddons stood listening, grey curls nodding politely, as Cynthia Danby maintained a ceaseless current of loud chatter while paying for her purchases.

'We must not rest on our laurels,' Cynthia insisted, 'or should I say, our Lobelia. Just because Nettlecombe has won the Village in Bloom title twice running does not make this year's result a foregone conclusion. I know for a fact that Upton Maytravers have enlisted the help of a garden designer. From London, if you please. How that sits with the spirit, if not the letter, of the rulebook I wonder, Miss Siddons, I really do. Oh, I'll have a packet of mints too. Thank you. Ah, Mrs Behr. How is Baby?' she squinted out of the window. 'There, slumbering happily. They are so sweet when they're asleep, aren't they?'

Somehow Rose communicated to the Post Mistress her need for a stamp, and the transaction was made without interrupting Cynthia. In fact, she was able to accomplish her mission wordlessly, wave goodbye, and hurry back to Baby.

As she released the brake she glimpsed Neville as he entered the shop. She was aware of him pausing on the threshold, as if changing his mind, and then she heard Cynthia greet him enthusiastically. She wheeled away towards the snugness of her home, secretly excited at the thought of Baby being publicly acknowledged as Barnchester's Beautiful Babe.

For a fraction of a second Neville considered turning on his heel, but the unexpected sight of Cynthia at close range rooted him to the spot.

'Just the man I was hoping to see!' Cynthia moved towards him with such purpose that Neville flinched.

'Did you get my message? I have such exciting plans. I just know you'll want to be involved. This year's Nettlecombe Hatchet fundraiser will be the culinary event of the season.' Excitement tinged Cynthia's powdered visage with an unbecoming pinkness.

Neville fought for sensible words under the chemical warfare that was her perfume.

'Mrs Danby, I ...'

'Cynthia, please ...'

'Cynthia, I'm sure you don't need my help ...' he began to edge past her towards the relative safety of the cold cabinet.

'Oh but I do, *mon cher.*'

'I'm really very busy at work at the moment.' He focused on selecting semi-skimmed. 'I'm afraid I wouldn't have the time to make a commitment, I wouldn't want to be forever having to send apologies and put you to extra work covering for me, that sort of thing.'

'Forget about such details, dear boy, put them from your mind. No, what I need you for is your infallible instinct for what is right when it comes to food. Please, don't try to be modest,' she held up her hand, 'I have seen you in action in the kitchen.' She lowered her voice. 'I often think of the time we spent together at the Hardy House Country Hotel.'

Neville shot a nervous glance in the direction of Miss Siddons, but she was fully occupied shuffling yesterday's Bath Buns. He knew what lay ahead if he allowed himself to be dragooned into helping Cynthia – hours of meetings, all involving her, probably at her house. He must stand firm.

'It's very kind of you to consider me, but I really have to say no. As I said, I have to do lots of overtime. It wouldn't be fair to say yes and then never be available.' He stepped sideways towards the newspaper stand, but Cynthia gripped his arm.

'Work is all very well, Neville, but one must have balance. One cannot afford to neglect the heart, the soul. I know you share my passion. I see in you a kindred spirit. Do not deny your true self.'

Neville was horribly afraid the conversation was getting away from him. He opened his mouth to protest further, but Cynthia was in full flow now. He listened, his eyes beginning to glaze, unable to interject. Just as he began to feel the blossoming of a huge and vulgar yawn, the mention of a name brought him to his senses.

'What did you say? Who is going to be present?' he demanded.

'Claude Lambert! I know, isn't it thrilling! It's all down to a cousin of mine who knows a niece of his. Or her daughter was at school with his niece. Or something! Anyway, Sylvia, my cousin, mentioned to him at some do or other that I was looking for a chef of some renown for our humble little event, and voila, he agreed to take part. In fact, the whole thing has escalated. I met him in London last week ...'

'You've actually met Claude Lambert?' Neville was seriously impressed.

'Such a charming man, we talked about ideas he has for his new book, and how he might make the fundraiser a tie-in, as he is launching a new venture with our very own Withy Hill Farm. Their produce is top notch.'

Suddenly, as far as Neville was concerned, the whole project had taken on a golden glow. Claude Lambert, his chef of choice, his hero, was coming to Nettlecombe Hatchet, and he, Neville Meatcher, had the opportunity not only to meet the great man, but to work closely with him. Cynthia Danby or not, this was an experience far, far too special to miss.

'Well, of course, if I really can be of some use ...'

'So you'll do it? Marvellous! I knew I could count on you. It's going to be such fun! Now, there's a great deal to be done. I shall set up a meeting; we'll need a committee. I'll be in touch very soon.'

Scooping up her purchases Cynthia departed the shop a little breathless, leaving in her wake the smell of lavender and efficiency.

Back in the sanctuary of his kitchen Neville depressed the plunger on his cafetiere. He found it hard to believe that Cynthia could actually have secured the involvement of the chef of the moment, and yet he knew it must be true. Whatever the woman's peculiarities, she was not given to making up such things. Neville's head teemed with questions he would ask the great man. Of course, he had all his books, and had followed his recent TV series as an assiduous student. He poured himself a cup of Jamaican Blue Mountain and resolved to steep himself in Monsieur Lambert's recipes over the next few weeks. Sipping his coffee he wandered into the living room and looked out the window. The sun was already warm, and he decided a bike ride up to Bulbarrow Hill would make best use of the day. Below he saw a woman he didn't recognise walking lightly across the green, his attention caught by her splendid auburn hair. He watched her disappear down Brook Terrace, newspaper in hand.

Fliss, as always, found her mood lifted by the sunshine. She had slept well, the self-doubt of the night before had melted away under the sun's rays, and she was looking forward to Daniel's visit.

As she turned into the narrow street that was her new home she smiled to find his car parked outside number 3.

'Dan? You in there?' She called from the front door.

'In the kitchen, Babe. Kettle's on.'

She found him ferreting in a cupboard.

'Are we out of sugar?'

That 'we' further soothed Fliss's heart. She wanted always to be 'we' and 'us', rather than 'I' and 'me'.

'There's plenty of brown in the jar by the coffee.'

'Ah, brown. I meant real sugar. Honest to goodness white tooth rot.'

'You know I never buy it. We only have the stuff in the house if you smuggle it in.'

Daniel grinned, wrapping his arms around her and pulling her to him.

'And you know I have no greater pleasure than corrupting you, my angel. I live to help you sin.' He kissed her, long and slow. 'Did you miss me last night? All alone in that big old bed?'

'What makes you so sure I was alone? How d'you know I haven't got the hang of sinning, after all your expert coaching?' she kissed him back.

Daniel gasped. 'Tell me you weren't with that Teddy of yours again! Furry little bastard! No wonder he always looks so smug.'

'Poor Daniel – replaced so easily by a bit of stuffed fabric.'

'And he's only got one eye.'

'Hmmm, makes him sort of heroic and romantic, don't you think?' She wriggled free of his embrace and finished making the coffee.

Daniel sat at the table and flicked idly through the newspaper.

'Where's Rhian?' he asked.

'Where any self-respecting teenager would be at 10.30 in the morning – under her duvet!'

'God, do you remember what it was like to be able to lie in like that? I just can't do it any more. Body clock's screwed by years of nine to five.'

'Don't give me that – you love your job. I've never known anyone who enjoyed working more than you do.' She sat down opposite him and passed him his coffee. 'Flapjack?' she offered, nudging the tin in his direction.

'The ultimate hippy fodder, will you never stop trying to convert me to yoghurt and lentils?'

'Only when you stop spiking my coffee with poisonous white sugar.'

'Ah, but the difference is I do things like that through absent-mindedness. You, on the other hand, would love to change me, to win me over to your highly laudable if somewhat chewy lifestyle. With you it's premeditated. You hate it that I haven't had a day's illness in years. I am walking, talking, living proof that all your careful weeding out of this, and cutting down on that, and raw vegetables on the hour is totally unnecessary.'

'I can't help it if I care about the way you look after yourself. I have a vested interest in keeping you healthy, after all. Teddy's not available every night.' She nibbled pointedly on a flapjack. 'Besides,' she went on, 'I think secretly you want to be reformed. Otherwise why would you bother with me?'

'Oh, I can think of one or two activities we enjoy sharing,' he said, kicking her foot gently.

'I know you. I've worked it out. This arrangement is going to suit you perfectly. In London you can have your cutting edge, modern-man-who-doesn't-give-a-shit life, then down here you can breathe fresh air, eat decent food, play village cricket, and pretend you're doing it all for my benefit.'

'Clever bugger, aren't I?' He leant across the table. 'What say you we go upstairs and pretend to be teenagers for a couple of hours?'

Fliss smiled but shook her head.

'Tempting, but I have an interview to go to.'

'On a Saturday! For crying out loud, Babe. Not much point in my coming down here if you're going to be busy. When did all this happen, anyway?'

'Don't sulk. It'll only take an hour or so. I saw an ad in the local rag last night, they need a cleaner up at the big farm on the hill. They asked me to pop up and see them. I could hardly say no. Now put that bottom lip away before someone treads on it.' Fliss glanced at the kitchen clock. 'Look on the bright side,' she said standing up, 'if you walk with me as far as the Soldier's Arms they'll just be opening by the time you get there. I'll call in for you on my way back, okay?'

'I suppose I could force myself to drink a couple of pints. If it'll make you feel better.'

'You're too good to me.'

'Hmm, well, I've got to win you away from old fluff brain somehow. Come on, I can ruin my reputation in the village on day one by lurking in front of the pub if we're early.'

Outside the day continued to outdo itself, and the village was at its most photogenic. A sprinkling of children played on the swings at the far end of the green. From a distance they were timeless and harmonious. Somewhere nearby their parents were watching, but not worrying. Miss Siddons' elderly Jack Russell stretched his Queen Anne legs – twice round the duck pond slowly, his waddle matching that of the birds. Two teenage boys presented a study of boredom on the wooden bench, neither aware, despite the brass plate, that their backsides rested courtesy of the Nettlecombe Hatchet Soroptimists Society.

Fliss and Daniel made their way through the centre of the village and began to climb the hill that would lead them first to the pub, a little way beyond the church, and ultimately to Withy Hill Farm.

Daniel took Fliss's hand.

'We've got to make a decision about where we're going on holiday,' he said. 'We need to get something booked soon.'

Fliss did not answer immediately. She had always looked forward to their time away together but not after the previous year. 'Rhian won't come with us this time. Her mind is quite made up.'

'She's at that age.'

'She's only 14.'

'Exactly. It's just not cool to go on holiday with the oldies, is it?'

'Well she can't stay here on her own.'

'Perhaps your mum would have her,' Daniel suggested.

'For two weeks? They'd kill each other. One week, maybe, at a push. With the right mixture of bribery and threats. For each of them.'

'One week's no good, Babe.'

Daniel's tone was light, but Fliss knew when he was likely to be stubborn.

She sighed. 'I'll think of something,' she said. 'I suppose it'll be a saving – no point paying all that money for someone who doesn't want to go.'

The memory of their tense summer holiday in Greece as one of the longest fortnights of her life still refused to fade.

'You know I'm happy to pay. My treat,' Daniel reminded her.

'I like to pay my share.'

'Aren't I allowed to spoil you sometimes? Especially if it's just going to be the two of us. We could go somewhere really spectacular. Just this once couldn't you ease up on the whole independent female thing and be a kept woman? Just for a few days?'

They stopped outside the pub, its doors still solidly shut.

'I'll think about it,' Fliss promised, turning Daniel's hand in hers to check his watch. 'I'll be late. I'll leave you to loiter.'

Five minutes later she reached a bend in the lane. Turning, she could see Daniel still leaning against the pub wall, taking a packet of Camel Lights from his pocket. As she walked on she tried to convince herself that the holiday didn't have to be a big deal. Except she didn't like the idea of leaving Rhian behind or of being away from her for two whole weeks. It seemed too soon. She was still a child in so many ways. And Fliss herself would never be completely happy with Daniel paying her way, however well meant the gesture. Her ability to support herself and her daughter was vital to Fliss, and shaped the way she saw herself. It was the reason she was determined to earn her own living, even if that meant cleaning up somebody else's mess, despite all Daniel's offers of financial support. She knew he could afford it, but that wasn't the point.

Still, she consoled herself, her work as a crystal healer would pick up once she was known in the area. And the gem and crystal parties could be good money-spinners. One day she hoped to be able to make a living from doing the things she enjoyed and be able to hang up her Hoover for once and for all.

On arriving at the farm she was surprised to find the place buzzing. Two Withy Hill trucks swept passed her, hurrying towards the shiny new warehouses. It struck her as unusual to find so much going on on a Saturday.

She paused to steady her breathing after climbing the hill, and watched the activity. From where she stood in the original farmyard beside the house she had a clear view of the new storage buildings and office, but not the barns which housed the livestock. For a farm it was a scene curiously devoid of animals. Not even a solitary chicken, for which the farm was known countrywide, was visible. Not a feather. Fliss could hear the distant humming and drumming of tractors working somewhere in the fields, and glimpsed the human beings busying about, but did not spy so much as a yard cat.

Forgetting the time, she wandered over to the corner of the old stone hay barn, hoping for a better view of the chicken sheds behind, if sheds they could be called. These were enormous, gleaming, metal constructions, low and slinky, covering acres of ground. Fliss moved closer, curious to know what such buildings could be like inside.

'What in blazes do you think you're doing?'

The unexpected volume and ferocity of the man's voice sent Fliss's heart sprinting again.

'Oh, sorry,' she smiled weakly. 'I was looking for Mrs Christian.'

'My wife is in the house.'

Two Dobermans at his side tracked her smallest movement with piggy eyes. Mr Christian flicked his fingers as he walked on towards the barn. 'Eric, Vinnie, come!'

Fliss waited until the dogs had stopped staring at her before heading toward the house.

There were days, she allowed herself to acknowledge, when being a kept woman, as Daniel might have put it, seemed extremely attractive.

CHAPTER THREE

Blood surged through Neville's body and his breathing was deep and ragged. He lowered his head and redoubled his labours, the effort forcing from him short, undignified grunts. He tightened his grip on the handlebars. The top of the hill was close, and beyond it lay the sweet reward of fast freewheeling down the two miles to Barnchester.

By the time he reached the summit his bicycle was wobbling and zigging with every push of the pedals. A final spurt of effort achieved his goal, and with a modest whoop of delight he was careering down the slope, the air drying his briny face, while speed and triumph re-energised his body. His heart beat changed from the erratic salsa which accompanies exertion to the rock rhythm of exhilaration.

He did not, however, have long to enjoy this blissful state.

He was dimly aware of a vehicle approaching from behind. Gradually the timbre of its engine caused him sufficient concern to glance over his shoulder. He glimpsed the distinctive white and red livery of a Withy Hill lorry, and registered, too late, that it was descending at an unsafe speed. The lane was narrow, its path twisting, and its surface patchy. Neville attempted to hug the verge, felt his front wheel wobble perilously, overcorrected, hit an unnecessary kerbstone, and left the road. As the lorry swept past, Neville and his bicycle described a high arc through the air, the finishing point of which was at the centre of an impressive bramble thicket.

'Shit! Ow!' exclaimed Neville, and then 'Aah! Sod it!' as his hands grasped nettles.

It took him a full ten minutes to right himself and extricate his stinging, bleeding body from the vicious plants. He hauled his bike back onto the tarmac. It had fared better than he, but he feared punctures. His own wounds were not serious, but they were many and unattractive. He could feel blood dripping from a particularly nasty scratch on his cheek, and more from his throbbing nose. His hands were a mass of small cuts and stings. He spent a further ten minutes removing vegetation from himself and his bike before proceeding stiffly on his way. By the time he reached his sister's house, he was feeling quite unwell.

Sandra ushered him into her kitchen, the better to examine his injuries. 'For heaven's sake, Neville! Whatever happened?'

The twins bounded into the room with energy levels peculiar to seven-year-olds, plastic laser guns at the ready.

'Uncle Neville, you're a mess! Did you come off your bike?' they chorused.

Neville was spared the trouble of a reply by the appearance of his brother-in-law, Brian.

'Good grief, Neville. You look like you've been dragged through a hedge backwards!'

'Forwards, actually,' Neville corrected. 'And thrown rather than dragged. But otherwise your powers of deduction do you all credit. Ouch! That stuff stings.'

'Don't be such a baby.' Sandra continued to dab at him with something that smelled suspiciously like loo cleaner. 'Really, it's not a very dignified way to behave, flying about the countryside on that bike of yours, falling into hedges. At your age!'

Neville wondered how he had gone from baby to geriatric in the blink of his sister's eye.

'I'm 45,' he said.

'My point exactly. There, that's the worst of it off your face. When did you last have a tetanus jab?'

'Don't overreact, Sandra,' said Brian. 'It's only a few scratches. Nothing a stiff drink won't put right. Isn't that so, Neville?' he asked, heading for the brandy.

'You shouldn't give alcohol to people in shock,' Sandra told him.

'He's not in shock, are you Neville?'

'I don't think so.'

Sandra tutted and raised her eyes, apparently addressing the ceiling.

'People don't know they are in shock. That's the point. They're too shocked to be able to tell. Do try to be sensible, Brian.'

'What's tetanus?' asked one of the twins.

'Used to be called Lockjaw,' their father revealed with some relish. 'Very nasty. Patient goes rigid, can't open his mouth. Bites through his own tongue sometimes.'

'Wow, gross!' the twins agreed, jostling for a better view of their uncle.

Neville was sure they had never found him so interesting.

'I think I'll just go and wash my hands.' Neville made his way unsteadily to the toilet under the stairs.

Behind the firmly locked door he peered at his reflection in the mirror. It was not a reassuring sight. His face looked as if he had had an encounter with a rabid porcupine. It was clear the porcupine won. The longest gash, which had at last stopped bleeding, ran in an unflattering straight line across his cheek and over his nose. Not for him some rakish scar accentuating handsome bone structure. His nose, which must have briefly connected with something solid, was already swollen and pink. A series of nicks at the corner of his mouth gave him a sickly grin.

'Neville Meatcher,' he told himself, 'you are a pathetic sight.'

Once back in the kitchen he ignored Sandra's warnings of imminent coma and accepted Brian's brandy. The twins, sensing Neville was in fact in control of his jaw, tore off to be noisy and destructive elsewhere.

The first few gulps of Napoleon's finest began to spread a welcome numbness through Neville's body. He sat on a stool at the breakfast bar, watching his sister busying about in the kitchen, and started to feel better. The doorbell abruptly halted his recovery.

'That'll be Wendy,' Sandra spoke from the depths of the fridge. 'Let her in will you, Brian?'

Neville had forgotten about Wendy. He had to make a conscious effort to stop his shoulders sagging. He really did not feel up to making polite conversation with someone he couldn't ever remember meeting. Seconds later he was doing his best to smile at a particularly tall, skinny, yet unmissably full-bosomed young woman.

She held out a hand.

'Hello, Neville. We met at Brian and Sandra's New Year's do,' she laughed softly, 'I don't suppose you remember me. Oh dear, what has happened to your face?'

'Fell off his bike,' Brian enlightened her. 'Man's a speed freak, Wendy. Knows no fear. Lives for excitement. Isn't that so, Neville?'

Neville felt about as exciting as a candlewick bedspread, but tried not to show it. He took Wendy's hand, but then felt silly shaking it while still sitting down. Standing up, however, proved to be a mistake. Wendy was standing so close that there is now no space between them at all. Neville found his proximity to her cleavage, which was prettily framed in a floral summer dress, distinctly unnerving.

He squinted painfully at her, trying a brighter smile, but feared the cuts on his face turned it into a lunatic, lopsided leer.

'Of course I remember you, Wendy,' he lied. 'How could I not?' He unfortunately allowed his gaze to slide back to her chest.

'Brian,' Sandra snapped, 'for heaven's sake, take our guests into the lounge. Don't keep them hanging about in the kitchen. You haven't even offered Wendy a drink yet. Sorry, Wendy. You'd think we never had visitors. Now off you go. Make yourselves comfortable next door. I'll be in soon as I've seen to the parsnips.'

Neville experienced a flashback to a previous encounter with some of his sister's parsnips and made a mental note to give them a miss.

Brian did as he was told before disappearing upstairs to quell quarrelling twins. Neville and Wendy were left sitting uncomfortably on comfortable chairs.

'Do you race?' Wendy asked.

'Sorry?'

'Your bike, Brian said ...'

'Oh, no,' Neville shook his head, causing the room to spin a little. 'It's just my way of getting around really. Quite tame. I don't often end up like this.'

'How did you come to fall off?' Wendy crossed her long, thin legs, her dress moving to reveal a length of thigh.

Neville found himself thinking of scaffolding poles.

'Actually, I was forced off the road,' he explained. 'By a lorry.'

'Oh, how awful.'

'Had the bad luck to land in brambles.'

'Poor you.' Wendy looked genuinely distressed by his suffering. 'I don't think they should allow lorries on country lanes,' she decided, raising her chin. 'Not on Sundays.'

Whilst Neville considered this a somewhat idealistic vision, it occurred to him that it was strange to meet a Withy Hill truck on the road at the weekend – particularly on a Sunday.

Wendy appeared to have run out of questions on the subject, and a prickly silence sat between them. After a full painful minute Neville could stand it no longer.

'Do you do any sports yourself?' he asked desperately.

'Me? Goodness, no!' Wendy laughed. 'I only ended up at Sandra's aerobics class because I'd got the nights mixed up. Thought it was pottery.'

'Ah, arts and crafts more your thing, then?' he pressed her.

'Not really. Just thought I'd give it a go.'

Neville sensed another chasm opening up in the conversation. His head was now unpleasantly fuzzy, and all manner of aches and bruises were surfacing. He caught himself mid sigh, prepared to admit defeat and accept the fact that he was socially crippled, useless at the whole getting-to-know-you thing, destined to remain a bachelor, and would quite happily have done so if only his sister would give up her clumsy attempts at matchmaking. He was shocked to find himself so keen to bring the tortuous tête-à-tête to an end that he actually couldn't wait to get to Sandra's Sunday roast.

Noon at Honeysuckle Cottage found the Behrs presenting a tableau of happy family life. Mummy and Baby sat on a rug on the front lawn surrounded by the prettiness and colour of the little garden. In the driveway Ryan stood by his car, sponge raised, about to apply copious amounts of Gleam Foam. To the passer-by nothing could have appeared more tranquil; a perfect example of a young English family on a Sunday afternoon. The dependable husband providing the good life for his good wife and his infant. One unit. One family. One team. Living the rural dream in their rose-covered cottage. Here surely was love, trust, contentment, security, safety, harmony, a matrimonial symphony where three was company.

In truth, however, the Behrs were parts of two different pictures. They were experiencing two different moments. Rose was completely absorbed in gazing at the true object of her affections, and Ryan saw nothing but his. While Rose delighted in the slightest movement or response from her baby, her husband was enjoying a near sensual pleasure from bathing his car. For him, the pearlessent vehicle was the apotheosis of his ambitions. This car did not simply enable him to go places; it showed the world that he had arrived. This Japanese automobile with Italian pretensions said all there was to say about its owner.

Rose allowed her gaze of adoration to rest long and loving on her golden child. She was lost in contemplation of the culmination of her own wishes and desires.

They continued in their own little worlds for a further hour, the citrus scent of the car shampoo their only shared experience.

Rose studied Baby closely and decided it was time for his lunch. She picked him up and walked over to Ryan.

'I'm taking him in for something to eat now,' she told his back. 'Do you want anything?'

She already knew the answer, but was unable to stop herself asking just the same.

Years ago Ryan had announced he did not wish to be tied down to the routine of a proper Sunday lunch, so they now they ate their meal in the evening. Quite why he required such flexibility Rose couldn't fathom, as his Sundays continued to follow the exact same pattern, month in, month out. He would invariably go out, with his mates, on a Saturday night, arriving home late and drunk. He would lie-in the following morning until his hangover forced him into the kitchen, where he would expect a full English breakfast. He would refuse lunch, only to raid the fridge without fail at about three o'clock, having renewed his appetite by washing the car. Sunday afternoons he could be found dozing in front of the television, waking in time to bounce the baby on his knee for ten minutes before declaring himself more than ready for a drink.

'I don't need lunch,' he told her without looking up from his suds. 'Wouldn't do you any harm to skip the odd meal, either' he added.

Rose, who never ate breakfast, deflected his barbed remark by squeezing Baby just a little tighter, then turned for the house. Stepping along the path she brushed passed a budding fuchsia bush. The feel of its light tickly leaves transported her back to childhood and a thousand happy hours spent in this garden, with these very plants. She thought back to how patiently her grandmother had taught her all their names; shown her how to tend and get the best out of each flower or shrub or little tree; impressed upon her which ones had healing properties, and which were poisonous, and how sometimes these were one and the same, the different result dependent upon the quantities used. She plucked a short spike of lavender by the front door and held it for baby to sniff, watching his little eyes widen in surprise. Happy now, Ryan for the moment forgotten, she continued towards the kitchen.

In the hot kitchen of 3 Brook Terrace, Fliss grasped the bird's legs and prised them apart. The heat burnt her fingers. She fought a wave of nausea at the smell of cooking meat as she reached for a fork and began jamming the stuffing into the chicken's steaming cavity. But the limbs were greasy as well as hot, and she had difficulty maintaining her grip. Casting around the room for help she spotted the rubber gloves. They did indeed improve her purchase on the slippery bones, though more than once she was aware she had stabbed through the pink rubber with the fork.

Daniel appeared in search of ice for the gin-and-tonics he was assembling. He stood behind her and peered over her shoulder.

'Aren't you supposed to stuff it before it goes in the oven?' he asked.

Fliss considered this to be a wholly unnecessary question, and was tempted to pretend she had learned some modern and trendy technique regarding the cooking of fowl, but she couldn't be bothered.

'I forgot.'

'Ah. I like the rubber gloves. Nice touch. Makes the whole procedure look very surgical. Very ER.'

'Where's that gin-and-tonic I was promised?' Fliss wanted to know. She was hot and flustered and fed up and would rather have been anywhere than in her smelly, steamy kitchen on such a beautiful day. Every Sunday she went through the ordeal of preparing a roast dinner, and every Sunday she asked herself why she bothered. Being vegetarian, she would make do with the vegetables. Rhian would always find something to complain about, and would never be persuaded to help with the clearing up. Daniel would begin to prowl and pace as the day went on, complaining that it had all got very late and he had work to do before Monday came. Fliss would be left with an Alpine range of washing up which would rob her of the remainder of the weekend.

She slammed the oven door on the somewhat misshapen chicken and wiped the back of a gloved hand across her brow, depositing small lumps of stuffing in her hair.

'Here you are, Chef,' Daniel handed her a drink, glancing at his watch as he did so. 'What time d'you think it'll be ready?'

'Oh, usual time' Fliss tried to sound nonchalant, but was having trouble not snapping at him. The added stress of having to cook in an unfamiliar kitchen full of unlabelled boxes was beginning to get to her.

'Usual time being ...?'

'When it's cooked.'

'Right. About two? Did you know you've got stuffing in your hair? Mmm, good G and T, if I say so myself. Now, where's the Review section of the paper got to? Ah here it is. Garden for me, I think.' He walked towards the back door, pausing and asking, clearly as an after thought, 'You going to join me?'

'In a minute,' she told him. 'Just want to get the gravy done.'

'Oh. Need any help?'

'I can manage, thank you,' she replied through gritted teeth, snapping off her gloves.

Once alone she sat at the kitchen table and swigged off half her drink. The worst thing about the hairball of irritation inside her was that most of it was caused by her own feebleness. She knew if she were firmer with Rhian, and Daniel for that matter, she would get more help. Some help! But it was never worth the battle.

Through the window she could see Daniel sitting on the patio reading, his back to the house. He was leaning forward on his chair studying the paper on the table, so that Fliss could see the nape of his neck and the strong line of his shoulders. She enjoyed an echo of pleasure as she remembered the night before. Even after two years they were still hungry for each other, still hot, as Daniel liked to put it.

She smiled, thinking of the way he made her feel. When they were together she had no doubts about him, no fears or insecurities. It was only when they were apart that the woodworm of fear began its work on her self-esteem. For now she was content to remind herself that whatever he lacked as a house-husband he made up for as a lover.

She finished her drink and went out to join her man, deciding to make the most of the peace and calm before lunch.

An hour later Daniel helped her lay the table.

'Rhian!' Fliss shouted up the stairs. 'Lunch is ready. Get yourself down here.'

'Yeh, coming.'

'Now, please!'

'This smells delicious, Babe,' Daniel said. 'And those roasties are a triumph, as always.' He slipped his arm around her waist as she passed, planting a kiss on her throat.

'Dan!' she laughed, wriggling from his grasp. 'The gravy's going to boil over. Let go.' She removed the pan from the heat and called Rhian again, 'It's on the table!'

'No need to shout,' her daughter said as she appeared at the door. She had the air of one being forced to do something hugely unreasonable. Whilst not actually frowning, there was a darkness shading her young features that suggested intense disapproval of everything and everyone.

'Ah, there you are. Hope you're hungry, there's loads here.'

'Drinks, Ladies?' Daniel asked. 'A nice clean Pinot Grigio perhaps, to complement the meal?' With a flourish he took the wine from the fridge and made a point of offering it to Rhian for inspection.

'I'll have water,' she said, reaching past him for a bottle of Evian.

'Fliss? You'll join me in a glass, won't you?'

'Yes, please, mind your backs, chicken coming through.' She placed the meat on the table, relieved to have got the cooking over with.

Rhian frowned at the awkward angle of the bird's limbs.

'What happened to it?'

'Nothing. What do you mean?'

'Well look at it. Its legs are all wonky.'

Daniel moved over for a closer look.

'Hmm, does look a bit dodgy. More battered hen than battery, I'd say.'

Fliss saw nothing remotely funny in the situation.

'It most certainly is not a battery chicken, nor has it suffered any ill treatment whatsoever, alive or dead. This sort of thing is unavoidable sometimes when you are stuffing fowl, as the two of you would know if you'd ever done it. Now sit down and let's eat.'

'I'm sure it'll be scrumptious, Babe. You know I love your cooking. Here,' he poured her a generous glass of wine, 'get some of this down your lovely neck.'

Fliss fortified herself with a few gulps of her drink, then did her best to carve. She wished the others wouldn't watch so closely while she was doing it.

'Dan, help yourself to veg. Rhian, come on, don't let it get cold. Stuffing, anyone?'

At last they were all seated in front of platefuls of food. Fliss nibbled at a roasted yam. She noticed Rhian eyeing her chicken suspiciously.

'There's nothing wrong with it, I told you.'

'Why can't we have organic chicken? Sharon's Mum always buys organic.'

'Sharon's Mum has an enormous divorce settlement to squander. She can afford to eat organic, sadly we cannot.'

'It's embarrassing, being poor,' complained Rhian.

'Then don't tell anyone.' Fliss replied.

'Everyone knows.'

'I don't see how. And anyway, who is "everyone"? And why do you care what they think?'

'It's obvious,' Rhian stabbed at a potato but didn't eat it. 'For a start we don't even have a car.'

'We don't need a car.'

'Yes, we do. I'll have to cadge lifts and get my friends' mums to take me places now that we live out here. Assuming I ever make any friends in this Hicksville place. It'll be humiliating.'

Daniel tried to lighten the tone.

'Is this where I'm supposed to say things like, "good for the soul" and "character forming"?'

'No,' Fliss warned him. 'This is where you're supposed to top up my glass and say nothing.'

'Fair enough.'

'Anyway,' Rhian tried another angle, 'I think it's hypocritical of you, feeding me this. You're always banging on about healthy food, you don't eat this stuff, but it's okay for me to.'

'I don't eat any meat, expensively organic or otherwise. And this is perfectly good food, Withy Hill chickens ...'

'Are full of God knows what,' Rhian interrupted. 'And we're only eating it because you've taken a cleaning job up there and your new boss gave you a freebie.'

'All the staff get a discount, and I told you the farm has a reputation for quality food. They supply posh restaurants in London, for heaven's sake. I wouldn't feed you anything questionable. Now can we just eat, please?'

But Rhian pointedly put down her knife and fork.

'Daniel could pay for decent meat,' she declared. 'He can afford it.'

There was a crackling pause where most of the oxygen seemed to disappear from the air in the kitchen. Fliss knew the best course of action would be to ignore the remark, but she could see Daniel about to defend himself.

'Don't be rude, Rhian,' she said quickly.

'I'm just stating facts. It was the same in London, he's happy enough to stay with us at weekends, he could pay something towards ...'

'Daniel contributes exactly what I ask him for.'

'Huh, a few bottles of gnat's piss wine and the odd pub lunch. Big deal!'

Daniel could stay silent no longer. 'I'd willingly give more, really, it's your mother who ...'

'Shut up, Daniel,' said Fliss, rather more sharply than she had intended. 'Rhian, get on with your lunch. When you contribute to the housekeeping, then you can have a say in how it's spent. Okay?'

'Oh great!' Rhian stood up, noisily pushing her chair back. 'I'm supposed to get a job now as well as school just so we don't have to eat crap food. Well fuck it! You can keep your toxic chicken!'

'Rhian! Don't speak to me like that ...'

But Fliss was talking to an empty space, her words lost in the slamming of doors as her daughter charged back to her room. Fliss felt her already flimsy appetite evaporate entirely. She looked at Daniel beseechingly.

'Don't take any notice, Babe,' he told her. 'Hormones.'

Fliss had been going to alert him to the flap of rubber glove he was about to eat with his mouthful of stuffing, but changed her mind and watched him chew.

CHAPTER FOUR

Fliss considered the supine body in front of her. It was a body that had seen too many good meals; enjoyed too many large vodka and tonics; survived too many late nights; inhaled too many cigarettes; and been a stranger to exercise all its 59 years. It passed through Fliss's mind that women are judged harshly for such a lifestyle, and that had Pam been a man she could have been proud of her world-weary physique, letting it speak of high living and adventure. The cruel truth Pam had to live with was that no amount of lippy and mascara applied myopically, mouth stretched and eyes surprised, would ever again cause heads to turn - unless they turned away!

Fliss knew Pam was hoping for a miracle transformation. Which was why she was lying on the bar an hour before opening time letting Fliss place crystals all over her. As if she could do anything about a career of smoking and drinking and overeating. Fliss tried to focus. In her mind she ran through the lengthy list of aches and minor ailments Pam had given her at the start of the session. She selected a large amethyst from her collection. It was heavy and surprisingly warm in her hand. The purple of the stone was darker at the base, diluting to clear crystal at the spiky tips, reminding Fliss of a swiftly sucked Popsicle. She gently placed the gemstone on Pam's brow knowing the corresponding chakra to be the same colour, allowing a connection.

Fliss consulted her reference book, checking her theories, trying not to let the pages make telltale noises. Amethyst for centring, she read, for confidence and general healing. And garnet, of course, garnet!

She was finding it hard to concentrate. The week had been a long one, preceded by a weekend without Daniel. Heavy workload, he had claimed. Needed time to get on top of things paperwork-wise, he said. Reasonable enough, she told herself. But still she harboured suspicions that his absence might have something to do with Rhian's behaviour the week before. Her increasing rudeness towards Daniel was reaching an unpleasant level, and Fliss was unsure what to do about it. Still, it made a change from worrying about money. Having secured two cleaning jobs in the village within a week of moving in at least she had something which could be called an income. And the odd Crystal Healing session was a little extra cash.

Her attention was dragged back to her uncomplaining client by a low rumbling, which Fliss eventually identified as the sound of Pam snoring.

'Pam?' Fliss gently squeezed the older woman's shoulder. The snoring stuttered and hiccupped, rounding off with a loud snort.

'What? What's that? Finished already?' Pam sat up stiffly. 'Well done, Fliss. Christ I feel better for that. You can work magic with those stones of yours, my girl. Magic!' She swung her legs around and sat heavily on the edge of the bar. 'You wait till Pete has a go. He's gonna love this. Now, how about a coffee before you start on the Gents?'

Fliss winced at the mention of her least favourite cleaning task. Somehow the job felt even more revolting following so closely the gentle activity of working with crystals.

'I'll have a rosehip thanks, Pam. I've got a some with me.' She fished a box of herbal teas from her bag.

Fliss gazed wearily at the lounge bar as her drink infused in a mug declaring itself to be a present from Mallorca. Pam had told her of all the plans she and Pete had for the place when they bought it; how they were going to transform it from a modest boozer to an up beat, happening place with live music and quality bar food. They had not reckoned on the entrenched preferences of the locals, the lack of passing trade, or the dwindling numbers of patrons generally due to stringently enforced drink-driving laws. The designer bottled lagers had gathered dust in the cellar. The chrome and leather barstools had not been appreciated by the undiscerning bums that buffed them. The green Thai curry with wild rice had failed to excite interest. Even the live music had left the ungrateful clientele unimpressed. Still they had persevered until a spontaneous piece of market research in the public bar had revealed all but one band to be considered second best to silence. Pam had finally thrown up her hands, installed a huge TV for football matches, and doubled the orders of pork scratchings, her dreams of a high-class eatery disappearing as swiftly as the specials on the chalk smudged board.

As she headed for the urinals, Fliss wondered if her own hopes and aspirations would suffer the same fate.

At Honeysuckle Cottage, Rose was, by contrast, enjoying her cleaning tasks. It had only been an hour since Ryan left for his overnight trip, and already the house felt lighter, bigger, and friendlier. Of course, Rose no more believed in the existence of the Manchester Estate Agents Conference than she did the existence of the tooth fairy, but she would not challenge her husband about it. He made up conferences to excuse his absences when it suited him. She knew he lied, and that whichever girl from the office, or one of the nightclubs in Barnchester, was currently in favour would be enjoying his company. She also knew he would deny it with his dying breath. She knew too that there was nothing she could say or do to stop him going. In any case, she had become accustomed to his behaviour. It was simply the way things were; the way things had been in their marriage for some time. Except for one crucial difference; now she had Baby.

As she sprayed the mahogany-look nest of tables with BeesKnees she planned how she and Baby would spend their 48 hours of precious uninterrupted time together. While he was having his morning nap she would cook a batch of sweet potato puree, freezing it in ice cube trays, saving some for his lunch. When he woke up she would sit with him on his tartan rug in the sitting room and together they would explore things that rattled and squeaked and rustled. She would coax from him smiles and gurgles and tell him she loved him, speaking aloud words she could never in her life say to another adult. After lunch she would take him out in the pram so that he could benefit from the spring air, and so that the world, (or at least her small corner of it) could see how lucky she was. Tonight she would take time pressing his little clothes, and she would sleep in the single bed next to his cot, so that she could watch him sleep.

The ringing of the telephone startled her, catching her in such indulgent thoughts.

'Mrs Behr? It's Martin Cripps here, from the Barnchester Echo.'

'Oh, hello.'

'I'm ringing to let you know that you are the lucky winner of our Barnchester Bonnie Baby Competition. Or rather, your baby is!' Mr Cripps laughed at his own little joke.

'Yes, I see. Thank you.' Rose did not sound surprised because she was not. She, after all, knew Baby to be the most beautiful infant in all the land. It was only natural to her that, given a glimpse of him, everyone else should agree.

Mr Cripps was a little deflated by her muted response.

'This means that Baby Behr is automatically entered into the regional final, and as part of your prize we will be sending along the Echo's very own photographer to create a wonderful portrait of the little chap. This will be yours to keep, along with the £100 cash, of course. And you are free to order as many copies as you like.'

'Oh, thank you very much.'

Mr Cripps gave up trying.

'So, when would be a convenient time for our photographer to call? Say Tuesday of next week?'

Rose did not need to consult a non-existent diary to tell her she had no other engagements next Tuesday.

'Can he come at about eleven?' She knew Baby would have finished his morning nap by then, and would be at his dimpling best.

As she resumed her polishing Rose smiled to herself and began to sing a nursery rhyme in a clear, high voice that seldom ventured out.

Neville pedalled slowly, and more than a little reluctantly, towards The Vicarage. The evening was already a sweet one, and he could think of any number of better things to be doing than heading for a meeting at Cynthia Danby's house. His bike was still not running as smoothly as it should have been, following the previous week's crash, and the idea of tinkering with it in the little sunny yard behind his flat was a tempting one. But he knew he could not escape Cynthia and her plans so easily. He reminded himself why he agreed to get involved in her fundraising event in the first place.

'Claude Lambert,' he said aloud, adding a silent prayer that the great chef would stick by his promise to be the main attraction, and not lose his nerve and remember a prior engagement after a few more doses of Cynthia.

Neville's bicycle crunched gravel beneath its slim wheels as he steered up the drive which curved to the front of the house. He has always thought the building particularly unattractive but undeniably imposing. Its spires, pointy windows and angular lines were softened a little by the warmth of the local stone, but not enough to stop it being a foreboding dwelling.

As always when reaching the threshold of The Vicarage, however, there was something which exercised Neville's mind far more than Victorian Gothic Architecture. And it was with dread that he heard the unmistakable sound of that something approaching. He dismounted, hastily leaned his bike against the wall, and hammered on the door. He even yanked on the rusting bell-pull, though he knew this to be a reliably futile activity. Had the bell still been attached to the thing, its ringing would in any case have been drowned out by the monstrous rasping bark of Cynthia's revolting dog.

Neville could hear the creature thundering around the side of the house and knew in another moment it would be upon him. He tried the handle, but the door was locked. Cursing Neighbourhood Watch and all its crime prevention leaflets he turned to face the inevitable.

Cynthia's Great Dane may once have lived up to that description, but in its sunset years it was a sorry excuse for its breed. Being called Hamlet seemed a cruel joke now. Arthritis had slowed its gait to a stiff-legged shamble. The steely grey of its coat had acquired rust patches of eczema. It blundered about squinting through matching cataracts, guided mostly by its nose, which had mercifully become immune to its own fearful pong.

'Good boy, Hamlet. It's only me,' Neville knew the terrible hound to be friendly, but wished to prevent the usual enthusiastic greeting in all its wet smelliness. He held his hand out to be sniffed. Hamlet failed to notice and advanced, wagging and panting, jaws wide open, so that Neville's hand disappeared into its fetid mouth. Neville gasped as the dog chewed playfully before letting him go.

'Oh for pity's sake! Get down, Hamlet! You disgusting creature. No, I don't want to be licked. Where is your mistress? Cynthia!' He thumped on the door again, dog drool running down his arm.

Hamlet moved in for an embrace, standing to place a heavy paw on each of Neville's shoulders, pinning him against the door. At the same moment Cynthia could be heard unbolting the door. Neville struggled free of Hamlet's clutches just in time to avoid the indignity of falling flat on his back at Cynthia's feet.

'Ah, Neville! There you are. Come in, come in, darling boy. You've no time to play with Hamlet now. Come along, follow me. We're in the dining room.'

Neville quickly caught Cynthia up, hoping Hamlet would lose interest in him, but the dog, like its owner, was more than a little keen on Neville.

In the dining room the shutters were still open, so that low sunbeams fell across the room allowing a fine display of dancing dust. Half way down the landing strip of a table sat Sally Siddons, looking uncomfortably out of place. How much better suited she was to her more usual surroundings of the village Post Office. Her smallness and frailty fitted among the bitty detail of chocolate bars, penny chews, envelopes and stamps. Here she was somehow not drawn to scale, set against the muscular furniture, high ceilings, gigantic paintings, and lawn-sized Persian rugs.

'Now, we've made a start on things,' Cynthia returned to her seat at the head of the table. 'It's breaking with protocol to carry on with people missing, but needs must. And given the disappointingly short list of volunteers there is not a moment to be wasted. Miss Siddons has kindly agreed to act as Secretary for the Nettlecombe Hatchet Event Committee – which we will refer to as NHEC for simplicity's sake.'

Miss Siddons smiled sweetly and nodded her bouncing grey curls in Neville's direction.

Neville knew exactly why the harmless woman had been press ganged into service. She would have sooner fallen on her neatly sharpened pencil than have disagreed with their host. This effectively gave Cynthia two votes on anything and everything, just to be extra sure that things were done her way. Neville took a seat as far from Cynthia as politeness would allow. Hamlet sat heavily beside him.

'Is anyone else coming?' he asked.

'We are expecting Pamela from the Soldier's Arms – she expressed an interest, being in a catering business of sorts herself. Then of course Mr Christian is keen to be involved, as Withy Hill Farm is to be the venue for our event. However, he is an exceptionally busy man, so we may not see much of him. We will have to content ourselves with the use of his facilities, and of course the not inconsiderable benefit of the Withy Hill reputation for fine food. Monsieur Lambert will not be able to attend our meetings in person, though I understand he may send his Personal Assistant on occasion. He wishes to be kept informed of our progress. I must say it is a coup indeed to have such a well-known and highly respected chef as the main attraction for our fundraising occasion. I'm certain he will draw a good crowd.' She fixed

Neville with a meaningful stare. 'There are others who share our passion, *mon cher.*'

Neville was determined to steer a strictly business course through the stormy waters of Cynthia's infatuation with him.

'So,' he cleared his throat, reluctantly scratching Hamlet's ears to keep him from climbing onto his lap, 'it would seem to me that we need to make a plan. A countdown to the big day, with tasks identified and allotted, so that everyone knows what they are supposed to be doing and when they are supposed to be doing it.'

'Quite so ...'

'And we should decide what shape the day itself is going to take, down to the smallest detail.' Neville surprised himself with his own boldness. Not many people would dare to interrupt Cynthia. He quickly lost his nerve, however, 'Don't you think so?' he added.

Miss Siddons nodded again, resembling more and more a toy dog on a car parcel shelf.

'I do indeed,' Cynthia enthused, 'which is why I have jotted down one or two points which I believe will ensure the day runs smoothly.' She launched into a lengthy description of the Nettlecombe Hatchet Event, starring Monsieur Claude Lambert.

It was a vision of such detail that Neville wondered why she was bothering with a committee. Clearly the involvement of anyone else was for form's sake. He listened to her increasingly excited portrayal of the planned day. There was to be a 'Food Hall' selling local produce; entertainments and activities for children (to include a bouncy castle and pony rides); a refreshment tent; music provided by a local string quartet (Neville had particular misgivings about this); and, of course, the cookery demonstration by their celebrity chef, followed by a question and answer session, and book signing. As if this weren't more excitement than a person could stand, the competition for the best local recipe (to be included in Monsieur Lambert's next book) would be judged on the day.

Neville was seriously beginning to question Cynthia's motives for having him involved at all, when all sensible thought was rendered impossible by Hamlet suddenly entering into a frenzy of wheezy barking. Cynthia added to the din by bellowing at the dog as it lumbered towards the hall. It was brought to a sudden halt in the doorway by the equally solid frame of Pam, who repelled its advances with a stealthy slap.

'Sorry I'm late, Cynthia. Gents flooded again. Still, I'm not the only one who can't make it here on time. Look who I found on your doorstep.'

She moved aside. Neville craned his neck to get a better view, and into the room stepped the loveliest, sexiest, most beautiful, most elegant, most delectable, and all-round most gorgeous woman he had ever seen.

CHAPTER FIVE

When a remarkably beautiful woman walks into a room two
things happen. The first is that she is noticed – by everyone!
Noticed and appraised. The second is that the people in the
room are affected. They all undergo subtle changes. The men
instinctively suck in their stomachs and puff out their chests.
The women lift their chins. The presence of great beauty does
not impact so hard on others who inhabit extreme positions
on the scale of gorgeousness. Other fantastically beautiful
people know they are just that, do not doubt their own
fabulousness for one second, and so are not threatened.
Such loveliness is the norm for them. Fearsomely
unattractive people are also only too aware of their place on
the spectrum of loveliness.

It is everybody in between who will wiggle and squirm.

The fifty-something woman on her way down as her looks
crumble could do without another *momento mori.*

The balding man who was the college Romeo two decades
ago can only look, sigh, and run his fingers through the
memory of his hair.

The young girl on her way up licks her finger to tidy an
eyebrow and gets ready to stand comparison.

The new mother strokes her now empty belly and
determines to start those sit ups again.

The very old man who still hears air-raid sirens licks his
parchment lips and tries to remember a time when he wasn't
invisible.

In this particular room, the immediate result of such
gorgeousness was silence. A moment later Cynthia came to.

'Aah, Miss Ferris-Brown, so glad you were able to join us.
Everyone, this is Monsieur Lambert's personal assistant,
Lucy Ferris-Brown who has kindly agreed to assist us on
behalf of the great man himself.'

There was much nodding and hello-ing and shuffling
about through introductions.

'And this is Neville Meatcher,' Cynthia told the lovely
Lucy, 'our local culinary expert.'

Although passably good-looking in a harmless, forgettable
way, Neville had never enjoyed much success with women.

He had had his moments, and of course there had been his engagement to Catherine, but on the whole he found relationships with females to be more trouble than they were worth. He was used to being pretty much ignored by any young and gorgeous women, should they happen to stray into his orbit. It didn't bother him. Being ignored was infinitely preferable to receiving the type of attention he suffered from Cynthia.

It came as something of a surprise, therefore, to find Lucy greeting him with a warm, lingering handshake, gazing at him intently, and apparently hanging on his every word.

'Pleased to meet you,' he said awkwardly.

'Anyone sitting here?' Lucy arranged herself elegantly on the chair next to him, the skirt of her exquisitely cut suit revealing yards of silky leg.

Neville tried to focus on what Cynthia was saying, but his attention kept getting tweaked back to Lucy, as wafts of Something Classy and Expensive reached him.

The meeting meandered on, consisting mostly of Cynthia telling everyone how things would be, Lucy saying what a good idea everything was, Pam's tummy rumbling, and Miss Siddons nodding earnestly.

On Neville's left, Hamlet came and settled himself, leaning heavily against his leg. On his right Lucy sat light as an angel, her own thigh occasionally making a whispering contact with Neville's. Hamlet's malodorous breath did battle with Lucy's sweet perfume somewhere over Neville's head. He found himself leaning away from the stinking dog and therefore towards Lucy. Experience told him to expect her to shift in the other direction, but she did not. Instead she seemed to enjoy the proximity, and laughed softly if Neville made even the feeblest of witty remarks.

So unused was Neville to being flirted with that he took most of the evening to realise what was going on.

When the meeting came to a close Cynthia announced she would make coffee.

Lucy spoke quietly.

'Bet it's instant,' she said.

Neville nodded. 'More than likely,' he said.

'I do hate cheap coffee, don't you? Rather not have anything at all. At home I always use Jamaican Blue Mountain. Beans, of course,' she said.

'Really? Me too,' said Neville. 'There's no finer coffee, in my opinion. And the fabulous smell when you grind those beans ...'

'Mmmmm,' Lucy closed her eyes in rapture. 'I'd love a cup of that. Right now,' she said, eyes still closed.

'Oh well, I could organise that.'

'You could?' her eyes sprang open, bright and beaming at Neville.

'No problem. I've got my bike outside. I'll nip back to the flat and get some.'

'Oh,' something approaching a frown flitted across Lucy's face. It was quickly replaced by a little smile. 'Wouldn't it be so much nicer if we went to your place, just the two of us. You and me.' She stepped forwards and ran a beautifully manicured finger down his lapel.

Neville opened his mouth to speak but nothing came out, so he shut it again.

'You can tell me all about your little village,' Lucy went on, 'so I can tell Claude. I know he'll want all the details.'

'Oh yes, of course.' Neville began to blush. 'I suppose we'd better say goodbye to Cynthia.'

'Oh, let's not bother her. Let's just slip away quietly.'

'Right. Good idea.'

Neville led the way down the hall to the front door. Hamlet insisted on following them, and more than once sniffed Neville's crotch noisily.

'Look, will you sod off, Hamlet. Go on.' Neville pushed the dog back into the house and edged outside. 'There. Sorry about him. He's harmless, but, well, you can see ...'

'Yes. Never could see the point of dogs,' said Lucy. 'Especially when they get old and smelly like that one. Oh, is this your bicycle?'

'Yes.' Neville had never wished more in his life for a sports car.

'Hmm, you must be incredibly fit, riding this everywhere. Does it go very fast?'

Neville raised his eyebrows. Fond as he was of his bike, he had never considered it a babe magnet.

'Do you want a go?' he found himself asking.

Lucy laughed prettily.

'In these shoes? I don't think pedals were designed for kitten heels. But you could drive the thing. I'll sit on the handlebars, like they do in romantic movies.'

'Are you sure? They're quite narrow, and the bell's not in the ideal place.'

'Oh come on, it'll be a hoot,' said Lucy, buttoning up her jacket.

'OK,' Neville whipped his bicycle clips from his pocket and fumbled to put them in place, a curious nervousness making him clumsy. He straddled the bike then turned to Lucy.

'I'm not sure ...'

'Just hoik me up. I'm quite light,' she told him.

She was indeed no weight at all. Neville was able to lift her onto the handlebars quite easily, her short skirt allowing her legs to dangle on either side of the front wheel.

'Oooh!' she squealed as they set off. 'You were right about that bell!'

Neville concentrated on pedalling and steering the worryingly unstable bike. The gravel drive wasn't the best surface for such an exercise. Just when he more or less had things under control Cynthia's shrill voice put him off his stride.

'Neville?' she cried out from the front doorstep. 'Neville, what on earth are you doing? There are things I need to discuss with Miss Ferris-Brown. Bring her back!'

'Quick!' urged Lucy. 'Let's get out of here before she drags us back inside and forces us to drink foul coffee.'

Neville kept his head down and pedalled hard. Cynthia's entreaties were drowned out by the bellowing bark of Hamlet, who, now released, was giving chase.

'Bugger,' said Neville.

'Faster!' cried Lucy.

Hamlet was closing on them when they reached the end of the drive and broke free of the snare of the gravel. The wheels found smooth tarmac and a downward slope and the bike shot forwards. Too late Neville discovered that Lucy was hampering his access to the rear brake. As they gathered speed down the hill into the village he did not dare apply the front brake for fear of catapulting his passenger into the middle distance.

'Wheee!' she cried, holding up her legs and sticking them straight out in front. 'This is lovely!'

The night was clear and well lit by a pearly moon, so that Neville could not pretend to himself that the spectacle he and Lucy now presented would not be enjoyed by most of the village.

Without brakes they did not come to a halt until well beyond the far side of the green.

Lucy was pink cheeked and glowing, her tousled hair and broad smile making her even more beautiful.

'That was fantastic, Neville,' she slipped nimbly off the bike. 'You certainly know how to show a girl a good time,' she said, tugging her skirt back into place.

They walked back through the village to Neville's flat. Lucy was more than polite about his little home. They talked as he set about making the coffee.

'You know,' she told him, 'Claude is terribly excited about the new partnership with Withy Hill Farm. It's very important to him.' She drifted around the kitchen idly inspecting things.

'I'm sure it'll be a success,' said Neville. 'Anything with Claude Lambert's name on it has got to be a winner.'

Conversation paused while Neville ground the beans.

'Mmm, smell that,' he said to her a moment later.

Lucy stood close to him and inhaled deeply, watching him pour boiling water over the coffee grinds.

'Shall we have some brandy while we're waiting?' she asked.

'Oh. Yes. If you like?'

'I noticed you have some rather good Cognac. We can still have the coffee. Later.'

There was something about the way Lucy said 'later' that made Neville prick up his ears. It smacked of 'afterwards'. Of dot, dot, dot.

Things were happening too fast for Neville to understand. The evening had started with Cynthia and Miss Siddons and boring details of the fundraising event to be chewed over. Now here he had a stunningly gorgeous woman in his flat smouldering at him and requesting brandy.

He poured them generous measures. She downed hers where she stood and handed back the glass for a refill. She sipped the second drink more slowly.

'Of course,' she said, 'for the business venture to be truly successful Withy Hill will have to expand – considerably! Claude has huge plans.'

'I'm sure he does.' Neville swigged away in an effort to catch up.

'They will need new offices, new buildings at the farm. Bigger production facilities. And, of course, somewhere for research and development.'

'It all sounds very ambitious and exciting.'

'Oh it is. Claude is a man of ideas. Of vision. You'll see that when you meet him.'

'I'm looking forward to it very much.'

'The two of you will get on so well, I know you will. You share a passion for food. You believe in excellence. Nothing but the best. No room for compromise.'

'Exactly,' Neville enthused, draining his glass. 'Another?'

Lucy hesitated, then nodded and offered her glass.

'The problem is,' she said, 'not everyone understands that sort of single-minded dedication. They have no vision, and they are suspicious of those who do.'

'Sad people leading sad lives,' Neville pronounced, emboldened by brandy and more than ready to agree with anything Lucy said.

'And people like that want to see great people fail. Sometimes they will even go out of their way to condemn and obstruct, just out of spite. As if they can't stand to see a man realise his dreams.' Lucy swigged more brandy and hiccupped gently.

'Pitiful,' said Neville.

'Isn't it? But I know, Neville, I just know we can count on you, and on your unfailing support.'

'Of course. Abso-bloody-lutely.'

Neville was standing so close to Lucy now he could see the pulse beating in her deliciously smooth throat.

'That's why I know you'll see that the planning applications for Withy Hill go through unopposed.'

'Oh well, you know that sort of thing really isn't up to me.'

'Oh Neville, don't be coy. I've heard you are a powerful man,' she purred, swaying a little, the drink seemingly having a strong and immediate effect on her.

'There's really not much I can do,' he told her.

'Really?' Lucy put down her glass and began to play with Neville's tie. 'Are you sure? Not even for little me?' She licked her perfect lips and stepped back, still holding his tie. She wriggled up onto the kitchen table and slowly reeled Neville in.

'Maybe there's some way I could make you change your mind,' she said.

In the cold, unsexy light of day Neville had once had an argument with his brother-in-law about scruples. Then, when nothing remotely fanciable was at stake, it had been easy to take a lofty view and to accuse Brian of being not moral but scared, in that it was acceptable to fiddle your expense account as long as you didn't get caught. Neville had insisted that every right-thinking man knew instinctively when something was fair and decent and when it was not. A man of scruples would naturally choose the right path; honour demanded it. A black and white situation every time.

Now, however, a certain greyness had descended. Perhaps it was an alcoholic fog, or, more likely, the murky mist of lust. Either way, what was being offered to Neville seemed so very much more worthwhile, and desirable and important than what was being asked of him. In any case, he could later rationalise, he truly could not influence planning decisions one way or the other, whether he wanted to or not. That this meant he would be doubly taking advantage of The Lovely Lucy was a point he chose to shut his mind to, as she began to unbutton her blouse and all sensible thought fled.

It had been some considerable time since Neville had had sex with anyone other than himself. He was pleased to find the idea sending the necessary signals to parts of his body which had been living something of a half-life. The sight of Lucy hitching up her Chanel skirt to reveal suspender clad creamy thighs had him fumbling frantically with his belt buckle. This was, by any man's standards, an ideal sexual encounter. A beautiful woman, and just enough brandy, and sexy underwear, and no commitment and no questions asked. No weeks of tedious dating. No having to say the right thing, or take an interest, or remember birthdays and star signs and pets' names. Not even any sensitive seduction or tricky foreplay required.

Sex on a plate – which somehow mixed sex with food in a way that particularly appealed to Neville.

As his trousers dropped to his ankles he became cruelly aware that he was still wearing his bicycle clips. Effectively hobbled, Neville teetered for a second or two before falling forwards into the open arms of the Siren on the table before him.

'Ooh, so you like things a bit rough, do you, Neville darling?' said Lucy, taking his lunge as a signal. 'Oh yes, that works for me too!' she told him huskily, flinging up her legs and hooking her feet around his back.

'Oh Lucy,' moaned Neville, kissing her hard. She kissed him back so enthusiastically his lip began to bleed.

Suddenly, into this maelstrom of lust came the insistent buzzing of Neville's doorbell.

'What? For pity's sake,' he hissed. 'Who can that be?'

'Never mind. Ignore it. They'll go away.' Lucy started kissing him again.

The buzzing continued. Then, just as Neville was on the point of adding Lucy to a short but memorable list in his autobiography, he was halted by the unmistakeable sound of Cynthia's voice.

'Neville? Neville!' she shouted through the letterbox. 'Neville, it's me, Cynthia.'

'Oh God, I don't believe it! That wretched bloody woman!'

'Don't answer. She'll go away,' panted Lucy.

'You don't know her – she'll never give up.' Neville disentangled himself from Lucy. Cynthia had an immediate and unmissable effect of him.

Lucy smiled sweetly.

'Never mind, darling. You take a moment to get your, er, breath back. I'll go and wait for you in the bedroom. Just get rid of the old bat.'

'I will. Sorry. Bedroom's through there. I'll be as quick as I can.'

'Neville?' Cynthia was hammering on the door now.

'Coming!' Neville shouted, causing loud giggles from Lucy. 'Bloody woman,' he cursed Cynthia as he descended the stairs, hastily doing up his trousers. 'Why can't she leave me alone?'

As soon as he opened the door Cynthia stepped through. Neville all but leapt in front of her to bar her route to the stairs.

'What is it, Cynthia? What do you want?'

'You left without these,' she held up the print outs from the meeting. 'I knew you would want them.'

'Couldn't it have waited until morning?'

'I suppose it could. I'm not interrupting anything, am I?' She peered up the stairs.

'No, I was just going to bed. Headache, you know.'

'Your lip is bleeding,' Cynthia told him.

'What? Oh, cut myself shaving I expect. Now if you don't mind ...'

'Where is Miss Ferris-Brown?'

'How should I know?'

'The last time I saw her she was perched on your bicycle,' Cynthia pointed out.

'I gave her a lift.'

'To?'

'The telephone box on the green. To call a taxi. To take her to the station. To catch a train.'

'She could have used my telephone. And anyway, don't all young people have mobile phones these days?'

'No signal here, apparently. Look, it was good of you to bring these round, but as I think I mentioned, I have got a headache, so ...'

'Shall I come up and make you some cocoa?'

Neville stared at the plain, lightly moustached, overweight, middle-aged, bossy woman in front of him and had no trouble declining her kind offer. With a gentle shove he bid her goodnight and firmly shut and bolted the door, then hurried back upstairs. This time he removed his bicycle clips and shoes before going in search of Lucy.

He found her, lovely as ever, quite naked save for his Egyptian cotton sheets, draped diagonally across his bed, and deeply, soundly, heavily asleep.

'Sod it,' said Neville.

Baby beamed at the photographer. Rose stood back, glowing. Here was surely a true star. The sitting room had been transformed into a photographer's studio and Baby was positioned on a sheepskin rug, a backdrop of blue sky and fluffy clouds showing off his sparkling little eyes to perfection. All around were lights, umbrellas, reflectors and gadgets and gizmos. Unfazed by any of it, the infant smiled and chortled and held poses beautifully.

'He's a natural, Mrs Behr,' said the photographer. 'A joy to work with. Wish they were all as co-operative as this. That's it, big smile, look this way, little fella. Lovely.'

Snap, snap. Flash, flash.

'Just the ticket, young 'un.' The photographer squinted back into his view finder.   'Lovely, lovely. Yes, like I say, my job would be a thousand times easier, if they were all like your little man here.'

Rose smiled. Having people praise Baby was high on her list of Things She Really Liked. And the photographer was clearly right – Baby was revelling in the attention, not a bit camera shy or unsettled by all the bright lights and flashes. He appeared to be thoroughly enjoying himself.

As if to confirm this, Baby let out a tuneful and spontaneous giggle.

'Reckon you've got a winner here, Mrs Behr,' the photographer continued to talk as he clicked. 'I've done hundreds of these baby shoots in my time, seen some corkers, and some down right pug-uglies, don't mind telling you. You'd be amazed.'

Click, click. Pop, flash, whirr.

'Now junior here, he's got star quality. Spotted it the minute I saw him. And he loves the camera. That's lovely, hold that ... Crucial, for this sort of thing. No good looking cute and cuddly if they start screaming at the sight of my tripod.'

Rose, by now quite pink with pleasure, waved an encouraging rattle at Baby. Any misgivings she may have had about subjecting the twinkling little light of her life to being photographed had long since vanished. Baby was loving every second of the fuss and focus.

The unexpected slamming of the front door caused both Rose and Baby to jump.

'Rose? Rose!' Ryan shouted as he stomped down the hall to the kitchen. 'Where the fuck's she got to now?'

Seconds later he arrived in the sitting room.

'There you are. Didn't you hear me calling for you? Why didn't you answer? My day's already pear sodding shaped enough without you playing silly buggers.'

All smiles vanished from the room. Baby stopped cooing and gurgling and gazed mutely at his father. The photographer paused, shutter release cable in hand, for once with nothing to say. Rose took a step towards Baby. She opened her mouth, but Ryan gave her little opportunity to speak.

'I've lost my bastard mobile,' he told her, pulling cushions of the sofa. 'Got all the way to the office before I realised it wasn't in the car.'

'Have you tried your briefcase?' Rose asked.

'Of course I've tried my sodding briefcase. D'you think I'm stupid?' He abandoned wrecking the sofa and started on the CD rack.

'I don't think it will be in there,' said Rose.

'Oh don't you?' Ryan's fury was reaching dangerous levels. 'Well where do you think it is, then, if you're so clever all of a sudden? Eh? You tell me where the bastard thing is.'

Baby began to whimper. Rose scooped him up and jiggled him gently. She made no attempt to answer Ryan.

'You're bloody useless, woman,' he said, storming out of the room. 'I can't waste any more time, some of us have to go to work. Just look for it, will you, if you're not too busy,' he yelled back at her as he thumped out of the house.

It took some moments for Ryan's turbulence to leave the room. Eventually the photographer found his voice again.

'Well, I think I've got what I need,' he said brightly. 'Yes, I think we've some cracking shots of our new little superstar here. You wait and see.'

He busied himself dismantling, disconnecting, and packing, chatting away all the while.

Still holding Baby close, Rose turned to the window so that this stranger who had witnessed her humiliation should not also see the lone tear she failed to hold back.

At Withy Hill Farm Fliss was at last nearing the end of her cleaning stint. The Christian's had hosted a drinks party the night before, and she had spent nearly an hour on her knees battling with red wine stains, cursing the sadist who dreamt up 'wheaten whisper' as a carpet colour.

'Ten more minutes,' she told herself, 'then freedom. Thank God.'

She stood up and checked the room for any grubbiness she might have missed.

'Pretty good,' she announced. 'Perfect, in fact. Should keep even Mrs Christian happy.'

'Ahh, Fliss, here you are,' Mrs Christian appeared as if from nowhere. 'Who were you talking to?'

'Oh, no-one. Just humming.'

'I see. Well, when you've finished in here, could you do the study. Michael is out today, so you won't be disturbing him.'

'That's alright then.'

'I'm sorry?'

'I said, that's no problem, Mrs Christian.'

'Good. I'm going into Barnchester. See you on Friday.'

Fliss snatched up her duster and hauled the Hoover into the study.

'Right,' she addressed the leather and mahogany. 'What can't be done in here in ten minutes doesn't get done.'

She vacuumed briefly, not bothering to move any furniture, then set about tidying the desk, flicking her duster over executive toys. As she shuffled papers into a neat pile the words 'planning application' caught her eye.

She looked over her shoulder to check Mrs Christian wasn't about to surprise her again. Pulling out the document, she read further. First glance revealed a straightforward application for a small new office building, and two new chicken sheds. Closer inspection, however, revealed something altogether more sinister.

A fourth building, positioned behind the others, had not one single window, and its title made Fliss pale. Clearly written beneath the architect's drawings were the words 'Proposed Laboratory.'

CHAPTER SIX

Neville landed heavily on the chair behind his desk. It was not yet nine, and already the morning had a sluggardly feel to it. Things weren't helped by the water still trickling down the back of his neck. He had grown blasé about the dry sunny days, and so had not bothered to pack his waterproof cycling poncho and had been caught napping by the weather Gods who Neville considered had a singularly schoolboy type of humour.

He had arrived at work looking sufficiently pathetic to send Mrs Appleby hurrying to find him a towel. Women of a certain age fussing around him were becoming a defining feature in his life. Still, as he rubbed at his hair in the merciful privacy of his little room, Neville was glad of this particular motherly act by the rosy-cheeked receptionist. He draped the towel over his head for a minute and removed his squelching shoes, placing them upside down on the radiator. Not for the first time he thanked his luck, and Bertie Willis's retirement, for giving him the sanctuary of his own office, rather than having to crouch behind a pegboard partition with the rest of the sorry souls in open-plan. He took off his sodden socks and draped them next to the shoes. Steam rose.

Barefoot and damp Neville tried to focus on his post, but found there was little, and what there was had 'pending' written all over it and could be ignored for some time. He looked at his watch. 9.05 am. He wanted a hot drink, but couldn't walk through the building without his shoes. He switched on his computer and tried to shake himself out of the lethargy which was threatening to triple the length of his working day.

'Pull yourself together, Meatcher,' he spoke to his reflection on the screen. 'Got to keep busy.'

This was hardly the work ethic speaking. His desire to be occupied and diverted had little to do with wanting to be productive, and a lot to do with wanting to avoid replaying the embarrassing events of the night before in his rather hung over head.

An idea came to him; he started tapping keys with something approaching enthusiasm. *Medieval Cooking,* he typed, then hit 'search'. A long list of sites presented itself.

He chose one and read an extract from a medieval recipe.

Kutte a swan in the rove of the mouthe toward the brayne elonge and lete him blede, and kepe the blode for chawdewyn; or elles knytte a knot on his nek.

'Yeuch,' said Neville. 'Somehow I don't think slashed swan would be well received in Nettlecombe.'

He searched on. In no time at all he was transported back, away from his mundane surroundings, to another world, a world where poverty and excess could be seen on the same page. Where feast day banquets sat beside concoctions of the basest ingredients flavoured with longing and stirred with desperation. No creature was too grand or too humble to be considered inedible. From the whale to the snail through a crispy pig's tail and a bucket of tripe in a potent cocktail of blood and entrails – everything was a potential comestible. Swan and peacock, gull and woodcock, flattened to spatchcock or brought to the table with feathers in place, garlanded and paraded, and carried shoulder high on pewter platters to the Lord and his cohorts. Meanwhile, down in the stifling kitchens, maids and boys supped boiled blood and vinegar, seasoned with their own sweat. On luckier days the lowly might dine on pudding of capon neck, whilst their masters sliced slivers of seal in a meal of noise and carousing, with strong ale arousing the revellers, spurring them on to lewdness and dancing. Every day the cooks would strive to invent yet more glorious dishes and ingenious menus to display their skills and disguise the truth of what they were eating. They coddled and curdled and spiced and diced and chopped and devilled and stuffed and dreamed up an endless variety of fare. Honey toasts, raspberry soups, comfits and daryoles, all as labour spending as was possible.

Neville was yanked back to the present day by a brisk rapping on his door, followed by the arrival of Luke Philips. Had he been blindfolded, Neville could have swiftly identified the youth by his trademark aftershave. Looking at the boy in front of him Neville doubted he actually shaved at all.

'The point of knocking,' Neville told him, 'is to wait for a response before entering the room. Did you miss that module at management school?'

'Sor-reee!' said Luke. He stood frowning at Neville, then his gaze shifted to the radiator.

Neville saw him notice the shoes and socks. He straightened his back.

'You've never worked in Japan, have you Philips?' he asked.

'No. Why, have you?'

'Oh yes, a few years ago. Before I came here,' Neville lied. 'Fascinating place. Know a thing or two about business, the Japanese. I was lucky enough to meet one of the true masters of the Shinto Way of Planning Management. And you know the first thing he taught me? The most crucial thing?'

Luke shook his head, leaning forwards a little.

'Feet,' said Neville. 'No real businessman in Japan would dream of keeping his shoes on in the office. *"He who traps the sole entombs the soul"*. That's what they believe. Only with the feet bare can a man truly utilise his management skills. Remember that, Philips. Remember and learn.'

'Really? Amazing,' said Luke. There was a short pause then he asked, 'And do they also say *"He who wears a wet towel on his head looks a complete twat."*?'

Neville scowled.

'What do you want, Philips?'

'Mr Harris asked me to give you this,' he lobbed a brown folder onto the desk. 'It's the planning application for the development at Withy Hill Farm.'

'Yes, thank you. I can read.' Neville pushed the file to one side, and went back to his computer. Without looking up he said, 'With all your qualifications you won't need a map to find your way out, will you, Philips?'

Alone again, Neville peered at the plans on his desk. A quick browse revealed them to be detailed and well prepared. He experienced a sudden flashback to the lovely Lucy lying beneath him on his kitchen table. With a sigh he closed the folder and returned to studying his monitor.

'Give me Medieval England any day,' he said.

At Honeysuckle Cottage, Rose and Baby were going about their daily chores. Baby lay on his tartan rug on the living room floor practicing passing a rattle from one hand to the other, while his mother dusted. Not that there was any dust. The flicking of a clean damp cloth was purely preventative. The miniature cottages on the mantelpiece gleamed; the permanently empty crystal vase sparkled; the television screen shone. No corners were cut. Rose crouched down to run her duster along the stripped pine skirting boards. As she did so, something caught her eye. She peered closer. A small silver object was wedge behind the radiator. Using the ornamental brass poker from the hearth she managed to free what turned out to be Ryan's missing mobile phone. She turned the unfamiliar object over in her hands. Ryan never let her use it.

Don't touch it,' he had warned her. 'It's not made for clumsy great hands like yours. You'll only break it. Have you any idea how much this thing cost? No, of course you haven't.'

Rose risked wiping it gently with her cloth and even allowed herself a little smile. Surely he would be pleased she had found it, after all the fuss he had made about it being lost. But somehow it would be her fault that it had slipped behind the radiator; something she had done. Better not to be the one who found it. Better to put it somewhere safe where he could find it himself later. She decided to place it on the mantelpiece beside the clock.

She was about to do just that when Baby let out a sharp cry, having managed to smack himself smartly on the nose with his rattle. Rose hurried to him, picking him up and making soothing noises. His sobs subsided and he began to gurgle happily again as she held him. It was only then that she noticed he had got hold of the phone and was squeezing buttons with his busy little fingers.

'Oh no! You mustn't do that, sweetheart. Here, give it back to Mummy, there's a good boy.'

Baby was not keen to give up his new toy, so that by the time Rose rescued it from his clutches the thing was bleeping and flashing. She returned Baby to his rug and stared at the phone, frantically searching for a way to switch it off. As she squinted at the small screen she saw there was something written. *Saved message,* it said at the top, and then underneath words scrolled by.

Hi Hotstuff. Can u get away again Friday night? If so, meet me @ The Larches @ 8. I'll bring Champagne, u bring fab body of yours. Love Sugarplum.

Rose read the message again. And again. Of course she knew about Ryan's infidelities but had always managed to close her mind to them. This one could not so easily be ignored. It was right there, in her house, in her hand. Too close to Baby. Too close.

She chose what turned out to be the right button to switch off the phone, then carefully wedged it back behind the radiator. She looked at Baby playing so innocently on his rug. She knelt down beside him and held his dear little hand.

'Something will have to be done, Baby,' she told him. 'Something will have to be done.'

But what?

She picked him up and wandered through the house and eventually into the back garden. She completed a slow circuit, pausing to show Baby the bright new ferns in the bottom hedge. Returning across the lawn the door into the garage caught her eye. She went inside. The space was spotless and empty, save for a pressure hose, a toolbox, and a workbench. A book lay on top of the workbench. She read the title, *Haynes Manual – Subaru Impreza*. She picked it up, giving Baby a little smile, and together they headed back into the house, just in time to hear the post landing on the doormat.

Under the usual entreaties from charities and bargain offers from a nearby DIY store was a slim white envelope addressed to Rose. She turned it over in her hand several times before opening it and unfolding the crisp cream paper.

Dear Mrs Behr,

We are delighted to inform you that your Baby has been judged the winner of the regional final of the Beautiful Babes Competition. We therefore have pleasure in enclosing a cheque for £500, shopping vouchers for Horrocks Department Store, Bournemouth, to the value of £500, and entry details for the National Final, which is to be held in London the week after next....

Rose gasped and beamed at Baby, who gave a gummy grin in reply.

'Oh goodness, Baby! London! Imagine that. Imagine.'

Fliss sat at the kitchen table and dialled Daniel's number. She rarely troubled him at work, but hadn't been able to get the idea of a laboratory at Withy Hill Farm out of her head. Daniel could do some digging for her.

'Hi, Babe,' he answered the phone quickly, but Fliss could hear him tapping away at his keyboard.

'Hi, Dan. Look, I know you're busy, but I've got a favour to ask.'

'For you, my sweet, anything. Shoot.'

'I want you to find out all you can about Withy Hill Farm Enterprises. There must be stuff on the Internet.'

'No problem. What exactly am I trying to discover?'

'I'm not sure yet. Something's not right up there.'

'Ooh, sounds spooky.'

'I saw some plans. They want to build a laboratory.'

'On a chicken farm?'

'Quite.'

'Just a sec, I'll do a quick search. Looking forward to this weekend, by the way. Should be able to get away early for a change, well in time for nosh on Friday, so get your best frock ironed and I'll take you out somewhere.'

'I'm not sure I possess a frock.'

'OK, just your underwear and a mink coat, then.'

'Ha, ha.'

'A man can dream, can't he?'

'Not if it involves me and fur, he can't.'

'Ah, here we are. Withy Hill info. Hmm, nothing obviously sinister, they are part of a group. I'll look up the parent company later and download some stuff for you. All looks pretty innocent so far.'

'Keep looking. I smell a rat.'

'That would be a lab rat, I suppose?'

'You are so much less funny than you think you are, Dan.'

'But you love me anyway, right?'

'See you Friday.'

As she finished her call the back door burst open and Rhian appeared.

'What are you doing home?' Fliss wanted to know.

'I live here.'

'You know what I mean, it's not three o'clock yet. Why aren't you at school?'

'The scuzzy teacher called in sick and they couldn't find a replacement, so we got an early bus. Okay?'

'We?'

'Yeah, I brought a friend home with me. I suppose that is allowed?'

'Of course, you know I like to meet your friends, especially new ones.'

Rhian called back through the door.

'Mum's cool, come in Sam.'

Sam turned out to be a short, dark haired, solemn looking girl, with heavy brows and thick-rimmed glasses. She stood out from Rhian's previous friends by her extreme and unexpected squareness. She even offered Fliss a firm handshake.

'Pleased to meet you, Mrs Horton.'

'Please call me Fliss. It's very good to meet you, too, Sam. Is that short for Samantha?'

'It's just Sam.'

'Right. Do you live in Barnchester, Sam? Have you let your Mum know where you are? You're welcome to stay for supper, or for the night if you like.'

'Yes, I do live in Barnchester. And yes, I have informed my parents of my whereabouts. And yes, I would like to stay if it's not inconvenient.'

'Not at all. What sort of thing do you like to eat? I'll rustle up come tea.'

'My family is committed to a vegan diet.'

'Oh, I see. I'm a vegetarian myself...'

'Mum, Sam's not just a veggie, she's a proper vegan.'

'I know, don't panic, I'll make a batch of nut burgers and I'll be really careful about what I put in them.'

'Thank you very much, Mrs Horton.'

There was a short silence. Fliss noticed Rhian was grinning, clearly impressed by her new friend's strangeness.

'Sam's mother was at Greenham Common, Mum. Her oldest brother was born there. How cool is that? And Sam's been on six demonstrations. Six!'

'Well, that's wonderful,' said Fliss. 'What were you protesting against?'

'A variety of things. We believe in action, be it a march, a silent protest, or something more direct.'

'Direct? You mean tying yourself to the railings outside 10 Downing Street, or throwing yourself under a horse?' Fliss risked finding out if Sam had a sense of humour.

'If the cause warrants it.'

Clearly she did not.

'Well, better not let you two go to the races then.'

'Mum, do you have to be so flippant?' Rhian was cringing. 'Just because Sam actually believes in stuff ...'

'I don't doubt her sincerity, Rhian, I just don't want you doing anything rash.'

'No-one said we were going to do anything.'

'True, but Sam here is clearly an old hand, having been on six marches ...'

'Demonstrations,' Sam corrected.

'I beg your pardon, six demonstrations. You're new to all this. I'm your mother, I get to do the worrying and fussing; you get to be embarrassed and frustrated. That's the way it works.'

'Sam's parents go with her on the demos, they don't fuss.'

'OK, next outraged uprising of the population we'll all go. I'll make vegan sandwiches, how about that?'

'Mrs Horton,' Sam adjusted her glasses and regarded Fliss with a long suffering face. 'We believe demonstrations to be manifestations of the collective subconscious. Indeed, the French for a public demonstration is *une manifestation*. As such it is up to the individual to give voice to that subconscious whenever the need arises. This may not necessarily be in the context of a nationwide protest.'

'Well, I can't argue with that,' said Fliss.

'C'mon, Sam, let's go upstairs.' Rhian took her friend's bag and led the way. 'Give us a shout when grub's ready, Mum.'

CHAPTER SEVEN

Rose waited until Baby was properly asleep before she changed. She had spent time earlier in the day selecting suitable clothes. Now she struggled into an old pair of dark grey jogging pants and slipped on a black hoodie of Ryan's. She pulled the hood up and closed the zip to her chin. She tiptoed into Baby's room to check on him one more time before going downstairs.

In the sitting room she positioned the portable part of the baby alarm beside the telephone. Next she retrieved Ryan's mobile from behind the gas fire where she had hidden it. With great care she switched it on and dialled her own number. When the house phone rang she answered it at once, checked the connection, then placed the receiver on the table next to the baby monitor. She picked up the cotton wool pad she had ready and taped it over the keypad of the mobile to safeguard against pressing some crucial button by mistake.

At the front door she paused, hand on the latch, and looked anxiously up the stairs. No sound came from Baby's room, and he rarely woke in the evenings, but still she hesitated at the idea of leaving him, even for twenty minutes. But go she must. Her mind was made up. The mobile would allow her to listen in via the baby monitor, and she could be home again in less than ten minutes if necessary. She picked up the small bag of things she would need later, then left quietly.

Outside the air was thick with the promise of thunder. At nearly ten o'clock summer dusk was darkening to night. Rose walked briskly, head down, skirting the green so as to be less noticeable. She turned left past Brook Terrace, then climbed the stile onto the footpath that would take her across the meadows. The field was level and recently cropped by cattle. Rose knew the route well from childhood. The path headed west towards the neighbouring village of Mile Compton, and emerged on the lane directly opposite the gravel drive of Holme View.

Rose's breath became ragged as she pressed on. She was unaccustomed to such a brisk pace but didn't want to be away from Baby a moment longer than was absolutely necessary.

In a few short minutes she arrived at the house. From the front it appeared uninhabited, but as Rose crept past the *For Sale* sign and, around to the back, she could see light thrown down through a rear bedroom window. Fortunately, Ryan's Impreza was parked tight against the house and so remained in helpful darkness.

Rose paused to look up at the open window. Voices, unclear but identifiable, could be heard. The occasional laugh, a swear word, a giggle. In the background, the music was slow and smoochy.

At that moment a figure appeared at the window. It was Ryan, wearing only his boxer shorts. The designer ones he had recently treated himself to. Rose froze, breath held. Ryan threw out a cigarette stub, declared the night sticky as you like, then disappeared back into the room.

Rose breathed again, then turned her attention to Ryan's beloved car. She took the spare keys from her bag, pointed them at the car, and squeezed. The car chirruped and flashed once, then was mercifully silent again. Rose carefully opened the driver's door. There were two sunken screws on the underneath of the seat which secured a small panel. These she removed to expose the workings of the seat-heating system. Next she pulled from her bag a small plastic tub. Even though the prawn and crab mix was fresh it was already beginning to smell. She tipped the fish into the inside of the seat, taking care not to spill any on the floor, then replaced the panel.

The sounds from the bedroom had taken on a more basic and animal nature by now. Rose's mouth set in a determined line. She reached across the dashboard and shone her torch into the demisting vent at the bottom of the windscreen. From her bag she took the pea-sized bead she had removed from one of Baby's rattles. She dropped it into the vent, listening to it bounce through its bagatelle journey to the lowest point possible.

She was in the process of putting away her things when a muffled sound made her heart thump and milk surge through her breasts. She clamped the mobile phone to her ear. Baby stirred, murmured, belched lightly, sighed, then slept quietly once more.

Rose moved quickly now. She was able to firmly close the door and reset the alarm without fear of being heard, the noises from the bedroom assuring her that Ryan's attention was elsewhere.

She pulled the hood of her top tight over her head and hurried away without bothering to glance up at the bedroom window. Once on the footpath she risked using her torch, and was able to return to happily sleeping Baby in no time at all.

The threatened thunderstorms of the night before had not yet materialised, and in Neville's flat the sultry heat of the day outside was merging with the steamy heat of the cooking inside, producing an unpleasant level of humidity. Even Cilla had decamped to the relative cool of the bedroom. Neville, however, was a man with a mission, and as such he barely noticed his uncomfortable working conditions.

'Now let's see, "For the Daryole," ' he read, ' "take marrow, cloves, mace, ginger and wine and let it boil and add some cream ..." hmm. Well, we're doing without the marrow, and let's try nutmeg proper. Sod it, where did I put my grater?'

As he gathered ingredients and weighed and measured and mixed he hummed along to Purcell's *Fairy Queen*, being the best he could do in the way of medieval music. It was the only time Neville ever hummed - when he was cooking, and when it was going well. He was excited at the prospect of recreating a centuries old dish *à la Meatcher*, and was secretly confident about his chances in the fundraiser recipe competition. The thought of being included in one of Claude Lambert's books was, for him, the ultimate motivation. He had barely started assembling his new pudding, however, when he was interrupted by the buzz of his doorbell.

'What now?' he wiped his hands and stomped crossly down the stairs to the front door. His mood was not improved by the sight of Cynthia in an alarming summer dress.

'Neville, my dear boy, I am so relieved to find you alive and well.'

She pushed past him and thudded up the stairs before he had a chance to stop her.

'Of course I'm alive, why wouldn't I be?'

'I haven't been able to raise you on the telephone, either here or at your office. They said you were busy there, naturally, but as time went by I began to wonder if they were not hiding some terrible truth. I simply had to come and seek you out.'

'Your concern is touching, Cynthia, but as you can see I am in one piece ...'

'I think,' Cynthia adopted a coquettish tone and wagged a playful finger at him, 'that you have been a naughty boy, Neville.'

'Naughty?'

'Why yes, you haven't been returning my calls. I think you've been playing games with little Cynthia.'

Neville struggled to marry the words 'little' and 'Cynthia'.

'I think,' she went on, a coy smile rearranging her too pink lipstick, 'that you wanted me to come and find you. Is that so, Neville?' She leaned back a little against the kitchen table and toyed with her pearls.

It was difficult not to draw comparisons between the solid, ruddy-cheeked woman in front of Neville, and the luscious, peachy-skinned girl who had stood in the same spot only a few days before. It was not a fair contest, and Cynthia did not come out of the encounter well.

'Look,' said Neville,' I'm sorry if I haven't called, I have been very busy at work. And at home, as you can see.' He gestured towards the paraphernalia about them, then regretted doing so.

'Oh, Neville, are you working on your entry for the fundraiser? How wonderful. Let me see what you're doing. Do tell me what it's going to be.' She turned and began peering into bowls.

'I'd really rather not discuss it at this stage,' Neville forced himself between her and the table.

'Oh, is it a secret?' Cynthia made no attempt to take the hint and move back.

'Not a secret, just, well, I'm still experimenting,' Neville mustered a smile and took Cynthia's arm, turning her gently towards the sitting room.

'Why don't you sit down for a minute. I'll make some tea.' Much as he wanted rid of the woman, Neville had first to deal with the immediate problem of getting her away from his Daryole. She was right about him being secretive. He most certainly did not want anyone, especially Cynthia, getting sneak previews of his creation.

Cynthia was more than willing to take to the sofa.

'This is cosy,' she said, stroking the old leather and leaning back in a relaxed fashion. 'You make some tea, Neville, then hurry back and tell me what you're dreaming up to impress Monsieur Lambert.'

As Neville clattered about with cups and saucers back in the kitchen he began to feel more and more trapped. He so wanted to be perfecting his recipe, and he so did not want to be having tea with Cynthia, who already looked as if she had settled onto his sofa for the rest of the day. He carried the tray of tea things in and set it on the coffee table.

'Shall I be mother?' Cynthia didn't wait for a reply, but sat forward and arranged the cups. As she shifted position her petunia-patterned dress gaped dangerously at the front, displaying more than was sensible in the way of vintage cleavage.

Neville hesitated before sitting down next to her. Opposite would have left him nowhere to look other than her startling bosom.

'Now,' Cynthia patted his knee as she handed him his tea, 'at least give me a clue or two. Is it a meat dish? Something with fish, perhaps?'

'All I'm prepared to say at this stage is that it is a pudding.'

'A pudding! Oh, how marvellous. I can't wait. I myself toyed with the idea of something based on chocolate, but I decided against. Too much temptation. I'd be forever picking and nibbling while I tried it out, and a girl has to look after her figure, you know.' She gave a little laugh.

Neville swigged his tea.

'Anyway,' Cynthia went on, 'the reason I've been trying so urgently to contact you this week is that I have news. There's to be an extraordinary meeting of NHEC, next week, Thursday evening, up at Withy Hill Farm. I know you'll be as excited as I am for Claude himself has promised to attend. Isn't that wonderful?'

'Really? He's really coming to the meeting?' Neville was impressed.

'He wants to meet all the key players in the event. Check that we're doing a good job, I shouldn't wonder. I must say I'm looking forward to it. Can I count on you to be there?'

'Cynthia, wild horses wouldn't keep me away.'

'Splendid. Now, one lump or two?'

The back garden of 3 Brook Terrace shimmered in the afternoon heat. The sun's rays blasted through the hazy air, stripped of their brilliance, but losing none of their warmth. Fliss stretched out on her threadbare lounger. It wasn't perfect sunbathing weather, but she was content to be outside, lying down, and with the prospect of two cleaning-free days ahead of her. The musical sound of ice cubes in a long drink tempted her to open one eye.

'Here you are, my gorgeousness,' Daniel handed her a brimming glass, 'One expertly assembled, medium-strength, maximum refreshment guaranteed, Pimms. Very healthy – more fruit than you could shake a stick at.' He sat down on the wooden deck chair next to her.

'Mmm, thanks Dan.' She sipped her drink and savoured the moment. The weekend was going well. Daniel had, as promised, arrived early enough the previous evening to take her out to dinner. They had enjoyed a delicious meal at the Thai restaurant in Barnchester, and an equally delectable night of sex, followed by a rare lie-in. Even Rhian had been uncharacteristically mellow. Moments such as these gave Fliss hope that maybe, just maybe, she and Daniel had a workable relationship, and that one day the three of them could actually amount to a family of some sort. She sat up and smiled at her lover.

'Not so bad is it, this weekend country retreat routine?'

'Can't complain,' Daniel agreed. 'Good food, good company, dangerous amounts of fresh air, flowers flowering, bees buzzing, all charmingly bucolic and stress free.'

'See, told you it could work.'

'Never doubted it for a nano-second. Even Rhian seems to be coming round to the idea.'

'You noticed the difference in her?'

'She hasn't tried to bite me once this weekend. A person notices a thing like that.' He glugged his Pimms. 'What did you do? Bribe her? Put happy pills in her meusli?'

'She's made a friend – Sam. A girl, before you ask. They're in the same class at school. She's coming over today, so if you're lucky you'll get a glimpse of her.'

'Easy on the eye, is she?'

'Not exactly. She has her own special appeal. Main thing is Rhian thinks she's wonderful, she doesn't appear to be into drugs, or drink, or boys, she's very polite, and helps Rhi with her homework.'

'Sounds too good to be true. What's the catch?'

'I'm not sure that there is one, but she is a bit, well, strange.'

'How strange?'

'She's very serious. Her parents sound like lifelong activists, and it's certainly rubbed off on her.' Fliss shrugged, 'Might be a good thing, I suppose.'

'Can't wait to meet her.' He leant forward and ran a finger down Fliss's bare, brown arm. 'Does this mean they'll be going out together later and giving us the opportunity to run naked through the house?'

'You can run, I'll watch. I feel far too lazy for anything so energetic.' She drained her glass. 'Now, fetch me another one of those, will you, and bring the stuff you dug out on Withy Hill, I want to read it.'

Fifteen minutes later Fliss was pacing up and down the garden, print-outs in hand, too furious to keep still.

'This is terrible, it's a nightmare.' She waved the papers in the air to reinforce her point. 'I can't believe it. We leave London and move down here for a better, healthier, safer, more natural way of life only to find we're in Frankenstein's sodding back yard. How can something like this be going on and nobody know about it?'

Fliss, Babe, calm down. Don't you think you might be jumping to conclusions a bit here? I read all that stuff and I didn't see anything so terrible.'

'What? You are joking! Withy Hill Farm is owned by Jefferson Inc, a humungous American corporation who, and I quote, "lead the field in the quest for new and innovative methods of bio diverse gene development and hybridised farming." That's genetic engineering, Dan. That's cloning, or mixing pigs with sheep, or God knows what.'

'You don't know that for sure. And anyway, just because the parent company might be into dodgy stuff doesn't mean anything like that is going on at Withy Hill Farm, does it?'

'Oh no? So why are they building a laboratory, then?'

'New types of chicken feed?' he offered.

'Daniel, why are you refusing to see this? It's here in black and white, why won't you admit it?'

'Look, I just think a little information can be misleading. There's probably nothing sinister going on, and I refuse to have our weekend ruined by something that might not even be happening.'

'Sod the weekend! There are more important things than having a good time, you know.'

'I know, I know. All I'm saying is, don't let it stress you out. I'm sure there's nothing to worry about, but ...' he held up his hands to fend off her interruption, '... on Monday I will try and find out more for you. Just to put your mind at rest.'

Fliss narrowed her eyes at him.

'And would you tell me if you found something you knew I wouldn't like?'

'Of course I would, sweetness.'

'Promise?'

'Promise,' he went over to her and slipped his arm around her waist. 'Now come and sit down and stop getting your thong in a twist.'

'I never wear a thong.'

'Bloomers then. Knickers. Panties.'

'Please, not panties. Panties are what drooling men of a certain age call them.'

Daniel kissed her lightly.

'What you need, young Lady, is a holiday.'

The tension quickly returned to Fliss's body.

'You're not going to bully me about holidays again, not now, please Dan.'

Now it was Daniel's turn to bristle. He stepped away from her.

'Well excuse me. Here's me thinking you might actually like to go on holiday with me, and all the time I'm just "bullying" you.'

'You know we can't agree on how long, or where, or when, or what to do about Rhian. And I've got other things to think about right now.'

'When haven't you? If you go on avoiding talking about it much longer there won't be any holidays left to choose from. I'm beginning to think that would quite suit you. Oh dear, everywhere is booked up. Problem solved. Forget the whole thing. Stay at home instead.'

'Oh, Dan ...'

'I'm getting a little tired of this, to tell you the truth. All I want is to take you somewhere warm and wonderful for a couple of weeks in the summer. What the hell is so wrong with that?'

'Nothing. But my life is a bit more complicated than that. I'm sorry, but that's just how it is.'

'If Rhian doesn't want to come with us, that's fine by me. She sulked her way through the entire fortnight last year anyway. She's a big girl now. Surely she could stay with a friend. She'd probably love it – a bit of independence. Or is that what really bothers you? That maybe she might be able to manage without you for a few days. Enjoy it even. Your baby's growing up, Fliss. Get over it.'

Fliss opened her mouth to reply, but missed her chance. Rhian came bouncing out of the house, followed by Sam.

'Sam's here, Mum. Okay if we make some pancakes? She's brought soya-milk.'

'Sure, why not? Hello there, Sam, how are you?'

'Very well thank you, Mrs Horton.'

Rhian gestured towards Daniel.

'Oh, this is Daniel. My mother's boyfriend.'

Sam held out her hand.

'Pleased to meet you,' she said.

'Hello, Sam,' Daniel was all smiles again. 'I've heard a lot about you. Fliss tells me you're quite the anarchist.'

'Actually, I said activist ...' Fliss corrected him.

Daniel laughed.

'Well, which are you, Sam?'

She considered the question for a moment, then said 'There are a number of crucial differences between being anti-establishment and being anarchic. Indeed, the state of anarchy is at odds with social progression, which I believe comes from a base of stability.'

'Yeah, right,' Daniel and Fliss exchanged glances.

Rhian pulled at Sam's arm.

'C'mon, Sam. I'm starving.'

'Do you want a lift into town later?' Fliss called after them.

'No thanks, Mum. We'll be in my room. We've got stuff to do.'

After they had gone Daniel flopped back in his chair.

'See what you mean about her,' he said. 'Seriously weird.'

'Hhmmm,' Fliss agreed. 'Odd they don't want to go out. They spend hours squirrelled away.'

'Homework?'

'I'm not so sure. I may be wrong, but I have a strong hunch that those two are up to something.'

CHAPTER EIGHT

When Fliss felt the first fat drops of rain she turned her face up to the sky. The day had been tryingly hot, with groans of thunder becoming more frequent and pronounced with each passing hour. Two cleaning shifts had left her drained and grumpy.

'Go on then!' she shouted up at the clouds. 'You've been burping and growling all bloody day. Let's have some rain!'

She stood in the middle of the lane at the top of the hill and waited. Seconds later she got what she asked for. It rained so hard that the water bounced off the tarmac and soaked her a second time on the way back up. Fliss laughed and shook her head, holding out her arms as the water coursed over her body.

'Yes! That's more like it!' she cried, whooping with glee as the rain washed away the dust of two sitting rooms, a lounge bar, and a study. Not to mention the lingering odour of the gents' loo.

'That feels fantastic!' she shouted, allowing herself a little dance in the swiftly forming puddles at her feet.

It was some moments before she noticed the car which had stopped behind her. It sat, engine running, wipers wiping, driver squinting out at the mad woman blocking the road.

'Oh, sorry!' Fliss called. She trotted over to the driver's door and peered in. 'Sorry,' she said again.

The window lowered six inches and Ryan Behr looked up at her. Fliss recognised him as the estate agent who had found her the cottage.

'Hi!' She smiled at him and received a vague look that told her he barely recognised her.

'You alright?' he asked.

'Fine, thanks. Just on my way home.'

There was a painful silence. After a sigh and a nervous glance around the interior of his car Ryan spoke again.

'Want a lift, then?'

'Oh, yes. Yes please' Fliss hurried round to the other side of the car and climbed in. 'Phew, this is really very good of you. Oops, sorry, I'm dripping all over the place.' She smiled at Ryan, but his expression was one of ill concealed horror at the amount of water being squelched into his leather upholstery.

'Lucky for me you came along when you did,' Fliss went on. 'Quite refreshing, the rain, for a minute or two, but I'd have been pretty fed up with it by the time I'd walked home.'

Ryan silently put the car into gear and sped away, causing Fliss to remember to buckle up.

'Wow! My goodness, this goes fast, doesn't it? Hope there aren't any cyclists about. Suppose there wouldn't be in this weather.' Fliss paused, frowning, then sniffed carefully.

Ryan shot her a glance.

'What can you smell?' he demanded.

'Oh, nothing really ...'

'No, go on. You were sniffing. You can smell something, I know you can.' Ryan was plainly agitated.

'Well, I don't know. I thought maybe I could detect just the slightest whiff of ...'

'Yes?'

' ...fish?' Fliss offered.

Ryan slapped the steering wheel hard, making Fliss jump in her seat.

'I sodding knew it! Fish! It is fish.'

'It's really very faint.'

'That's not the point, is it? What's it doing in here? That's the point.'

'Maybe someone ate fish and chips in here,' Fliss suggested.

'No-one eats in my car,' said Ryan coldly.

'Ah, no, of course not.'

Ryan began sniffing energetically.

It's been in here for two days now, and it's getting worse. Thought I was imagining it, but you can smell it. So where the fuck is it coming from?'

Fliss offered no more suggestions.

'Oh, just drop me on the corner here, that'll be fine,' she said.

As quickly as it had started, the rain stopped. Ryan pulled up on a slight slope.

'Did you hear that?' He almost shouted at Fliss.

'What?'

'That rattling noise. There was a rattle. Somewhere in the dashboard.'

'I didn't hear anything.'

'It happens when I turn a certain type of corner, or go up a certain type of hill. Listen.' Ryan knocked the car back into gear and roared off once more, completing a dizzying circuit of the green before coming to a halt again.

'There! There, did you hear it that time?'

'No,' said Fliss, 'Sorry. Nothing.'

Ryan's knuckles tightened to white on the steering wheel.

'There is a sodding rattle somewhere. I know there is.'

'Well, thanks for the lift,' Fliss climbed out of the car quickly before Ryan could decide to go round again. 'Bye.'

She shut the door and stepped back to avoid a further soaking from the wake of the speeding car. Shaking her head she walked down the narrow road that took her to Brook Terrace.

Inside the house was in gloom. The storm clouds still blotted out the sun, and the lights weren't working.

'Great, a power cut. Just what I need.'

She dropped her bag on the kitchen table and called out.

'Rhian? Rhi, are you in?' Silence answered her question.

Fliss climbed the stairs and fumbled for a towel in the half-light of the bathroom. She rubbed her wet hair, then stepped out of her soggy clothes and put on a pink towelling robe of Rhian's. It was not yet six o'clock, but the afternoon had been a tedious, sticky one, and Fliss headed back downstairs to the fridge in search of wine. The mostly empty shelves were a sorry sight without their perky little light.

'Teenagers,' Fliss said aloud, squinting at the spaces where there had once been food. 'How can anyone eat so much and still have legs like pipe cleaners? At least she's not interested in my wine. Prefers Pooch, apparently.'

She took the bottle and a glass and made her way to the peace and comfort of the little sitting room. She had just enough energy left to light a candle to lift the gloom before subsiding into her favourite chair. She put her feet up on a beanbag and wriggled into her seat with a sigh. Eyes closed she sipped her drink.

'Fliss,' she told herself, 'this is bliss.'

Suddenly a tension stiffened her body. She lowered her feet to the floor very slowly and sat up. She opened her eyes and tugged the bathrobe down over her knees in the self-conscious movement of someone who senses they are not alone.

Cautiously she turned her head and peered across the room to the curtain rail over the low window. The small, shiny eyes which blinked back at her belonged to a very large, very orange, and very baffled looking chicken.

The automatic doors of the large, ultra-modern hotel glided open and Rose wheeled Baby through in his buggy.   This was not the sort of place she was used to. There was a strange sound level in the foyer; a curious mixture of business shoes on holiday carpet, with voices pitched somewhere between a laugh and a whisper. Everything that wasn't glass was chrome, so that each surface shone and gleamed and reflected distorted pictures of passing people.

Rose and Baby paused to take it all in. Their journey up to London on the train had been swift and trouble free, so that they were both quite calm and relaxed, given such an exciting day.   Rose had tried to speak to Ryan about Baby reaching the national finals of the competition, but she could tell he wasn't listening. Maybe if she had mentioned that they would have to go to London, or told him just how much the prize money was, perhaps then he would have paid attention. It had been obvious he was more concerned with his car and its peculiar problems. In any case Rose was satisfied that she wasn't keeping Baby's success a secret from him. It was up to him if he could not be bothered to be involved and therefore may have missed one or two interesting details.

Rose looked around for clues as to where she was supposed to go next. Everybody else seemed to know where they were going and to be striding about with such confidence and purpose and style. Rose caught sight of a blurred version of herself peering out from a piece of metal wall behind a potted palm. She straightened her shoulders and adjusted the collar of her beige mackintosh. She hoped she wouldn't have to take it off, as it was, by a very long way, the most up-to-date garment she possessed.   At last she spotted a notice board which directed Baby Competition contestants to the Wessex Room. Fifty yards more of blue speckled carpet brought her to heavy double doors.

Inside the enormous room all was barely controlled chaos. The space was divided into dozens of open-fronted cubicles, each containing a small table, and each displaying glamorous photographs of the occupying infant. Mothers, fathers, grandmothers and nannies fussed and fiddled with their babies, arranging them atop their tables variously on sheepskin rugs, satin quilts, or tartan throws. The adults bustled about, all noise and seriousness and barely contained excitement, while their offspring either sat mute and dazed, or shrieked and screamed at full volume.

'Can I see your entry card?'

A voice at Rose's shoulder broke through the cacophony.

'Sorry?'

'Your entry card,' the smart suited young woman stood, clipboard poised. The plastic tag on her sharp lapel stated her name as Beverly. 'I need your contestant number.'

Rose fumbled in her bag and found what was required.

'Lovely. Follow me, I'll show you to your booth.' She set off at a brisk pace and Rose hurried along behind, pushing Baby through the slalom of parked buggies and kit bags.

'Here we are. This is you – 43J.' Beverly stopped and looked at the dumbstruck Rose. 'Have you got everything you need? Hmmm? Something to put Baby on, a rug, perhaps? Some props?'

'Props?' Rose was gazing at the beautiful photos of Baby which had been supplied by the newspaper photographer.

'Yes, balloons, ribbons, banners, teddies. You know the sort of thing.'

'Oh, I'm not sure. He has brought his blue rabbit ...'

'Good. Lovely! You get yourself set up then, and I'll pop back and see you again in a mo. Okay?' Beverly turned on an impossibly high heel and sped back towards the door.

Rose stood where she was left, transfixed. Everyone in the room except her seemed to know what they were supposed to do. Ribbons and bows festooned the little tables, where babies sat dressed in gorgeous dresses or immaculate sailor suits. Parents cooed and cajoled their children into pretty poses. Hangers-on dashed here and there fetching extra equipment and refreshments. It all looked very professional and daunting, and not at all what Rose had expected. She stared at the woefully bare table next to her.

The tannoy squeaked into action.

'Ladies and Gentlemen,' a voice boomed, 'judging will commence in fifteen minutes. Fifteen minutes to judging.'

Rose looked down at Baby sitting so placidly in his buggy.

'Right, little one,' she took a deep breath. 'Let's see what we can do, shall we?'

Claude Lambert was a man whose appearance denied his profession. It wasn't simply that he was underweight (downright skinny, truth be told), it was more than that. His body looked somehow starved – undernourished! What little flesh he had clung limply to his bones. His face was equally spare and angular. Over all he gave the impression of being someone who had no interest in food whatsoever. A disadvantage for a chef, one might have thought. But not so, in this age of the Cult of Thin, Monsieur Lambert's emaciation sent a subliminal message to his fans – eat my food, and you won't get fat. Eat my sinful crab and lobster pate, my calorie-rich steak Diane, my sugar toxic fruit brulee, and you will not get fat. Eat as much as you like, don't hold back. Feast. Indulge. Eat, eat, eat! You will not get fat. Look at me!

So thinness, then, did not constitute a problem for our celebrity chef. What was seriously beginning to be a cause for concern amongst his entourage was another aspect of his appearance. It had to do with his skin. No matter that he was pale – what sensible person does not protect himself from the destructive rays of the sun? No matter that his skin appeared so taut over his frame, or so hairless on his limbs and chest, or so slightly soft and feminine. The man was dedicated to his art, after all, spending his time in a kitchen, and working so terribly hard. All this could be explained away and forgiven. What was harder to ignore with every passing day was the unlikely but undeniable blueness of his skin. Blueness in regards to flesh is not good, however you look at it. And blueness coupled with skinny spells cadaverous. And death is not health, is it? Eat my food and it could be the last thing you ever do is not an attractive sales pitch.

Naturally, any photographs of Claude, such as those on the jackets of his best-selling books, or on the walls of his restaurant, had been skilfully manipulated to remove all traces of blueness. Some went even so far as to give him a rosy glow. So it came as a surprise to Neville to come face to face with his hero at last and discover him indigo tinged.

Standing in the drawing room of Withy Hill Farm he stared at Claude as the two engaged in a bony handshake. He was aware of Michael Christian's voice beside him.

'Neville is quite the gourmet. A great fan of yours, Claude. Good man to have on our team for the fundraiser.'

Claude managed a tight smile, a dry sniff, and a nod.

Neville stopped staring.

'It's an honour, a privilege, to meet you, Mr Lambert,' he said.

'Claude' muttered Claude.

'I'm sorry?'

'Claude. Call me Claude,' repeated the chef only a fraction louder.

He had a curious accent. His French origins were clearly evident, particularly in the strangled diphthongs. What was unexpected was the cockney twang, acquired from teenage years spent living with an uncle in Mile End. This collision of cultures put his name somewhere between 'cloud' and 'cleared'. On top of this, the man spoke so softly, as if every breath was an effort, that whatever he said was hard to make out.

Michael poured drinks. 'Sadly, the lovely Lucy cannot be with us tonight. I think you've met her, Neville? Claude's PA, yes?'

Neville began to blush, his memories of Lucy still all too fresh in his mind.

'However,' Michael went on, handing round whiskies, 'We are, of course, expecting Cynthia.' He paused to take a large swig of his drink. 'Not sure who else, still,' he slapped Neville on the back, 'as long as the three of us are here we can get this thing sorted, no trouble at all. Isn't that right, Nev?'

Neville winced. He disliked his name being shortened, particularly by people he barely knew. It surprised him that Michael Christian should be so apparently keen to have him involved. He had never given him the time of day before.

As if by way of an answer Michael said to Claude, 'I believe I mentioned Neville's an important guy hereabouts. He's in planning at County Hall in Barnchester, a man of influence.'

'Actually,' Neville interrupted, 'I really don't have any influence at all. Not over planning decisions. Not my responsibility.'

'Ahh, you're too modest, Nev.'

'It's true.'

'Don't sell yourself short, man.'

'I'm just saying ...'

'I understand,' Michael tapped the side of his nose, 'Can't be seen to be playing favourites. Don't have to spell it out. We know where you're coming from.' His wink had all the subtlety of a pantomime.

The rapping of a brass knocker, followed by distant, contained barking from Eric and Vinnie, heralded Cynthia's arrival. She came full of apologies and explanations.

'So sorry I'm late, everyone, unforgivable of me. Ah! Monsieur Lambert, we meet again. Please believe me, I would have been here on time had I not first called for Miss Siddons only to find she has been laid low by a summer cold, and sends her apologies. Ditto from Pam, my second stop *en route*. Pressure of work, she tells me. Why people cannot organise themselves properly I shall never understand. But there it is, *et voila, j'arrive toute seule,*' she gave a girlish laugh in Neville's direction. 'At least I know I can count on you, dear Neville. So good to have a friend one can rely on.' She stepped forwards and laid a hand on his arm.

Neville smiled weakly and moved to the table, drawing out a chair for Cynthia by way of an excuse for evading further physical contact.

'Shall we get started?' he suggested.

'Ah, enthusiasm! Marvellous!' Cynthia actually batted her eyelids at him as she sat down.

Neville was about to escape to the safety of the far side of the table, but Cynthia patted the seat next to her firmly.

'Come, come, *mon cher*. I need my right hand man at my right hand, after all.'

Michael and Claude joined them at the table, Michael replenishing glasses.

'Drink for you, Cynthia?' he asked.

'No thank you. I prefer to keep a clear head. Though I see, Claude, that you enjoy our Scottish beverage,' she said, watching Claude knock back another double.

Claude sniffed twice.

'I believe a little liquor is a fine digestive,' he said.

'Quite,' said Cynthia, putting on her glasses. 'Now, to business. We have made some progress during our earlier meetings, and, after several lengthy telephone conversations with your assistant, Claude, I believe the definitive outline for the event now exists.'

'Well done, Cynthie,' Michael congratulated her. 'Good news, eh, Claude?'

Claude gave an edgy Gallic shrug and another sniff.

Cynthia peered at him over her glasses.

'Do you have a cold, Monsieur?'

'Eh? Non.' He shook his head, fidgeting in his seat and rubbing his eyes. 'I am maybe a little tired.'

'Of course. I understand. Neville, would you be so kind as to hand these out?'

Neville took the neatly stapled piles of paper and did as he was told. It did not escape his notice that Claude took no interest in the details in front of him.

'I must say, Claude,' he said as he sat down again, 'I'm surprised you can find time in your busy schedule to fit in a humble little do like ours. Delighted, of course, but surprised.'

Michael was quick to answer for him.

'Oh, Claude knows what a fantastic opportunity this is for him to meet his public. Go hands on with his fans. It's great publicity for his new book, his restaurant, and for Withy Hill Farm, of course, to launch our partnership.'

Claude shifted uncomfortably in his chair. 'Yes,' he confirmed, 'it is for this reason I do it.'

'Right,' said Neville, 'great. London, Paris, Nettlecombe Hatchet – an obvious combination of venues for your enterprises.'

'What does he say?' Claude demanded hoarsely of Michael, who ignored him.

'Claude is an astute business man,' he told Neville, 'he knows what he's doing.'

Cynthia rustled her papers pointedly.

'Of course he does. Now, shall we get on?'

'I have to use the WC,' Claude announced suddenly, getting to his feet.

'What? Oh, Okay.' Michael ushered him out of the room. 'I'll show you where it is.'

After they had gone Cynthia tutted loudly.

'Really, artistic temperament. I do hope Monsieur Lambert will be able to deliver on the day. The man doesn't look at all well.'

'You noticed that too?' said Neville.

'He is rather an odd colour, don't you think? And all that sniffing, perhaps he suffers from hay fever.'

'I've never known hay fever turn anyone blue. He looks terrible. Not what I expected at all. He seems so ... flat. Where's the enthusiasm, the drive, the fire I've seen in him when he cooks on TV?' Neville shook his head. 'He's not the man I thought he was.'

Cynthia leant closer to Neville and gently patted his leg.

'*Courage, mon brave,* it is never easy to discover that one's heroes have feet of clay.'

Neville tensed with the effort of stopping himself removing Cynthia's hand from where it now rested on his thigh.

'I suppose it doesn't really matter,' he talked to cover his discomfort, 'It's his cooking that counts, his inspired recipes. Not how he looks.'

'Precisely. That is the reason people will flock to see him.'

'Even so,' Neville focussed intently on unfolding a paper clip, 'It's a shame we have a celebrity who appears devoid of personality. He's hardly the sort to make the party go with a swing, is he?'

Moments later Claude and Michael reappeared.

'Ahh, good,' said Cynthia, 'Now to business.'

'Yes, indeed, Madame,' said Claude, 'I am keen to know every little thing that you have planned. I truly believe this can be a fantastic day. For all of us, *formidable!*' He picked up the proposed schedule in front of him and studied it.

Neville, once again, found himself staring at Claude. The man seemed transformed. True, he was still blue, but now his eyes shone and his movements were quick, his gestures expansive and energetic, his whole demeanour altered.

'Yes, yes,' Claude enthused as he read. 'I can see how this will work. Wonderful, Madame Cynthia, together with the lovely Lucy you have created a masterpiece of the organising. I think it can be magnificent!' He reached across the table, grabbed her hand, and kissed it noisily. 'I salute you!'

'Oh, *Monsieur!*' Cynthia giggled and wriggled on her chair.

Neville kept his hands well out of reach in case this new improved version of Claude started kissing everyone. The man's transformation from warm corpse to *bon viveur* was startling, and, more than a little worrying.

CHAPTER NINE

Fliss walked purposefully along the pot-holed pavement, carrying the increasingly heavy box. Rhian and Sam trailed behind her, their bad moods slowing them down. They were now in the middle of the sizeable housing estate which was cruelly named Sunny Meadow. There was neither sun nor meadow. Teenagers roamed in packs like feral dogs. Smaller children swung on the remains of garden gates. Two of the pollarded plane trees were blackened stumps, the remainder looked scarred and sickly.

Fliss squinted at the number on the door in front of them.

'48 – is this it, Sam?'

Sam nodded.

Fliss put the box down and knocked on the door. After some time it was opened six inches, chain firmly in place. A large, middle-aged, male face looked out.

'Good morning,' said Fliss, a little too brightly.

'Not today!' growled the face before slamming the door.

Fliss tried again.

'No, wait. I'm not selling anything.' There was no reply so she pressed on. 'I, um, I've got something here which I believe belongs to you. You do keep one or two chickens, don't you?'

The door inched open once more.

Fliss pointed at the box.

'You see, my daughter and her friend, well, they're very fond of animals, and they were a little concerned that maybe this, er, this hen wasn't, well, very happy in her surroundings. Of course, I'm sure you know all about keeping chickens. Anyway, I'm afraid the girls got a bit carried away and sort of rescued the bird. Not that she needed rescuing.'

The face at last shifted his glare from Fliss to the box.

'Anyway, we've talked about it, and the girls have come to realise that what they did was wrong. So we've brought it back. I am sorry if you were worried. You know how impulsive teenagers can be.' She tried a weak smile.

The door closed again. There was a rattling before it opened once more. The heavy man stepped forward with surprising speed, snatched up the box, and disappeared inside without a word.

Fliss found herself staring at the re-slammed door. She turned to the girls.

'Satisfied?' Rhian's scowl was entrenched.

'We've done the right thing,' said Fliss.

'He didn't even say thank you for bringing her back, ignorant git! You didn't see the state of the place he's keeping those chickens. You've sent the poor thing back to die of some terrible disease.'

'Come on,' Fliss steered the girls back the way they had come. 'We've already had this argument. And this is not the place to discuss it further.'

They walked in silence, the argument following overhead. Not that there was anything much to be said – they had spent a long and exhausting evening hammering things out the night before. Even when Rhian had announced she was going to become a vegan like Sam, Fliss had been unable to be pleased. She had been a vegetarian for years, and her daughter had always refused to give up meat. Now she was friends with someone who persuaded her to break into garden sheds when she should be at school, and suddenly she wanted to live on Soya milk and sunflower seeds.

It wasn't until they were all on the bus heading out of Barnchester in the direction of Nettlecombe that Fliss tried once again to get Rhian to talk about the wrongs of chicken-napping.

'I know you feel very strongly about what you did, both of you,' she said. 'But you must see that you can't simply go around stealing things.'

'Liberating,' Sam corrected her.

'I'm afraid Mr Forty-Eight Sunny Meadows might not have seen it quite like that.'

'Sod the old fart.'

'Rhian, I was hoping you were going to take a more adult approach to this. Anyway, the conditions couldn't have been that bad – look how fat that chicken was. She must have been well-fed, at least.'

'That, Mrs Horton,' said Sam, 'is because she was a table bird.'

'Sorry?'

'Poultry bred for eating. That's what it's called. The reason she was so obese is that she had been stuffed with toxic amounts of unsuitable food to put more meat on her. Her housing was not the main issue here.'

'Oh, yes, I do see that's not very nice, but there are ways of registering your protest. Ways that don't involve breaking the law.'

'Right, Mum, like we could have talked to the creep and he'd have put her on the Atkins diet. I don't think so.'

'You could have talked to me. We could have come up with something together.'

Both girls gave Fliss a look of such scorn that she started to blush.

'I'd like to help. Surely you know that? If there's something that matters to you so much I want to know about it, to be involved. Just occasionally, can't you forget I'm your mother, Rhi, and see me as a human being? If nothing else, I might be useful, hmm? Might be able to do something?'

'Do something?' Rhian gave a derisive little laugh. 'You work at Withy Hill Farm, for that creep Christian. It's a chicken farm, in case you hadn't noticed. You'd hardly be my first choice of someone to help liberate exploited animals.'

Fliss shifted uncomfortably on the worn seat.

'Withy Hill has a reputation for looking after its livestock,' she said, though the words lacked conviction. Since discovering the plans for the laboratory and the truth about the farm's parent company, Fliss had been finding it increasingly difficult to justify earning money at the place.

Sam appeared to read her thoughts.

'As a matter of fact, my parents were discussing Withy Hill only the other night,' Sam said. 'Information has reached them that there are plans for new buildings on the site.'

'How did you know about that?' Fliss asked.

'Mum, do you mean to say that you knew about this?' Rhian rounded on her.

Sam went on. 'All local planning applications are subject to public scrutiny, although some notices are not posted as prominently as they should be. As part of our family policy of endeavouring to be guardians of our environment, we make it our business to monitor all new construction projects in the area.'

'Do you know what they're building?' Fliss asked.

'Our information is not that detailed,' Sam told her. 'However, given the nature and usual business of the conglomerate to which the farm belongs, we have reason to suspect they may be planning a research laboratory.'

'Did you know about this, Mum? Did you?' Rhian demanded.

Fliss hesitated just a fraction of a second too long before answering.

'Well, not exactly ...'

'How could you! How could you know what they were up to and still be a part of the place?'

'Now wait a minute. First, we don't know exactly what they are going to do with the new building – they could be developing new types of chicken feed for all we know. Second, maybe they won't get permission to build. Nothing has been decided.'

'That's true,' Sam agreed, 'but it can only be a matter of time.'

'What makes you say that?'

'The person who works at the planning office and oversees applications like this is known to us. He is also known to have attended meetings at Withy Hill, at night time. It's obvious there is collusion.' She turned to Fliss. 'As a matter of fact, he lives in your village.'

'In Nettlecombe? Well, who is he?'

'His name is Neville Meatcher. He lives in the flat above the Post Office.'

'I know which one he is,' cried Rhian, 'I've seen him coming out the front door. You know, Mum, the anorak on the battered bike.'

'Oh, yes, I think I know who you mean. But why would he ...'

'Why would anyone, Mrs Horton?' Sam's voice was grave as she turned to gaze out the window. 'They do say every man has his price.'

'Mum, you could talk to him.'

'What?'

'Go on, it'd be easy to bump into him – he only lives across the road,' Rhian's mouth was setting in that thin determined line Fliss dreaded. 'You said you wanted to be involved. You said you wanted to help. Okay, prove it.'

Rose cooked, as Baby sat happily in his bouncy chair, watching. It was nearly six o'clock and Ryan would be home soon. He would be tired and hungry and expect his tea. She chopped carrots and added them to the mince simmering on the hob. Shepherd's pie was always well received, which meant he wouldn't complain or make nasty remarks. Rose's own small salad was already waiting in the fridge.

She smiled at Baby. He didn't seem a bit tired after the exciting events of the previous day. The late afternoon sun slanted through the window and bounced off the shiny silver cup on the dresser. Rose couldn't resist pausing to read the inscription one more time.

Most Beautiful Babe

She still couldn't believe they had actually won the competition. Of course, she knew Baby was the most scrumptious child on the planet, but she had been so unprepared for the size of the event. All those people. All those cameras. And everybody else with beautiful shawls, rugs, balloons, ribbons and all sorts; and Baby sitting on that plain table with his nothing but his blue rabbit. The judges had liked that, they had told her so. Said something about simplicity, and the essence of being an infant, whatever that meant. And as if winning hadn't been enough – the cup, the cheering, the enormous amount of prize money, the jostling photographers – the lady from the modelling agency had been so nice, said such lovely things about Baby. Told Rose he had an exciting career ahead of him.

The rumble of the Subaru in the driveway shook Rose from her thoughts and sent her back to her cooking.

Ryan called from the hallway. 'Rose, tea ready yet?'

'About ten minutes.'

'I'll have a shower then,' he yelled.

Rose waited until she could hear the power shower working and then took down a small, unlabelled jar from the back of the herb shelf. She shook a small quantity of the curly, green leaves onto a board and chopped carefully. The more she chopped, the less they resembled the unfurling ferns by the compost heap. When they were fine as pixie dust she measured half a level teaspoon into the mince and stirred well. Three good shakes of Worcester sauce should cover any unfamiliar taste.

Rose found herself humming as she covered the meat with mashed potato and then placed the dish beneath the grill to brown.

A short time later the three of them were seated at their table, each with their own suppers. Rose nibbled her salad, Baby yummed down creamed carrots, and Ryan shovelled in the shepherd's pie.

'I've got to leave early tomorrow morning,' he told her through a mouthful of mash, 'got to take the car in to be checked.'

'Oh,' said Rose. 'Is there something wrong with it?'

'No, I just like getting up at the crack of sparrow sodding fart and wasting my time at the garage. Of course there's something wrong with it.'

'Oh dear, is it serious?'

Ryan did not answer straight away. He swigged at his bottle of lager for a moment.

'Dunno,' he said at last. 'Could be, I can't get to the bottom of it, but something's got to be done. Can't drive around with that ...' he glanced at Rose. 'Never mind, you don't understand about cars.'

Rose nodded and helped baby to some water from his beaker.

Ryan looked at his son, as he sometimes did.

'So, a winner, eh? First bloody prize, that's my boy.'

He punched Baby lightly on the shoulder in a rare gesture of playfulness.

'Mind you, not sure I like you two going up to London like that.'

'I did tell you ...'

'You told me he was in the finals, didn't say where, though, did you? Like to keep your little secrets, don't you, eh?'

'I didn't think you'd be interested.'

'Of course I'm interested – I'm paying for the sodding train tickets, aren't I? Or did the organisers cough up for your expenses? I don't think so.' He turned to look at the cup, then back to Rose. 'What about the prize money, anyway? That should cover the train fares. How much was it?'

'Didn't I say?' Rose began to go a little pink.

'No, as it happens, you did not say, another of your secrets. Come on, let's have it.'

Rose walked over to the drawer in the dresser and pulled out a slim envelope. Slowly, without meeting his eye, she handed it to Ryan.

He took out the contents.

'Vouchers!' he spat the word. 'Where's the real money? What good are sodding vouchers to me?'

'They are for that big department store in Bournemouth. They sell the shirts you like, you know, the ones with the button-down collars. And shoes, they have expensive shoes too,' she told him.

'Hmm, I suppose you might be right. Could do with some new gear. Here you go, lad,' he handed one to Baby, 'you did all the hard work. You get yourself something. Bet they have a toy department. Get yourself a ... a train, yeah,' he put the rest of the vouchers in his pocket and went back to his food. 'Buy the kid a train.'

'Oh, okay.' Rose waited, but it seemed the subject was closed, so she sat down again and stopped Baby eating his voucher.

Ryan held up a forkful of meat.

'You put something in this?'

'What?' Rose stiffened in her chair.

'Something different? It tastes different.'

Rose froze for a few seconds, not daring to look at Ryan. She busied herself wiping Baby's face.

'Sage,' she said, 'I put sage in it, that's all.'

Ryan shrugged.

'Tastes okay,' he said, clearing his plate, before leaning back in his chair and letting out a long, loud belch.

By seven o'clock Neville had reduced his sister's orderly little kitchen to something resembling a crime scene. There was not a clear inch of work surface to be seen, and every pan, jug, mug, pot and container seemed to be in use. The windows were opaque with steam, and the humidity in the room was well beyond comfortable.

'For pity's sake, Neville,' said Sandra, coming in from the garden, 'open a window before you pass out. There's no air in here.'

'What? Oh, I hadn't noticed. I'm too busy to worry about that sort of thing.'

'Clearly. I've never seen such a mess.' She moved towards the sink and reached for the rubber gloves.

'Oh don't bother with that now, Sandra. I'll clear up later.' Neville carefully spooned the creamy pudding mixture into a pastry case, tongue between teeth as he tried to remain focused on the task in hand.

'It won't take a minute. Don't worry, I won't interfere.'

Neville didn't reply. He was struggling with the unfamiliar kitchen, inferior gadgets, a woefully inadequate store cupboard, constant interruptions and irritating questions from the twins, and well-meaning fussing from Sandra. Still, he had known it would be like this, and he had made up his mind to deal with the difficulties. A lot was at stake. He was fairly sure he had, at last, perfected the Daryole recipe, but he needed to try it out on someone before the competition. It had been galling to realise the only potential guinea pigs were

Sandra, Brian, and the boys. A less discerning collection of palettes it would be hard to find. But who else could he ask? Cynthia would no doubt have leapt at the opportunity, but would also have read all sorts of inaccurate things into the invitation. The possible consequences were not worth the risk. There was no one at work whom Neville liked enough to invite to dinner, however desperate he was. He briefly flirted with the idea of contacting Lucy, but his nerve failed him. And so he found himself in Sandra's kitchen, battling to do his recipe justice, ready to submit to the judgements of two adults whose idea of *haute cuisine* was the local Harvester, and two children who spent more time dropping food than eating it.

Brian appeared in the kitchen carrying two bottles of wine.

'Now then, chef, red or white?' he asked.

Neville winced. What the choice actually consisted of was something claiming to be a Bulgarian Bordeaux, or a supermarket white so sweet it would make his teeth ache.

'All taken care of, Brian. I've brought a couple of bottles of Pinot Noir. Thanks, all the same.'

Neville stooped to slide the precious pudding into the oven, gently closed the door, checked his watch, and then allowed himself a sigh of relief.

'Right you are,' said Brian. 'What time's kick off, then?'

'Dinner should be ready in five minutes.'

'OK. I'll drag the twins to the table. Boys!' he headed out into the garden in search of his children.

There was much whining and shouting and forcible washing of hands and demands for lemonade and chips and television but finally everyone was seated at the fine, reproduction Regency table in the dining room.

'Well,' smiled Sandra, 'isn't this lovely, a delicious meal cooked for us by Uncle Neville.'

The twins were unconvinced.

'What is it?' asked one.

'I don't like that,' said the other.

'The main course,' Neville told them, 'is a simple steak and kidney casserole...'

'Urgh!'

'Don't like kidneys!'

'... which is a suitably traditional recipe to have before the rather special pudding I've prepared. There are green beans, carrots, and minted new potatoes.'

'Don't want beans!'

'Don't like carrots!'

'Now boys,' Sandra reached for their plates, 'I'm sure it will all be very tasty. Just try a little.' She spooned out miniscule portions.

'That's too much!'

'Don't like it.'

Neville's own appetite began to dwindle.

Sandra continued to cajole.

'Just give it a try, boys, Uncle Neville's gone to so much trouble.'

The boys sniffed their plates suspiciously.

'Don't like it,' said one.

'Smells disgusting,' said the other.

'That's enough!' boomed Brian, slamming his hand down hard on the table. 'Sit still, be quiet, and eat!'

Two mouths opened to protest. He cut them short.

'Or there will be no paddling pool in the garden this afternoon and you can spend the rest of the day tidying your bedrooms instead. I mean it. Now, eat!' He banged the table once more.

The tense silence that followed was punctuated by the occasional sniff.

'Really, Brian,' Sandra gave him a look.

Brian continued as if barking at his children and bullying them into compliance was a regular happening not worthy of mention.

'Nev, or should I say, Chef, this looks fantastic. Real food, none of that two bits of lettuce and a twig of something with a dollop of goo. Proper stuff! Good man.' He helped himself to large quantities of everything.

'Mmmm,' agreed Sandra, 'this is delicious, Neville. And your beans stay so green, how do you do that? I always have trouble there.'

Brain laughed.

'She's not kidding, Nev. Poor things look like they've been through a boil wash by the time Sandra's finished with them.'

Neville saw his sister shoot Brian a glance of such fury that for a moment he was whisked back to childhood squabbles. Which Sandra had always won, easily.

He tried to concentrate on his meal.

'It's all simple stuff, really,' he told them. 'It's the pudding that's new. That's what I'd really like your opinion on.'

'Ah yes,' Brian shook enough salt over his food to preserve it through winter. 'The mysterious competition entry. Can't wait to get stuck in to that. Pass the mustard, would you?'

Neville watched Brain obliterate any original flavour from his casserole, and looked on forlornly as Sandra avoided the kidneys and washed every mouthful down with diet tonic water. The boys squirmed on their seats emitting little squeaks and nibbling painfully at the odd carrot. Things did not look good for the pudding.

'I was wondering,' Sandra dabbed at her lips with a Monet print paper napkin, 'if you'd heard from Wendy at all.'

'Wendy?' Neville was at a loss.

Sandra tutted. 'You know who I mean. You met her here, just a few weeks ago. I thought she might have phoned. Or you might have called her.'

'Oh, no,' Neville shook his head. 'Not really my type, I'm afraid.'

'No! Pity, such a nice girl. We liked her, didn't we Brian?'

'Certainly did. Well, bits of her, anyway, eh Nev?' he laughed, shoulders shaking, at his own little joke.

The twins, baffled, but no doubt relieved to see their father's humour improve, laughed too.

'Really, Brian. Not in front ...' Sandra twitched her head in the direction of the children. 'Anyway, I'm sure Neville has interests in a possible new girlfriend other than just her ... well, I mean, he wants someone he can get on with. Someone pretty, someone nice to be around, someone to talk to.'

'Perhaps I should buy a budgie,' said Neville.

'Oh, you always sell yourself short,' she wagged an admonishing knife at him. 'That's always been your trouble. I'm sure there are lots of nice girls out there who would love to meet someone like you. You just need to make the effort to meet them, that's all.'

'Look, it's kind of you to take such an interest in my personal life, but really, there is no need.'

Brian passed the wine in Neville's direction.

'Why's that then, Nev? Taken a vow of chastity, have we? Or is it miles on the clock, eh? Taking its toll on the old libido? It's creeping up on all of us, you know, middle age.'

There were days when Neville felt middle age had indeed crept up on him, mugged him, and left him for dead in a dark alley. Even so, he disliked Brian making such jokes at his expense. After all, he couldn't imagine Sandra making heavy demands on her husband in their Scandinavian style bedroom.

'I say there's no need,' he told them, 'because that position is filled.'

Four astonished faces turned to stare at Neville. He attempted to ignore them and get on with his plateful.

Sandra was the first to speak. 'You mean, you've got a girlfriend?'

'I don't see why you should be so amazed. You've just said yourself, lots of women would consider me a good catch.' He sipped his wine and gave a nonchalant shrug. 'You were right,' he said, allowing himself a little smile at the effect of his pretence.

'That's my boy!' cried Brian, laughing again. 'Well, this is a turn up. What's she like, this secret woman of yours?'

'Now, Brian,' Sandra held up a hand as if halting traffic, 'I'm sure Neville will tell us all about her in his own good time.'

There was an expectant silence. Neville was already beginning to doubt the wisdom of the idea of inventing a girlfriend He ineffectually sought to change the subject.

'Oh, she's not anyone you know. More beans, Brian?'

'Someone from work, perhaps?' suggested Sandra.

'Work? No, not from work?'

'Not been dabbling in a bit of Internet dating, have you, brother-in-law? Loitering in the odd chat room or two, maybe?'

'I most certainly have not,' Neville drained his glass. 'She's someone I met in the village, that's all.'

The more Neville tried to knock the conversation on the head, the more uncontrollable it became.

'Ah, I see,' Sandra nodded. 'You did tell me you were on the committee for the recipe competition and so on. How lovely. Someone living in the village with the same interests as you, couldn't be better.'

'Now, I didn't say she actually lived in the village ...'

Brian was unstoppable.

'When do we get to meet her, then?' He helped himself to the last of the bottle of wine. 'Can't keep her hidden away for ever, you know.'

'I'm not hiding her.' Neville pulled at his collar which was beginning to feel unusually tight. 'She's a very busy woman, that's all. Doesn't have much time for socialising.'

Brian was impressed.

'A career girl?' He let out a low whistle. 'Good move, Nev. Expensive creatures to keep, women.'

'What's her name?'

'What?' Neville tried not to look as if this were an unreasonable question. 'Her name, yes, well, good grief,' he studied his watch pointedly. 'Look at the time, must rescue the pudding. Don't want to overcook it. Was the whole point of the meal, after all.'

He stood up in an effort to flee to the kitchen, but Sandra caught hold of his sleeve. She looked up at him dewy eyed, and when she spoke her words were breathless.

'Oh Neville, I'm so happy for you,' she squeaked.

He smiled wanly, wriggled free of her grasp and dashed for the kitchen.

The smaller twin spoke in a stage whisper, his words bringing a tiny sob from his mother.

'Dad, is Uncle Neville getting married?'

CHAPTER TEN

The early morning of the Nettlecombe Hatchet Cookery Demonstration and Fun Day, as the occasion had been snappily named, was blessed with the rosy sunshine of a very British summer. A wisp of mist rose from the brook, which could be tracked up and out of the village to its source at Withy Hill Farm. The scene was in soft focus, as the gentle light quivered in dew drops and diamond-strung webs, and glistened on leaves of viridian trees, which yawned and stretched their limbs as the day woke them up. The Farm itself had worked hard at hiding its true identity of rural industry, of factory, of place of business, and was instead carefully dressed in its bucolic summer best. All was rustic charm and Arcadian calm, contrived to disarm and beguile the observer into believing that God was in his heaven, and all was right with the world.

Tubs and troughs and hanging baskets overflowed with the brightest of blooms, all selected for their quality of relentless cheerfulness, and for the eye-smarting brilliance of their hues. Busy-Lizzies jostled for space with shameless pansies, blousy begonias, petulant petunias, strident geraniums, and the restless and hectic lobelia. Soon ladies in their good-weather frocks would pick up the theme, chameleon-like in their floral prints, competing with the flowers for the sunshine.

In the old meadow to the side of the farm, comfortably away from any hint of the modern and the new, stalls and stands and little tents and grand marquees had sprung up mushroom-like overnight. There was something here for everyone, and so in attempting to please all, nothing was exactly suited to anyone. The beautiful carousel with its transfixed horses would be ignored by thrill-addicted children, and was chiefly an expensive piece of decoration. The Treasure Hunt would attract the would-be gamblers, but had no entertainment value whatsoever for the spectators. And at the end of the day the trove would reveal a beauty parlour voucher, much to the bemusement of the lucky winner, Mr Albert Games, in his 90th year. Guess The Weight of the Lamb would start well, but become an increasingly malodorous stand as the day wore on, the focus of such scrutiny nervously and frequently relieving itself in its small pen. Perhaps it sensed its fate; perhaps it knew it was to be sacrificed on the altar of fun, and that its corpse would be first prize.

Parents would struggle for a few hours to convince their children that entertainment could come without a microchip. By four o'clock they would wonder why they bothered. By six o'clock every teenager would be home and plugged in once more.

Local food producers with unshakeable smiles would stand behind cheeses and pickles and sausages and hams, and yoghurts and cakes and biscuits and jams, knowing that they would barely cover their costs, but convincing themselves they were living the good life.

And however much effort was made to elevate the tone and appeal to the finer senses, most of the money would be made by the bouncy castle and the hot-dog stall.

By 9:30 Rose had Baby is his buggy and was wheeling in the direction of Withy Hill. She would be among the first to arrive, but she had Baby's routine to consider. Slung beneath the little chair was a fine picnic for the pair of them, along with plenty of bottles in cooling flasks, and one or two favourite toys. The prospect of an outing in the sunshine showing off Baby made Rose smile as she pushed along the lane. The day was already beginning to warm up, and showed signs of continuing the sultry heat that had been a feature of the weather for nearly ten days now. Rose adjusted the fringed parasol over Baby's bonneted head.

As they reached the entrance to the meadow they met Cynthia hurrying in the direction of the big marquee.

'Ahh, Mrs Behr, and little Baby Behr!' Cynthia swooped.

'Good morning, Mrs Danby. Beautiful morning, isn't it?'

'It certainly is. We are so fortunate to have the sun shine on our little party. And how is our local superstar, hmmm?' she bent over the buggy, causing Baby to stop gurgling and stretch his eyes. She stood up again and addressed Rose. 'I read about his success in the *Echo*. My dear, how thrilling! You must be so very proud.'

Rose blushed a little and smiled.

'He was such a good boy,' she said. 'We had to go to London, for the final, and he didn't mind a bit. Really, Mrs Danby, I think he enjoyed it all.'

'I'm sure he did. And will his daddy be joining us today?'

'I'm afraid not. He wasn't feeling very well this morning,' said Rose.

'Oh dear, I am sorry to hear that. Anyway, it's lovely to see you and Baby here. I know you'll have a fun-filled day. We're not quite up and running yet, though,' she checked her watch.

'Oh, we're always early for ...' Rose stopped, mouth open, and stared at the car pulling into the farmyard. It was a sleek, metallic blue Subaru Impreza – Ryan's car. And yet, as far as Rose knew, Ryan was in bed nursing a gripy tummy and a nasty bout of diarrhoea. She watched the car come to a halt and the engine stop. Her grip tightened on the buggy handles.

Cynthia turned to see what she could be staring at.

'Ahh, splendid, I see Claude Lambert has arrived. A little later than expected, but there we are. My goodness, I believe it's getting warmer by the minute. Please excuse me, I must go and see that he has everything he needs.' She strode away, a woman with more than enough to do.

Rose watched the celebrity chef and the beautiful woman climb out of the car as Cynthia approached. Her hold on the buggy relaxed once more and she pushed on towards the flower tent.

After Neville had pinched his fingers in the trestle table for the third time he decided it wasn't going to move another inch.

'It'll be fine here,' he told Pam.

'Didn't Cynthia say ...?'

'If Cynthia doesn't like it she can move it herself. God, look at the time. Let's get the cloths on, and then we can start bringing the equipment in. Where is everybody else, anyway? I wasn't expecting to have to do all the donkey work.' He adjusted the name badge which declared him 'Event Organiser'. One of Cynthia's daffier ideas, as far as he was concerned.

'You're lucky you've got me.' Pam reinforced her point by effortlessly picking up four folding chairs. 'The pub is going to be packed out on a steaming day like this. I won't be popular when I get home. Buggered if I know what's happened to the others.'

'We'll never be ready for the demonstration on time at this rate. Here, get the other end of this.'

They were in the process of unfolding a tablecloth the size of a small spinnaker when Cynthia arrived looking worried. One look at the state of Claude, and Neville knew why. The man appeared on the verge of collapse, and was indeed being all but held up by Lucy. Neville stared at them both, still clutching the tablecloth, then became aware Cynthia was saying something.

'Isn't that done yet?' she barked. 'Monsieur Lambert needs to inspect the equipment.'

Pam spoke in a low voice which was nevertheless clearly audible to all.

'Monsieur Lambert needs to lie down, if you ask me,' she said.

Cynthia glanced back at the wobbly chef, who sniffed twice, but was otherwise silent.

'Oh, yes. Perhaps you would like a few minutes to recover from your journey. Lucy, why don't you take Claude over to the farmhouse, perhaps a nice strong cup of tea ...? I'll let you know when we're ready for you here.'

Lucy smiled sweetly.

'What a good idea. Come along, Claude. Soon have you right as rain,' she said, steering him through the chairs. As she passed Neville her smile brightened a fraction. 'Lovely to see you again, Neville,' she breathed, 'Catch you later.'

Neville gazed after her.

'Oy,' yelled Pam, 'Are we going to stand like this all bloody day?'

'Sorry,' he lowered the cloth and turned to Cynthia. 'My God, he looks like death. He's bluer than ever.'

'What are we going to do, Neville? He can't go on stage in that condition.'

'St John's Ambulance will be thrilled. Bet they've never had to treat anything like that before.'

'Really, I don't see there is anything remotely funny about this situation,' snapped Cynthia. 'We have an expectant public arriving for the demonstration in less than an hour, and our star turn is not fit to be seen. I'm not sure he's capable of standing up unsupported. What are we going to do?' she wailed again.

Neville did his best to sound reassuring. A tearful Cynthia was more than he could cope with. 'Look, don't let's panic.

Maybe he gets carsick. I'm sure if anyone can sort him out, it's Lucy. He's in good hands.'

Cynthia's expression changed from feeble to frightening in an instant.

'Yes, well of course you would know all about that, I suppose.' She paused for a moment, seeming to take stock and pull herself together. 'Right, no point in standing about. Mr Christian has gone abroad, urgent business apparently, and Miss Siddons has shingles, so it's just us. Come along, we've work to do. Who on earth put this marquee up? Can anyone actually believe it is supposed to be at such an angle? And those two guy ropes aren't even tight. Can no one do anything properly? And I have to say, inside is not looking much better. That trestle needs moving, for a start.'

The three worked without pause for the next forty-five minutes. Neville spent most of the time biting his tongue as Cynthia yapped instructions and he and Pam did all the lifting and shifting. The heat outside was already considerable, turning the air inside the marquee into a canvas-flavoured fug. By the time Neville had struggled with a tabletop cooker, a sink unit, a small fridge, and boxes and boxes of essential items, he was a hot, sticky mess. At last all that could be done had been done, and the plumber arrived to sort out the temporary water supply.

Pam slumped into a folding chair, which gave a little creak of protest.

'I'm buggered,' she announced. 'I'm not doing another bloody thing until I get a long cold drink. How about it, Cynthia?'

'What? I'm afraid I have a million things to do. Someone has to check on Claude and make sure he's ready for the demonstration. Oh, very well, I'll have some drinks sent over.'

Further conversation was rendered impossible at that moment due to the Young Farmers Club Steel Band limbering up with a few lively numbers.

'Good heavens!' Cynthia cried above the noise. 'I said we should have had a string quartet. And they can't possibly set up there, it's entirely the wrong place,' she charged off towards the unsuspecting teenagers with a shout of 'What do you think you are doing?'

Neville sat heavily next to Pam.

'This is going to be a shambles,' he said. 'I feel it in my bones.' He stretched stiffly, joints clicking, 'Make that my aching muscles. How did we let ourselves get talked into this in the first place?'

'Our Cynthia can be very persuasive.'

'That's a generous word for it.' He allowed himself a long, heartfelt sigh. 'Actually, I did it because of Claude – he's my hero, you know, always admired his recipes. Inspired, some of them, truly inspired. But look at the state of him. He's like one of the living dead.'

'He did look a bit peaky.'

'Peaky! I tell you there's sod all chance he's going to be able to cook properly today. And as for judging the competition entries ...'

'Ah, worried he won't appreciate your little creation, eh?'

'I don't think he's capable of appreciating anything in that state. God, I hope Lucy's managed to sort him out.'

'Now's your chance to find out,' said Pam, standing up and nodding in the direction of Lucy, who had just breezed into the tent. 'I'm off to find that drink. See you later.'

Neville squinted up at Lucy as she stood in front of him, backlit by the sunshine, more beautiful than ever. He ran a hand through his sweat drenched hair, then wished he hadn't as she held out an exquisitely manicured paw to him. He stood up quickly, taking her hand and giving it a damp squeeze.

'Neville, it is so lovely to see you again.' She lent forwards and gave him the lightest of kisses on his salty cheek.

Neville breathed in her glorious perfume. It was like oxygen to a drowning man after the fetid atmosphere of the marquee.

'Lucy, I wasn't sure you'd be here. It's ... it's wonderful to see you again too.' He found himself staring, so tried to be business like. 'So, how is the great man? Walking unaided yet?'

'I'm afraid poor Claude is not feeling very well today.'

'You don't say.'

'I'm sure he'll be fine once he gets started. He's terribly professional, a true perfectionist, like yourself, Neville.'

She stepped a little closer.

Neville struggled with an urge to grab the woman and kiss her countered by an equally strong desire to run.

'You know,' Lucy began to fiddle with his lapel badge, 'I believe you and I have some unfinished business.'

A lazy grin slid round Neville's face. A second later it was replaced by an expression of horror, as Sandra and Brian wandered into the tent, twins fidgeting beside them.

'Sod it,' said Neville. 'That's all I need.'

'I'm sorry?' Lucy arched her perfectly plucked brows.

'Oh no, not you. It's my sister and her brood. I'm afraid they're looking for me.'

There was a deal of waving and smiling and cooey-ing.

'Looks like they've found you,' said Lucy.

Neville attempted to get past her to head off his family, but he wasn't quick enough.

'Neville,' Sandra insisted on a peck. 'This all looks very nice.'

'I didn't know you were planning to come,' he said, aware that Lucy still had her hand resting on his collar. He couldn't quite bring himself to wriggle free.

Brian gave Neville a conspiratorial wink.

'Thought we'd come and see what you were up to. You know, check things out.'

Neville tried to pretend his brother-in-law didn't exist.

'This is not a good moment really,' he appealed to Sandra.

'Say no more, Nev,' Brain winked again and leered at Lucy.

Sandra noticed his bizarre behaviour.

'Brian, have you got something in your eye?' She turned back to her brother. 'Aren't you going to introduced us, Neville?'

'Oh, yes. Lucy, my sister Sandra, and her husband Brian, and the twins. This is Lucy Ferris-Brown. She is Claude Lambert's personal assistant. Now, as I said, this is not a good moment. The demonstration is due to start. As you can see, people are beginning to take their seats, and ...'

'Don't mind us,' Sandra waved away his concerns. She gave Lucy her brightest smile, followed by a limp handshake. 'It is so nice to meet you at last. Neville's mentioned you, of course, and it's always nice to put a face to the name, isn't it?'

Brian chipped in. 'A name would have been a start. Plays his cards close to his chest, does our Nev.'

'Really?' Lucy gave Brian a dismissive look and refocused on Neville. 'I like a man with a bit of mystery about him.'

'I must say,' Sandra was getting into her stride, 'you're not at all what I expected. When Neville said he'd met someone in the village, well, most people around here are not very glamorous, are they? Lovely people, of course, but ...'

'Mum, Mum,' for once a twin made a welcome interruption. 'Can we go on the bouncy castle now? Can we?'

'Dad said we could,' the second child pointed out. 'He promised.'

'Yes, all right. Brian, give them some money. Fifteen minutes, boys, I don't want you both being sick all afternoon. Now, Lucy, you must promise you'll come and visit us. Dinner one night perhaps, hmm?'

Neville stepped in.

'Lucy's really terribly busy, Sandra ...'

'I'd love to,' Lucy purred. 'You can tell me all Neville's little secrets.'

Neville was spared the trouble of interrupting further as Cynthia arrived in full military commander mode.

'There you are, Lucy. This is no time to stand around chatting,' she wagged a dangerous looking finger, 'Claude is asking for you. For heavens sake get him to come out of the house. Tell him the marquee is full and the audience is getting restless.'

'Leave it to me,' Lucy was unfazed by Cynthia's brusqueness. 'Catch you later, Neville.' She gave a little wave as she left.

Cynthia squinted at Sandra and Brian.

'Have you got tickets?'

'Oh, no, I'm afraid not ...' said Sandra.

'This is my sister and her husband,' Neville explained.

Cynthia softened immediately.

'Oh, your family, Neville. Darling Boy, why didn't you say so?' She grasped first Sandra's hand, then Brian's. 'Cynthia Danby. So nice to meet you, I expect Neville's told you all about me.'

'Well, I ...' Sandra was confused.

'We've been seeing more and more of each other lately, so much to do for the fundraiser. Not that I'm complaining, of course. There is no one with whom I would rather spend my time. We are kindred spirits, your brother and I. We share a grand passion.'

'Good Lord,' said Brian. 'But I thought ...'

Sandra trod heavily on his foot.

'It's lovely to meet you, Cynthia.'

'Neville can be a naughty boy,' Cynthia grabbed his arm. 'He likes to have his little secrets. But we understand one another, don't we, *mon cher*?'

'Cooking,' Neville explained. 'Like me, Cynthia is very keen on cooking.'

'That's lovely, isn't it?' Sandra smiled 'A shared interest keeps a couple happy. We've always found that, haven't we, Brian?'

'We have? Oh yes, we have,' said Brian.

Cynthia gave one of her unnerving girlish giggles.

'Neville, find your family some seats. There are one or two left at the back, I think. Then you really must excuse us. The demonstration is about to begin, and ...'

'Blimey,' Brian stared past her. 'Is that your wonder chef? Whatever he's got I hope it's not catching.'

They turned to see a sickly looking Claude being propelled onto the stage by Lucy. He stood in front of the cheerfully clapping audience, blinking like a mole in a sunbeam, and teetering on unsteady feet.

A growl of not-too-distant thunder expressed Neville's thoughts.

'My God,' he said, 'he looks even worse than he did before.'

'I'm not sure I can bear to watch,' wailed Cynthia.

They stood, riveted by the unfolding disaster in front of them. The sky had darkened and now deafening thunder came nearer and grew louder, drowning out the pathetic little voice of the shambolic chef. Claude attempted to do what was expected of him, but it was obvious he was not up to it. He dropped things. He broke things. He muttered and mumbled and forgot what he was supposed to be doing. The longer it went on the more painful the experience became for everybody. The audience began to fidget. This embarrassing performance was not what they had come to see.

Ten long minutes into the demonstration Claude suddenly froze. All movement ceased, and he appeared incapable of speech. He stared out of the side door of the marquee, open-mouthed.

'Now what?' hissed Neville.

'Is he having some sort of seizure?' Cynthia asked.

Neville leaned forward to see what was having such an effect on the poor man. He could just make out Claude's car in the car park. Next to it stood two particularly large men in sombre suits. They were peering into the car and trying the doors.

'I think someone's trying to steal his car,' he told Cynthia.

'Never mind his car, look!' she shrieked.

Neville looked in time to see Claude fleeing out of the back of the tent, showing a surprising turn of speed for one apparently so near death. In two seconds he was gone, leaving an empty stage, a crowd about to turn nasty, and a baffled Neville trying to placate a near hysterical Cynthia.

It was only a short walk from Brook Terrace to Withy Hill Farm, but by the time they arrived, Fliss was already wishing she hadn't talked Daniel into coming along.

'Oh look,' he pointed at the hot dog stall, 'good, wholesome country food. I was wondering why we'd come.'

Fliss glanced back at Rhian and Sam, walking a safe distance from anyone who might be identified as a parent, and continued to do her best to ignore Daniel's snide remarks.

'I want to go to the flower tent,' she told him, 'see if I can pick up one or two things for the garden, bound to be healthier plants than in a garden centre.'

'Whatever, Babe, I'm just happy to soak up the atmosphere. Rural entertainment at its best, all the little village people coming together to bond over gladioli and strawberry jam.'

'I think things may have moved on a bit since your grandmother's day, Daniel. We may surprise you.'

'I love the "we", Babe. You're really getting into the whole village life experience.'

'I don't see the point in living here if you're not prepared to try things. This sort of event is important. It stops people feeling isolated; builds up a sense of community. Anyway, I don't want people thinking I'm just another Londoner who wants the space and fresh air, but isn't prepared to contribute anything.'

'Like me, you mean?'

'No, it's different for you. You're a part-timer.'

'Oh, is that how you see me? Your part-time boyfriend? Hmm, better have a good look round and see who I might be job-sharing with. Fancy a bit of rustic muscle mid-week do you?'

'Very funny, Dan. Almost as funny as all your other little jokes at everyone else's expense.'

'I only said the hog roast looked like a sacrifice at a black mass. And that the steel band appeared to be made up of care in the community rejects. And that ...'

'Yes, thank you, they didn't make me laugh the first time I heard them.'

'Come on, Babe, lighten up. Only having a bit of fun.'

'Well do you have to be so snippy about everything?'

'Sorree! If that's how you feel, think I'll leave you to it and check out the beer tent. That okay with you?'

'You do whatever you want, Daniel, you always do.'

'Right, I will then.'

'Right, see you later.'

Fliss watched him stomp off and wondered, not for the first time in the past few weeks, just whether or not her relationship with Daniel could have a future. All around her women in summer frocks and children clutching candy floss seemed to be genuinely happy and having a quietly normal good time. And here she was having a spat with the man she spent all week looking forward to seeing. Somehow, lately, the reality had not been living up to expectation. She sighed, annoyed at having her mood altered in a downward direction.

'Mum,' Rhian had caught her up. 'Can you bung us a few quid? I haven't got much pocket money left.'

'Good grief, Rhi, I only gave it to you yesterday. What do you do with it?'

'Am I supposed to keep accounts? Look it's really hot. I just wanted to get Sam and me a couple of frozen yoghurts, okay?'

'Can you eat that?' Fliss asked, surprised.

'Filmore Dairies do a range with Soya milk,' Sam explained. 'They have realised the potential of the vegan market.'

'Right, well, why not. Here you are. And that's it, there's no more, okay?'

'Thanks, Mum. Hey, look, there's that bloke Sam was telling us about. The nerdy one from the planning office,' she pointed to the entrance of the big marquee. Neville was standing in the doorway talking to a swarm of people. 'You said you'd speak to him, Mum. Now's your chance.'

'What? Now?'

'Go on, he's right there. You promised.'

Fliss took in the expression on her daughter's face and realised she had been issued a challenge. She turned back to Sam.

'What did you say his name was?'

'Meatcher, Neville Meatcher.'

'Right. Here goes,' said Fliss, taking a deep breath.

There were so many people trying to speak to the rather nervous looking man that for a minute Fliss doubted she was going to get to him. Then a whistling announcement over the Tannoy suggested ticket refunds might be available at the stage and the crowd moved as one body to the other end of the tent. Fliss saw her moment.

'Mr Meatcher, I wonder if I could speak with you?' Her words were obscured by a teeth-jarring crash of thunder.

'Look, I'm sorry, you'll have to queue with the other ticket holders to get your money back,' he told her.

'What? No, I didn't have a ticket. I want to talk to you,' she followed him inside the tent. 'My name is Fliss Horton.'

He studied her for a second or two.

'Sorry, should that mean anything to me?'

Fliss tried to respond but was drowned out again.

'You'll have to speak up,' he yelled at her. 'I can't hear a word you're saying.'

Fliss raised her voice to a shout, and the words came out angrier than she had intended, though actually befitting her mood.

'Planning! I want to know what's going on about the planning applications here at Withy Hill Farm! I hear you're the man in charge.'

'First, I am not in charge of planning applications!' he bellowed back. 'Second, even if I were I wouldn't discuss it with a complete stranger who has no interest in the project, and third,' he flinched as lightning bleached the sky for an instant, 'third, this is neither the time, nor the place.' Thunder boomed once more. 'Nor the sodding weather in which to discuss such matters. Now if you don't mind, I've got a monumental cock up to try to sort out!'

'Wait a minute! There's no need to be so bloody rude. Perhaps you don't want to talk about it because you've got something to hide!'

'What? Look, Mrs Norton ...'

'Horton!'

'Quite. I assure you ...'

But the weather Gods had other ideas. At last the sagging clouds overhead could carry their load no more. With an apocryphal rumble and ear-splitting crack of lightning the rain came down. It rained as if there had been years of drought, and as if it might not get a chance to rain ever again. The water speared through the sticky air, slicing its way to the ground with alarming force. A force that was more than a match for the hastily and inexpertly erected marquee. Outside, people ran for their cars, or for the shelter of the barns. Inside, aggrieved ticket holders forgot about their £3.50 and fled. Above them the canvas sagged and stretched. Around them the poles wobbled and the ropes creaked. In less than a minute the tent had emptied, save for Neville and Fliss standing in the middle of the chairs, and Cynthia on stage like a tragic heroine in a little known opera.

'I think we should continue our conversation somewhere else,' Neville shouted.

Fliss nodded, not attempting to speak further above the cacophony of the storm and the alarming groans of the marquee. She turned on her heel, causing her hair to spin round behind her. Unfortunately, she had been standing closer to Neville than she had realised, and her hair caught in his name badge at the precise moment he chose to try and exit in the opposite direction.

'Ouch!' Fliss screamed. 'Wait a minute!'

'What in God's name are you doing, woman? Keep still.'

Fliss had little choice but to do as she was told. For a second it seemed the structure of the tent would hold, but then the creaking of the ropes and the listing of the poles increased, and it was clear collapse was imminent.

'It's no use, we've got to get out!' she yelled, grabbing Neville's hand and hauling him after her through the snagging rows of chairs. Behind them she could hear shrieking from the stage as the roof came in. She made for the exit, but Neville tripped and brought them both heavily to the floor.

It occurred to Fliss, as she lay half drowned on the soaking ground, a strange man and a large tent on top of her, that she had had better days. After much struggling and floundering, and a little help from a couple outside, she and Neville were released from the tangle of canvas and rope. Still joined by Fliss's hair they lay, stunned, on the grass, spluttering as the rain continued to drench them.

'Neville?' A woman's voice broke through Fliss's thoughts.

'It's all right, Sandra, don't fuss, we're fine,' said Neville.

Fliss smiled feebly up at the worried looking woman, who tried to get them help.

'Don't just stand there, Brian,' she yapped, 'do something.'

'All under control,' said Brian, reaching down and taking Fliss's hand.

Of necessity, Neville hauled himself to his feet too, holding on to Fliss to prevent her losing a large chunk of hair.

Brian's grin could be seen even through the power-shower of water that coursed over his face. 'Well, Nev, a redhead too. The words 'dark' and 'horse' spring to mind, you old devil, you. I am impressed.'

Fliss turned to look at the saturated, mud-splattered, red-faced, bedraggled creature to which she was so annoyingly attached and saw very, very little to be impressed by.

CHAPTER ELEVEN

In the sunny front room of Honeysuckle cottage Rose hummed as she dusted. Baby had recently given up his mid morning nap and was enjoying the movements of the feather duster. Ryan was still in bed, which was not unusual for a Sunday morning. But this time he was not sleeping off a hangover. This time he wasn't recovering from the excesses of a late night out with the boys. Or with somebody else! This time he was laid low by stomach cramps, still suffering with diarrhoea, complaining of nausea, refusing food, and feebly demanding Lucozade.

Rose whipped out a soft yellow cloth and lovingly polished Baby's cup, which now had pride of place on the mantelpiece. She had enjoyed going to the fun day at Withy Hill, even if she had got a little wet on the walk home. Quite a number of people had read of Baby's success and come up to congratulate them. And Baby had smiled and gurgled and patiently put up with their silly faces and coo-ing and nonsense talk. Rose herself had never understood why people insisted on speaking to babies as if they were simple, when it was plain to see they were really very clever indeed. But Baby was good-natured, and seemed to know when people meant well.

'Rose? Rose?' Ryan's wail crept down stairs to her.

Instinct drove her towards the door, but then she paused and waited a little.

'Rose? Where the hell are you, woman? Are you sodding deaf?'

Rose's jaw tightened a fraction. She lifted her chin and narrowed her eyes, then picked Baby up and went into kitchen.

By the time Ryan appeared she was busy liquidizing meals for the freezer.

'I've been calling you, didn't you here me?'

'Oh, sorry. The blender is so noisy ... Are you feeling any better?'

'Do I look fucking better to you? Well do I?' He pulled his dressing gown tighter around him and slumped onto a chair. 'I feel like shit, if you must know.'

'I expect you've picked up a tummy bug.' Rose added cooked carrots to the liquidizer and whizzed for a second.

'Do you have to make that racket?' Ryan demanded once she had stopped. 'And anyway, if it's a bug why haven't you got it, eh? Why hasn't he?' He jerked his head in the direction of Baby in his highchair.

'I don't know. I suppose we don't go to the same places you do. We don't mix with the same people. Is there someone at work who's been ill, perhaps?' She spooned the lumpy orange mixture out of the jug and into small tubs for freezing.

Ryan paled visibly.

'If someone at work was ill they wouldn't be at work, would they? They'd be at home, being looked after. Unlike some of us, just left to sodding rot. I thought you were bringing me up a drink.'

Wordlessly Rose fetched him a glass of Lucozade and set it on the table before him. He sipped at it pathetically.

'Do you think you'll be going to work tomorrow?' she asked.

'You're having a laugh, aren't you? I can hardly stand up, how am I going to go to work?' He drank a little more then belched loudly. 'Anyway, the car's still not right.'

'Oh, won't it start?'

'It starts, nothing wrong with the engine. But there's this rattle, somewhere in the dashboard. I can't find where the bastard thing's coming from. It's getting on my tits, I don't mind telling you. Useless twats at the garage couldn't sort it out. I'll have to take it to the Subaru dealer in Bournemouth when I'm well enough.'

'I see,' said Rose. 'I don't suppose you'll be going out again this week then?'

'Out?'

'For one of your evening meetings. You know, like the ones you usually have on Thursdays.'

Ryan squinted up at Rose, trying to read her expression. She merely smiled back at him sweetly.

'No,' he said at last. 'I don't think I'm in any fit state for evening meetings at the moment.'

Rose nodded and set about washing up. As she stood at the sink she could see from Ryan's reflection in the window that he was looking at her.

'Have you lost some weight at last?' he asked after a while.

'No, I don't think so,' Rose didn't turn to speak.

'New dress then, is it?'

She shook her head, 'No, just one I haven't worn for a while, that's all.' She watched his reflection digest this information as he ran a hand through his unusually dishevelled hair. Then, very softly, she began to hum again.

The conservatory that was appended to The Old Vicarage had been built before the word 'makeover' was invented. It was more in the way of a leftover from an earlier fashion for glass and engineering and potted palms. In its day it might have been elegant and chic and modish, but this was not its day. Now it clung to the side of the house like the husk of a dead spider; spindly, frail, and only semi-transparent. The attentions of a window-cleaner might have helped. As would some judicious clearing out of the sickly and neglected plants inside. In particular the aged and fruitless vine deserved to be put out of its misery and consigned to a bonfire. It had outgrown its cracked terracotta pot many years ago, and now sagged on withered limbs as it hung from the decaying structure, which it would one day surely bring crashing to the ground if no action was taken.

Neville's mind, however, was on things other than the sorry condition of his surroundings. Against his better judgement he had let Cynthia persuade him to come for coffee to discuss the disaster of the day before. As she sat beside him on the small cane sofa, pouring cream into cups, he was only too aware that this was a woman on the brink of collapsing into tears and despair. And a lachrymose Cynthia was something he was entirely focussed on avoiding. So much so that for once he was grateful for Hamlet's pungent presence.

'He's looking very well, Cynthia,' he patted the dog, managing to find an area of skin less scrofulous than most. Hamlet responded with a low groan of pleasure.

Cynthia was not interested.

'Really, I don't know how I'll ever be able to show my face in the village,' she said in a voice cracking with emotion. 'I'll never be taken seriously again.'

'Cynthia, you mustn't let yourself get all worked up about what happened. People will soon forget ...'

'No they won't. They never forget when you make a mess of something. Oh, they're quick to forget all one's tireless years of service to the village; all the things that have gone right – the money made for the church roof, or the new playground, or the victory of the Pelican crossing. Oh yes, they soon forget about all that. But such a *debacle* as yesterday ... never!'

'But it wasn't your fault. You couldn't control the weather, or Claude, or the tent, people won't be blaming you.'

'Yes they will! They always want someone to blame.'

'But we gave everyone their money back.' Neville was beginning to regret having made any sort of fuss of Hamlet, as the dog now insisted on resting its head in his lap. The drool was already seeping into his trousers.

'Don't remind me!' Cynthia gulped her coffee. 'Do you realise how out of pocket NHEC is? Not only was the main event of the day a complete fiasco, not to mention the rest being a washout, but we have actually lost money. All our hard work, all our efforts and creativity, all wasted. All we have to show for it is an enormous hole in the bank balance and a ruined marquee. I have been totally humiliated.' She began to sniff.

Neville pushed the plate of Bourbons towards her.

'Have a biscuit. I expect your blood sugar's low. You haven't eaten since yesterday, have you?

The hint of concern in Neville's words was just sufficient to tip Cynthia over the edge. Tears brimmed from her eyes, accompanied by a sharp wail. The effect on Neville was that of fingernails on a blackboard.

'Please, don't cry, Cynthia, it'll only make you feel worse.' He winced as the wailing increased.

'Impossible!' she sobbed.

Even Hamlet was affected by Cynthia's distress. He stopped ruining Neville's trousers, lifted his nose, let his cankerous ears flop back, and started an eerie howl.

'Cynthia ...' Neville tried to make himself heard above the din, 'Please calm down.' He risked patting her hand lightly. It was all the encouragement Cynthia needed. She threw herself against him, lurching onto his lap and weeping on his shoulder, her arms fastened around his neck.

'Oh Neville,' she sobbed. 'What would I do without you? I knew you would understand. You are my soul mate, *mon cher.*'

Her tears soaked into his shirt, causing the second soggy patch on his clothing in the space of five minutes. Neville gently took hold of her hands in the hope of loosening her grip, but she clung on like a Koala in a bush fire, her whole body racked with sobs.

'It's so hard facing everything alone,' she squeaked. 'People don't realise; they think big, bossy Cynthia doesn't mind anything. They think I should be used to being a widow after all these years. But I am a woman, Neville.' She pulled back a little, keeping her face only a few inches from his. 'A woman as fragile and as vulnerable as any other.' Her ruddy nose was almost touching his now. 'You understand how a woman feels, my dearest, I know you do. That is why you are here now. I knew you would come to me in my hour of need.'

Fighting rising panic, Neville gently but firmly disentangled himself from Cynthia, though he was unable to dislodge her from his lap.

'Look,' he still had to compete with Hamlet's mournful noise, 'I really think you're blowing things out of all proportion here. You mustn't let it get to you so much. If people are determined to criticise, well, let them. What does it matter?' He took a deep breath, 'We know the truth. I know how much hard work you put into organising yesterday's ... um, yesterday. Let other people think what they like.'

Cynthia swallowed another sob and struggled to produce a wobbly smile. Given her wet, blotchy features, the effect was rather unfortunate.

'You're right, of course,' her voice was a whisper. 'Why should I care what others think when I have you?'

This was too much for Neville. Merely dragging himself to the Vicarage to deal with Cynthia had used up his year's supply of good deeds, and he could feel his patience coming to an end. On top of which, he was very afraid the woman was reading far too much into his few words of consolation. His trousers had been drooled on. His shirt had been sobbed over. His lap had been sat upon. Hamlet was still bellowing out strangled notes. And Cynthia's weight was beginning to put Neville's leg to sleep. It was time to go home. He stood up, ungallantly letting Cynthia grab hold of the table for support as she slid off his lap.

'Now I really think you should have a little lie down,' he said. Then, seeing the hopeful look on her face, he added, 'alone. I'm sure you'll feel much better after a rest.'

'Very well, darling boy, if you think it best.'

She straightened her crumpled dress and ineffectually patted at her hair.

'I'll see myself out,' said Neville, removing Hamlet's nose from his crotch.

'I'll call you,' Cynthia told him. 'Perhaps we could meet again, later in the week. We must be ready to present a united front to the committee before the day of reckoning.'

'Quite. Don't you worry about that now,' Neville walked backwards keeping both Hamlet and Cynthia at arm's length. When he reached the outer door of the conservatory he gave a curt wave before slamming the door on the dog and making hastily for his bike.

Neville pedalled quickly away, relieved to be heading for the safety and tranquillity of his flat. His relief was short-lived, however, when he found Fliss on his doorstep pressing the doorbell. As his bike squeaked to a halt she turned and saw him.

'Ah, Neville, I was hoping I'd find you at home.'

'Miss Horton ...' he began.

'Fliss, please. And before you say anything, there's no need to apologise for yesterday. Let's just put the whole thing down to an unfortunate accident and forget about it, shall we?'

'Me apologise?' Neville got off his bike and frowned at the woman who was blocking his path. 'I seem to remember you were the one haranguing me.'

'Rubbish, I was simply trying to get some information out of you.'

'At an entirely inappropriate time and place – as is this! Now if you don't mind, I'd like to enjoy what's left of my Sunday in peace.'

'How can you? How can you hide away up there in your little nest and pretend nothing is happening?'

Neville looked pointedly over first his left shoulder, then his right.

'As far as I can see nothing is happening.' He attempted to wheel past her but she refused to budge.

'There is something going on up at Withy Hill Farm, and you know about it. You must do. You're in charge of planning applications ...'

'For the hundredth time, I am not in charge.'

'... you must know they want to build some sort of laboratory up there. Why haven't there been public notices? The people who live here have a right to know what's going on in the village. We should have an opportunity to register our protest.'

'It strikes me you're managing to do that very well yourself. Look, if you have any queries about local planning issues you really should go through the proper channels.'

'Oh yes, and how long will that take? Meanwhile, everything gets rushed through and rubber stamped and before we even know what's going on it's all done and dusted.'

'You credit our department with far more stamping and dusting than ever gets done, I assure you.'

'Why won't you just answer a few questions? What are you trying to hide?'

'I beg your pardon!'

'I don't see why anyone who lived here would be happy for God knows what sort of experiments to be going on right on their doorstep. Unless there was something in it for them, of course.'

'What are you implying?'

'Well, it's obvious, you know the Christians pretty well. And that peculiar chef whose restaurant they supply. Perhaps you're all in cahoots.'

'Cahoots! I've had enough of this. You have the nerve to come here, to my home, on a Sunday, and accuse me of ... well, to be frank, I don't know what in God's name you are accusing me of but, whatever it is, I don't like it. And I resent your tone, and your assumptions.'

'What am I supposed to think? If you really don't have a clue what's going on under your nose, then that makes you culpably stupid.'

'A much more flattering option. Let's agree I'm an idiot and all go home. Now, if you'll excuse me ...' He all but shoved her off his doorstep and fumbled for his key.

'What if I get you proof?

'What on earth do you mean?' Neville turned the key in the lock and pushed the door open.

'Proof that there really is something to be concerned about. Proof that I'm not imagining all this just to spoil your weekend.'

Fliss put her hand on Neville's arm as he tried to manoeuvre his bike onto the doorstep. He saw her look at the damp patch on his shirt and then lower her gaze to the shiny wetness on his trousers. Slowly, she withdrew her hand. Neville rolled his eyes and sighed.

'OK. You bring me proof, whatever that looks like, of something ... untoward, and I'll look into it. Satisfied?'

'Promise?'

Neville met her stare now, surprised by the greenness of her eyes.

'I promise,' he said, and found himself meaning it.

As usual, by four o'clock Fliss was checking her watch. Her Monday afternoon cleaning stint at Withy Hill always seemed to drag, and this one was no exception. At least with the Christians away she didn't have anyone breathing down her neck or checking up on her. She also had the added incentive of being determined to find something to wave under Neville's patronizing nose. This had to be her best chance, with no one else in the house. She went through to the study and sat in Mr Christian's ludicrously large leather chair. She scoured his desk, but it had been cleared and yielded nothing. She swivelled slowly, taking in the whole room. The shelves had pretend books on them boasting smart embossed covers and no content. Here and there an object d'art of dubious taste filled a space. The walls were hung with photographs of motor yachts and racehorses. There were two filing cabinets beside the desk. Fliss got up and tried to open them. Locked! She tried the drawers in the desk in search of a key. Nothing! The only cabinet with anything in it was the one containing a whisky decanter and glasses.

Fliss crossed over to the window and looked outside. From here she had a clear view of the rear of the farm, where most of the chicken barns were. A farm labourer came out of one of them and went to the back door of the house. She watched him open it and let out Vinnie and Eric. The dogs had been shut up for some time and leapt and snapped at nothing in particular, practising their growls and sharp barks. Instinctively Fliss took a step back from the window. She watched as the man and the dogs headed off in the direction of the far fields.

'There must be something,' she told herself. 'Something somewhere.'

At that moment a small man in a suit came out of an unimportant looking building attached to the end of one of the barns. He started to lock the door, but was interrupted by his mobile phone. Fliss saw him answer it, then walk away from the building, still talking, climb into his car, and drive away. She squinted at the door. The keys were still in it.

It took her some time to walk out of the front door, around the side of the house, and over to the small outbuilding. As she walked she tried to look casual and confident in case anyone was watching, but all the time she kept a weather eye out for the return of the hateful dogs. By the time she reached the door her heart was thumping. With a quick glance behind her she went inside. The room was quite large, but so crowded with boxes and equipment and tables and cupboards that Fliss found it difficult to make her way across. It seemed to be something between an office and a storeroom.

She checked the small desk with the telephone on it, but the scribble pad was empty and the drawers locked. She opened one or two cupboards, but found nothing important. There were cartons of medicines for various chicken ailments; tubes of ointments; bottles of antiseptic; packets of bandages; and boxes of latex gloves. All legitimate veterinary products one might expect to find on a well-run poultry farm. On the far wall was a large metal cabinet, which appeared to be bolted to the wall. Fliss tried the handle, and was not surprised to find it locked.   As she looked around for something she might free the latch with, Fliss heard small scratching noises coming from behind a tall shelving unit. Cautiously, she walked towards the sound. Behind the shelves she saw a low table on which sat half a dozen or so metal cages. As she drew closer she could see there were small animals inside. She stood as close as she dared and peered inside the first cage.

To begin with she couldn't quite make out what was running about among the sawdust and hay. Then she saw it. Her hand flew to her mouth to stop a shriek of horror.

'Oh my God!' she said aloud, unable to stop staring at the creature in front of her.

She tried to focus. 'A box,' she told herself, taking one or two deep breaths. 'I need a small box.'

The room had seemed full of boxes when she first came in, but now she was having trouble finding one to suit her needs. A stout box, not too large, and with a firm, well-fitting lid. She found a walk-in store-cupboard at the back of the room. Inside she spied what she needed and started to empty it of its contents.

The sound of the door opening and shutting caused her to drop the box. She froze briefly, and then flattened herself behind the cupboard door. Someone was definitely moving about in the room. Fliss forced herself to peer through the tiny gap beneath the hinge to try and see who it was and what they were doing. The store cupboard door was not fully shut, so she peered through the space between it and the jam. A thin man searched through a number of keys on a ring. As he turned a little more to the side she saw his face.

'Claude Lambert!' she mouthed.

Claude selected a key and used it to open the large metal cabinet. Fliss watched him hurriedly take out a brown glass bottle and put it in his pocket. He locked the cabinet and turned to leave. As he did so Fliss leant forwards a fraction and just touched the door, which gave a grating little creak.

Claude stopped and looked around.

Fliss bit her lip and held her breath.

Claude walked towards the store cupboard, looking almost as nervous as Fliss felt. He reached out for the handle. Fliss closed her eyes. At that moment one of the inmates of the cages squeaked as it scuttled through its sawdust, distracting the chef. He paused for a moment, then shook his head and quickly left the building.

Fliss breathed heavily and waited for a full two minutes before venturing out of her hiding place. With shaking hands she returned to the cages. She forced open the nearest one, and slowly, carefully, gingerly reached inside.

'Come on, little one,' she said softly. 'There's someone I'd like you to meet.'

CHAPTER TWELVE

Fliss paced nervously as she waited for Neville. It was quite dark now, with a feeble moon. She slipped her rucksack off her shoulders and set it down carefully on the dry earth. Although it was a warm night, she pulled her jacket tight around her and did up another button. She squinted down the track, focussing on nothing for a full minute before Neville's bike light came into view.

'At last!' She failed to keep the edge out of her voice.

'I came as quickly as I could.' He dismounted. 'It's quite a pull from the village, you know. Why we couldn't simply meet at my place ...'

'Come here,' Fliss interrupted him. She bent over her rucksack and extracted a small cardboard box. She waited impatiently while Neville leant his bike against a tree.

'Hold that,' she handed him her torch.

'What is all this about? I was in the middle of a batch of scones. They'll be like rock cakes now; you can't just leave the mix sitting about.'

'Neville, shut up.'

'There's no need to be snippy.'

'I'm sorry, but will you please just look.' She held the box towards him and removed the lid.

Neville directed the torch beam inside.

'Shit!' he cried, stepping back. 'It's a rat! What are you doing with that?'

'I told you on the phone, I found it at Withy Hill.'

'You told me you'd found something, you didn't say it was a bloody rat. Don't they have pest control up there?'

'It's not that sort of rat. Look more closely.'

Gingerly, Neville peered in again.

'What's that? That thing on its back?' he asked.

'It's a leg.'

'A leg! That's disgusting. How did it get there?'

'The rat grew it.'

'You make it sound like a beard. For heaven's sake, rats don't grow spare legs on a whim.'

'Okay, I wasn't being accurate. I mean the rat was born with it, and the leg grew.'

'How?'

'Somebody ... engineered it,' Fliss told him.

'What in God's name for? Difficult enough catching the little buggers already, isn't it? Who wants faster rats?'

'Nobody! It's a guinea pig.'

'Look, I didn't come up here for a rodent Who's Who.'

'You know what I mean,' Fliss snapped. 'And have you noticed the colour. At first glance it looks white, but it's not, is it? It's blue.'

They watched the hapless creature as it twitched its whiskers and blinked in the strong light. Suddenly it scratched an urgent itch on the back of its head – with its fifth leg.

'Urgh!' said Neville. 'For pity's sake put the lid back on.'

Fliss was in the process of doing just that when she heard twigs snapping.

'There's someone coming!' she hissed. 'Quick! Behind this tree.'

They dropped to the floor and scuttled around the nearest oak.

'Can you see who it is?' Neville asked.

'No. But there's definitely someone there. Yes, I can see them,' Fliss told him. 'But I can't make out who it is. I wonder what they're doing out here at this time of night.'

'Bird watching? Badger baiting? Rat spotting? Who gives a flying fart? I can't stay crouched here like this much longer – my knees are seizing up.'

'Stop whining. I can't be sure, but I think it's a woman. Whoever it is has got a ... shovel.' Fliss swallowed. 'They seem to be burying something. Shhh!' She froze.

The dark shadow of a person stopped digging and turned in their direction. Whoever it was took a step forward and frowned into the gloom. Fliss and Neville held their breath. The figure turned, finished her task and left quickly.

'It's all right,' Fliss stood up. 'They've gone now.'

'Thank Christ for that.' Neville unfolded himself stiffly, brushing moss and twigs from his trousers.

'Who do you think it was? What do you think they were up to?' Fliss groped for the rucksack and lowered the box towards it.

'You are mistaking me for someone who cares.'

'Pretty odd, though, don't you think?' Fliss lifted the lid to check on the passenger. 'Oh, my God!'

'What now?'

'It's gone. The rat's gone.'

'Gone where?'

'How should I know? Don't just stand there, look for it.' She dropped to the ground again.

'Are you completely mad? If the thing's escaped, it's hardly likely to be hanging around waiting for us to catch it again, is it? Forget it, he's long gone.'

'She,' Fliss corrected him. 'It was a she.'

'No, sorry, that information makes me no keener to grovel in the dirt.'

Fliss stood up again and put her face close to Neville's so he could not ignore her.

'Think about it,' she said through gritted teeth. 'It's female. It's a lab rat. It's a mutant. It might well be pregnant, for all we know. Do you want to be responsible for infesting the Dorset countryside with blue five-legged rats? Well do you?'

'How is it my fault?'

'We don't have time to argue,' Fliss stomped into the undergrowth.

'Oh for goodness sake,' Neville picked up a stick and poked at a fallen log. 'Couldn't they have made it glow in the dark while they were at it. Nothing helpful like that, oh no.'

'Shut up, you'll frighten it away.'

'I'll frighten it!' He probed a patch of nettles carelessly. 'This is mission impossible. I've better things to do with my time than play hide and seek with Frankenstein's hamster.'

Fliss stood up, shoulders drooping with the hopelessness of it all. 'Bugger,' she said quietly. 'Bugger!'

As Rose opened the back door of Honeysuckle Cottage she was careful to make as little noise as possible. Baby would be sound asleep upstairs; his routine was sufficiently fixed for her to be sure of that. Ryan had decided he was well enough to get out of bed, however, and would most likely be watching TV. Rose didn't want to have to explain the mud on her shoes. Quickly and quietly she slipped them off and took them to the sink. She had just started running the tap to rinse off the soles when Ryan's voice behind her made her jump.

'You took your time.'

'I was as quick as I could be. Did Baby wake up?'

'Course not. He's not the one with diar-bloody-rhea, is he? You said you'd only be twenty minutes.'

'Sorry.' She continued to clean her shoes, as it was too late to pretend she was doing anything else.

Ryan stepped forwards and peered over her shoulder.

'Where's all that mud come from? You said you were just popping round to check on old Sally Siddons. Looks more like you've been on a cross-country run,' he gave a derisive snort. 'Which is pretty sodding unlikely when you think about it.'

Rose swilled away the mud as quickly as she could.

'I took the dog out for her. Sally's shingles is no better, you know. She's not up to exercising him. He needed to go out.'

'You two must have been a sight – my missus and the fattest Jack Russell in the country. Where d'you take him to get in that state, anyway?'

'It's quite sticky by the pond. The ducks have been churning it up after the storm, I suppose.' Rose dried the shoes off with kitchen towel and put them by the back door. She turned to Ryan, doing her best to muster a bright and casual smile.

'Can I get you anything?'

'Oh, nice of you to ask – finally! All very well running off to pander to silly old women with a few spots, but what about your husband? Eh? How about looking after someone who's really ill? I could manage a bacon sarnie.'

'Oh, good, you're feeling a little better then?'

'Now, I am, at this moment. Give the thing an hour and who sodding knows.'

'Would you like me to make you an appointment to see the doctor? I could ring the surgery in the morning.' Rose set about grilling bacon.

'No way, I don't want any overpaid quack prodding and poking me. No thank you. You know I never go to the doctor's.' He left the kitchen, heading back to the TV. 'Just bring me my sandwich when it's ready. If it's not too much trouble.'

Rose jabbed at the bacon as she turned it. It had been a long day. She had trekked into Barnchester on the bus with Baby in the morning to go to the bank, and the crowds and traffic and noise had worn her out. But it was something that had to be done. She had opened an account with Baby's prize money cheque on their way home from London, but she never had any intention of leaving the money there. The girl behind the glass screen had looked quite shocked when Rose told her how much she wanted to take out. She had asked her three times if she really wanted to withdraw all the money. She looked to Rose like the sort of girl who would go to Dixie's on a Friday night. That was the trouble with such a small town. Everyone knew everyone and spoke to everyone, and that was where Ryan had his accounts. It would be too easy for him to find out about the winnings. Besides which Rose didn't trust banks. When her grandmother had left her Honeysuckle Cottage the local bank manager had tried to persuade her to sell and invest the money. He had even given her name to the local estate agent. Which was how Ryan had come to call. Which was how they met. Which led to them getting married. No, the money was safer in the woods. She had wrapped it well in Clingfilm and put it in a sturdy Tupperware box, so it would be alright where it was. Until later! Until she decided what to do with it.

It had been an unusually busy Tuesday morning in Neville's office, so that it was almost midday by the time he had a chance to log on to the Internet. He punched in Withy Hill Farm and waited. A cheery website appeared: red and white logo to the fore, photographs of smiling workers, happy little chickens all over the place – the very picture of normality, not a rat in sight, five-legged or otherwise. He slurped at his cold coffee and shuddered. He had been fighting a headache since breakfast, and it wasn't helping his tiresome day. The fact that he had barely slept the night before added to his bad mood. He clicked on the link to the farm's parent company. Again, no mutant rodents, no professors with busy hair and foreign accents and glassy eyes. True, there was mention of biotechnology and even genetic modification, but all the information was so vague as to be worthless.

He thought for a moment, and then punched in the name Claude Lambert. The scrawny chef stared out of the screen at him. There followed details of his restaurant, his books, and his culinary achievements to date. There was also a piece on his new venture with Withy Hill Farm, singing the praises of their conscientiously farmed produce.

'Hmm, back to square one,' Neville said to himself. He checked his desk for the Withy Hill planning application. It wasn't there. He looked in his drawers, his in-tray, his miscellaneous heap under the telephone, and the little-used filing cabinet by the window. Nothing. He buzzed his irksome underling, who sauntered through the door some minutes later.

'Philips, good of you to find the time. Have you, perchance, got the Withy Hill application?' Neville asked.

'Me? No, I gave it to you,' said Philips.

'Yes, I know that, but it's not here now. Someone must have taken it.'

'Not me.'

'Well, is that it? Have you nothing more constructive to say on the matter?'

'Not my problem if you can't keep track of stuff. You were supposed to look at it. You were supposed to attach your comments and pass it up. You ...'

'Yes, yes, yes, I know all that. The fact is I hadn't finished dealing with it and now it's missing.' Neville pointedly rifled through the pile of folders on his desk. 'See? Not here. Gone. Vanished. Vamoosed.'

'I don't know what you expect me to do about it,' said Philips.

'I never expect anything from you, Philips, but I do still harbour this mad notion that as you work here you must serve some useful purpose. One day I'll find out what it is. In the meantime, ask Sharon to step in here for a moment, would you? Do you think you could manage that?'

Philips scowled and left, and was quickly replaced by Sharon.

'You wanted to see me, Mr Meatcher?' asked the department secretary. If ever there was a girl born to be shared among half a dozen men, it was Sharon. Out in the real world she would pass unnoticed in a crowd of even moderately attractive people, such was the forgettable quality of her appearance, and her sharp, thin voice would deter all but the most drunk or desperate. At work, however, she was regularly the cause of macho posturing and squabbling. Here every man in the office wanted to claim her as his own. The fact that none of them could justify having a secretary of their own only made them more determined to monopolise her, so that her time was constantly taken up with trivial and pointless tasks.

'Sharon,' Neville did his best to muster a smile, 'do you have any knowledge of the whereabouts of the Withy Hill application?'

'The chicken farm, d'you mean? Yes, Mr Forbes phoned down for it yesterday. I took it up to him myself. Do you know he's got air conditioning in his office? Imagine. Don't suppose we'll ever get it down here, though. Have to make do with dangling out the window to get some air. It'd be all the same to him if one of us fell out one day.'

'Quite. Did he say why he wanted it?'

'Air conditioning?'

'The Withy Hill file.'

'Oh no, he just said it needed rubber stamping and he'd get it done and out the way.'

'You mean he passed it? Without waiting for me to look at it?'

'Well, I suppose he must have, yes.'

After Sharon left Neville sat for a moment, gazing blankly at the gaunt face of Claude Lambert on his monitor, pondering. He opened his top drawer and took out the copy of his Daryole recipe. With a sigh he screwed it up, tossed it into his waste paper basket, deleted Claude, picked up the phone, and dialled the number Fliss had given him.

'It's me, Neville,' he told her. 'I've been doing some digging on Withy Hill.'

'What have you found?' asked Fliss.

'Absolutely bugger all.'

'Oh. That's useful,' she sounded disappointed. 'I have to say I'm not surprised, though. They're hardly going to shout about what they're up to from the virtual rooftops, are they?'

'No. But there is something ... odd.'

'What?'

Neville lowered his voice to a husky whisper.

'You could be right about the rubber stamping.'

'What? Hello? I can't hear you. Neville?'

'Yes, I'm still here,' he reverted to speaking normally. 'I can't talk to you about it properly now.'

'Okay, come round to my house after work. Oh no, wait, it's Tuesday isn't it? I'm busy tonight. How about tomorrow? Six-ish?'

'Right. See you then.' Neville wasn't sure exactly what he was going to say to Fliss when he saw her, but he had been sufficiently disturbed by the rat to know something had to be done. And the fact that the planning application had been rushed through was worrying, very worrying. He was stirred from his thoughts by the ringing of his telephone. It was Sandra.

'How are you feeling, Neville?' she asked, all sisterly concern. 'I thought you might be a bit down after Saturday. I wanted to call you before, but Brian said not to fuss.'

Neville rubbed his eyes wearily.

'I'm fine, Sandra, really.'

'Such a shame the day was a disaster, after all your hard work. And you never even got to put your pudding in the competition, did you? We liked it. Well, I did, you know how children are about food.'

'I seem to remember Brian saying it reminded him of school dinners.'

'Oh you don't want to listen to Brian, I never do. What a strange man that chef of yours was. Did you ever find out what made him run off like that?'

'No. In fact, no-one has been able to speak to him since.'

'Oh well, that's creative types for you, I suppose.'

'Sandra, much as I'd like to sit here chatting ...'

'Yes, you're busy, of course you are. I'll get to the point. We were wondering if you'd like to bring your friend round for dinner?'

'Friend?'

'Yes, whichever one you like. We thought they were all lovely.'

'Who all?' asked Neville.

'Lucy and Cynthia and Fliss, silly, who did you think I meant?' She paused, and then added, 'Or are there others too?'

'Others? No, no, no. Sandra, you've got it all wrong.'

'Oh? I did wonder. I mean, there's no reason why you shouldn't have three girlfriends – how you live your life is up to you. But I said to Brian, "I bet there's one he's especially keen on." I'm right aren't I? A sister knows these things.'

Neville frowned into the telephone, at a loss as to where to begin to unravel the tangled web that was being woven about him. He knew his sister well enough to realise that once she had an idea in her head he would have trouble ridding her of it.

'Look, it's very sweet of you, but I think it might be a bit much so early in our ... friendship. I mean, meeting my family, the twins, your house, you know ...'

'Ahh, you could be right. Might be too much for her,' Sandra thought for a moment, then had an idea, 'I know! Let's meet at the Farmer's Lodge instead. That would be much better – don't know why I didn't think of it before. Neutral ground. And the food's so lovely, any girl would be impressed.'

Neville winced at the very idea of the microwaved, mass-produced fodder served at such a place.

Sandra was becoming more and more enthusiastic about the idea.

'It's not far from you – just a short walk up onto the A367. Imagine, strolling hand in hand on a beautiful summer's evening, then a lovely meal ...'

'Sandra, have you been lurking in the romantic novel section of the library again?'

'... Brian's treat, of course, seeing as we invited you.'

The Scrooge-like side of Neville pricked up its ears at the thought of dinner and booze at Brian's expense. If nothing else the place must surely offer a reasonable bottle of wine.

At that moment the door of his office opened and in came Richard Forbes, Neville's immediate superior, and least favourite person on the planet – against stiff competition.

'Look, sorry, I'll have to go,' Neville told his sister.

'Saturday night, then. Meet you there about seven thirty, okay?'

'Yes, yes, fine. Bye.' Neville hung up and braced himself to deal with his boss.

CHAPTER THIRTEEN

As Fliss stood outside the Old Vicarage waiting for Cynthia to let her in, she admired the scale and abundance of the garden. It was a few moments before dusk, and a light mandarin tinge was lending the scene a warm, soft-focus appearance. The blossoms of spring had passed, giving way to the brilliance of early summer shrubs and flowers. Here was a perfect example of the fittest surviving, as only the most robust and healthy plants had battled off the throttling weeds to claim their space and light. Although clearly neglected, the garden gave the impression of being more than capable of managing on its own, thank you very much.

At last the door creaked open and a bathrobed Cynthia appeared. Fliss had no time to wonder at her choice of garment, as Hamlet barged out from behind his mistress to introduce himself.

'Ahh, Fliss, so nice to find someone who understands the meaning of punctuality. Hamlet, let the poor girl in. Don't mind him, he's very friendly.'

'Yes, he is, isn't he,' said Fliss, edging past the monstrous hound with no hope of evading his fearsome tongue. She resigned herself to being licked. She could not get accustomed to dealing with Eric and Vinny up at the farm, but at least this dog didn't want to savage her.

'I'm so looking forward to this,' Cynthia spoke as she strode ahead. 'Pam tells me you have worked wonders for her. Wonders! I thought we'd use the sitting room. Will the *chaise longue* be suitable?'

She led Fliss into a high-ceilinged, draughty room. The fireplace harboured a dust-collecting arrangement of dried flowers. The mantelpiece was a muddle of ornaments and pieces of paperwork. Two table lamps gave off an ineffectual glow as the light through the enormous window began to fail. The *chaise longue* was covered in faded red velvet and dog hairs.

'It'll be fine,' said Fliss, setting her bag of crystals down on the floor. She straightened up to see a near naked Cynthia before her. A few wisps of startlingly transparent underwear were, ineffectually, maintaining the woman's modesty. 'Oh!

No, that's not necessary. I mean, you can keep your clothes on.'

'Really? Are you sure it will work like that?'

'Quite sure, you don't want to get cold. It's important you're able to relax,' Fliss told Cynthia as she pulled her robe back on. 'Just lie on your back and make yourself comfortable.'

Fliss knelt beside the *chaise* and pulled from her bag a large square of purple velvet. She spread it on the floor and began placing her crystals upon it. Hamlet sat next to her and watched, apparently fascinated. Fliss tried to avoid meeting his eye, as the slightest attention provoked a further bout of licking.

'I don't pretend to understand what you do with those things,' said Cynthia, waving a hand at the stones, 'I only know Pam strongly suggested I give it a try, and heaven knows I am in need of something.' She placed the back of her hand on her brow and closed her eyes. 'This has been a difficult time for me, as I'm sure you know.'

'Yes, I was in the marquee when ...'

'Please! Don't speak of it,' she sighed. 'Of course one often meets setbacks in life. I have had my share of disaster and calamity, not least losing Edmund so young. But somehow, this time, I simply do not seem able to pick myself up, dust myself off, and start all over again.' She stifled a small sob, removing her hand and turning, watery-eyed, to gaze at Fliss. 'Do you think you can help me?'

'I'll do my best. Try to relax.' Fliss lit a small cone of incense, then took out a notebook and pencil and sat cross legged on the floor. 'Close your eyes if you wish. I'm going to ask you a few questions, just to give me an idea of what might best work for you, okay?'

'My dear, I am entirely in your hands.'

'First, can you tell me about any physical problems you've been having? Any aches or pains at all?'

'I have enjoyed rude health all my life. My mother was the same. But lately I have felt a terrible weakness. A lethargy, as if everything and anything is simply too much effort.' Cynthia closed her eyes and shook her head. 'It's not like me, not like me at all.'

'I see,' Fliss made a note or two. Hamlet leaned over her shoulder to see what she was doing. She pushed him off firmly, taking care not to inhale his fetid breath. In response to being touched he thumped down heavily onto his side and lay slowly whipping his tail against the floor. Small clouds of dust puffed up from the rug.

Fliss tried to focus.

'You've told me you've had a difficult time just recently, would you describe yourself as depressed?' she asked.

Cynthia considered the question for a moment.

'It pains me to admit it, but I think that is precisely what I am. It seems too silly, doesn't it? All over something so unimportant.'

'I don't think it's silly at all. The fundraiser wasn't unimportant to you, and you'd worked very hard getting everything set up, I'm sure. It's only natural to feel a bit down when all your efforts ended in ... Well, I think it's totally understandable.'

'Do you really? You know, my dear, that is exactly what I need. Understanding. Aside from yourself there is really only one person who knows how I feel, who is *simpathetique*.'

'Oh?' Fliss made a few more notes, then put down her book and began to select stones.

'Yes. Dearest Neville, my soul mate. I would be lost without his support. Utterly lost, I tell you.'

Fliss looked again at her client. The worn candlewick bathrobe stretched lumpily over her short, solid, body. Cynthia's hair was greying, thinning, and unwashed. Her bare feet were strangers to a pumice stone. Her stout ankles bore a fuzz of hair that could not be blamed on Hamlet. Even given Fliss's scant acquaintance with Neville, it was difficult to imagine him being interested in Cynthia.

'You know Neville, don't you?' Cynthia asked.

'Oh, barely. I met him ... last Saturday. I can put a face to the name. Have you known him long?' Fliss gently placed a piece of rose quartz on Cynthia's solar plexus.

'We have both lived in the village for years, of course, but we met for the first time at a cookery weekend. We share a passion for all things culinary. Hence the fundraiser ...' she let the thought peter out.

'Aah, I see.' Fliss placed small pieces of tourmaline in each of Cynthia's upturned palms. 'That must be nice, to have a shared interest and somebody appreciative to cook for. I'm afraid my daughter doesn't think much of my cooking. Just tip your head back a little and keep nice and still. That's lovely.' She positioned a flat piece of turquoise on Cynthia's brow.

'Alas, poor Neville is such a busy man,' sighed Cynthia. 'He rarely has time for social engagements. That's why I valued the time he so selflessly gave to NHEC, and all for nothing.'

'Oh, not for nothing. I'm sure he enjoyed your company.'

'I like to think so, of course, but,' she opened her eyes and looked up at Fliss, 'I expect you consider me a silly old woman who is deluding herself.'

'Nonsense, you said yourself he understands you, that's important. Shows he cares enough to bother.' Fliss sat back on the floor. 'Now, try not to think about anything for a few minutes. Let your mind relax as much as your body.'

Cynthia sighed deeply, then closed her eyes once more and lay quiet and still. Fliss watched over her in the fading light of the neglected old room. Silence wrapped itself around them both; silence which was eventually broken by a low rumbling snore. Fliss frowned at the figure in front of her, checking the stones, and wondering how she had gone wrong again. It was as she tweaked the position of the small garnet on Cynthia's belly that she realised the noise was coming from behind her. She turned to see Hamlet, flat as a trophy rug, tail motionless, his whole body shuddering through deep, baritone snores.

Rose lifted Baby out of the car seat and turned to stare at the beautiful stately home in front of them. Milton-sub-Hubdan Hall was the sort of building designed to make people feel small. The broad flight of steps up to the columned portico alone was daunting enough to rivet Rose to the spot. The car which had been sent to collect her slipped away quietly, leaving mother and child alone. Rose contemplated strapping Baby into his buggy, but she would not be able to haul it up the steps to the front door. On the point of heading off down the drive, she was relieved to hear someone scrunching over the gravel. Baby's agent, Annabel, appeared, smiling enthusiastically. The bubbly young woman waved as she called out.

'Rose! Lovely to see you again. And Baby, looking gorgeous, as ever. We're in the orangery, around the back.' She grabbed the buggy with one hand and steered Rose with the other. 'Fabulous location for a shoot, but, my God, the heat! Warmest day of the year, I shouldn't wonder, and we have to spend it in a whopping great greenhouse!' She laughed loudly. 'Still, that's showbiz! Did you have a good journey? Car all right? Look at darling Baby, such a good

boy. And you're going to keep on being a good boy for
Mummy, aren't you? I can tell.' She hooked open the
conservatory door with her foot, pausing for a second to look
earnestly at Rose. 'You've got a little gem here, Rose, a star in
the making. Trust me,' she tapped the side of her fine,
hooked nose with a ruby nail, 'I know star quality when I find
it, and your little sweetheart has got it in spades. Marco!' she
bellowed. 'Marco, we need hairdressing and make-up here
please. Now would be good.'

Rose let out a small gasp of delight. Before her eyes was a
scene from another land. A far away place, a fairytale. The
orangery was spectacular to begin with, but now it was a
picture of fantasy. Sunbeams danced through the ivies and
ribbons and swags of voile which festooned the upper parts
of the room. Tiny silver stars and glass beads hung on wires,
spinning and shinning in the light. Huge palms and ferns in
pots the size of baby elephants gave an effect somewhere
between jungle and midsummer night's dream. Dotted
among the plants and decorations were little sparkling silver
chairs suspended on chains, with flowers woven into them.

The people in this wonderland were much more ordinary.
Harassed looking men and women hurried about. Some were
wearing headphones, others talking into telephones and still
more with clipboards. Everyone was hot and cross and busy.
Expensive and complicated cameras and equipment trailed
wires everywhere. In the far corner two small babies were
being prevented from dismantling anything they could reach.

Marco appeared, followed by a girl holding a tiny a
bumblebee outfit, and a boy with a tray of juice.

'Ah, here we are.' Annabel took a glass. 'Have a drink,
Rose, this is thirsty work. Pippa here has Baby's costume,
and in a minute she'll take you to his dressing room. First,
let Marco have a look at him. He'll have a chat with you
about doing Baby's hair and make-up. Okay? I'll see you
later, got to round up a missing toddler. His mother is
reliably unpunctual.'

Rose smiled nervously at Marco. He was not quite what
she had been expecting. In her experience hairdressers were
female, with complicated hairdos, and a tendency to be
bored-looking. Either that, or the ones on TV were gay and a
bit strange. Marco seemed reassuringly normal. He was big,
too. At least six foot, and broad shouldered, and more than a
little overweight. His voice was another surprise.

'Hiya, Rose, is it?' he asked in a soft Welsh baritone.

Rose nodded.

'Nice to meet you, my lovely. And what a handsome young man this is.' He took Baby's hand and gave it a little shake. 'Very pleased to meet you, too, *bach*. Welcome to the madhouse. No, I shouldn't really say that, but you'll see what I mean. There's a competition going on here to see who can be the most stressed.' He leant down to whisper in Rose's ear, 'I think our director's winning at the moment, but the bossy woman in the green dress is giving him a run for his money. There'll be a ginormous row, in a minute.'

Rose laughed, startling herself with the unfamiliar sound. It had been a very long time since anyone had made her laugh like that. She smiled at Marco, who responded with the biggest grin she had ever seen.

'Baby won't need much hairdressing as such,' he told her, 'although he does have plenty of the stuff, which makes a nice change. All some of these babies need is a wipe over with a damp cloth to bring up the shine! Anyway, I'll help fix his antennae, and sort out a bit of bumbly make-up for him. You pop off with Pippa and I'll catch up with you in five minutes, okay?'

In the cluttered space which had been turned into a dressing room Rose gently wriggled Baby into his costume. As always he was happy and uncomplaining, and particularly enjoyed playing with his new wings. Other mothers and their babies arrived and there was a deal of cajoling and crying and tempers being lost. Soon the room was full of butterflies, spiders, grasshoppers, snails and dragonflies. Baby was the only bee, and particular care had been taken with his outfit, which was all shimmering velvet and satin, with gossamer wings. Rose sat by the open window with Baby on her knee, hoping the cool air would stop him overheating.

'Here you are, my lovely.' Marco pushed his way through the crush of people. 'Thought for a minute you'd gone home. Not nervous, are you?'

'Oh, just a little. It's very hot. And so many people ...'

'New to this game, is it? Don't you worry, the filming won't take long, and then you can get outside for some fresh air. Take Baby for a ride around the grounds.'

'I'm glad I don't have to go in front of the cameras,' she said.

'You'd look gorgeous – that blue really suits you.'

Rose blushed.

'Oh, thank you. I bought the outfit specially. I'd never been to an expensive boutique before. The lady who owned the shop was so nice. She had so many good ideas. She helped me chose the dress, and the shoes, and the bag.'

'You want my advice, *cariad?* You buy all your clothes there from now on. Figure like yours, you want to show off those curves.'

Rose fidgeted in her seat uncomfortably.

'No,' Marco explained, 'I mean it. In this job I'm surrounded by women with pipe cleaners for legs, fried eggs for boobs, and no bums worth mentioning. It makes a very pleasant change to see a real woman, very pleasant.'

Rose stared at the big, strong, friendly man. That somebody might find her attractive was such an alien concept to her she was at a loss to know how to handle the idea. Ryan had done a very good job over the years of destroying her self-esteem. But lately she had been making more of an effort – for Baby. Now that they had to go out and about, she didn't want to show him up. And she knew she looked smart in her new outfit. When she had signed Baby up with the modelling agency Annabel had warned her she would need to be practical, organised, and reliable to make the most of his career. She knew that involved looking well turned out too.

'Right,' without further warning, Marco picked up Baby and lifted him gently into the air, 'come on, bumble bee *bach,* let's get you ready for your close up.'

Rose instinctively reached out a hand to take Baby back, then paused. She watched as Baby clapped his hands with glee, and listened as he broke into spontaneous, joyful laughter.

'I think he likes you,' she told Marco as they repositioned themselves by a highchair and a table of make-up.

'Course he does, why wouldn't he? He knows I'm just a big kid myself, don't you, my little superstar?'

Rose watched over Marco's shoulder as he applied tiny amounts of glitter to Baby's face, and a few dark smudgy lines. She glanced up at the mirror and saw her own reflection. Her hair was a mess, somehow managing to frizz and flop at the same time. She pushed it back off her face quickly.

Marco noticed the gesture.

'The woman with the boutique hasn't got a salon as well, I suppose?' he asked.

Rose shook her head.

'I'm afraid not. I can't do anything with it in this heat.'

'Let's have a look,' Marco swivelled round in his chair and softly stroked Rose's hair, gently straightening out a curl, then letting it spring back into place again. 'I can see where Baby gets his lovely locks from. I know people who would sell their grannies for curls like these. But you're not making the best of them, my lovely.'

Rose's face showed her discomfort.

'Not to worry,' he told her.' After the 'shoot' as we professionals call it,' he said with mock importance,' we'll be hanging around for ages before we can go home. I won't be busy then. We'll find a basin and a quiet corner, and I'll give you a do. How'd that be?'

'Oh, no, I couldn't ... it wouldn't ... I haven't ...'

'Great, that's settled then. Look out, Baby,' he turned his attention back to the make-up, 'we are going to make your Mam look fabulous.'

Neville knocked smartly on the door of number three Brook Terrace and waited. He was ten minutes early, having decided this was not a social engagement, as such, so that lateness would be inappropriate. He heard footsteps and the door opened. A skinny teenage girl eyed him suspiciously.

'Oh,' said Neville, 'I'm looking for Fliss. Fliss Horton. This is the right house, isn't it?'

'Yes. You're the man from the planning department, aren't you?'

'That's me,' Neville waited for a possible introduction or an invitation to step inside. Neither came. 'She is expecting me,' he explained.

'You'd better come in then.'

Neville was led through the tiny hallway and into the kitchen where Fliss appeared.

'Ah, Neville, I see you've met my daughter, Rhian. Great. Would you like a drink? A glass of wine, perhaps?' she headed towards the fridge.

'Well, why not,' he peered past her, trying to see what was on offer.

Fliss turned and showed him the bottle.

'Pinot Grigio do you?'

'Oh,' Neville was pleasantly surprised, 'yes, thank you.'

'Come on,' Fliss grabbed a couple of glasses and a corkscrew and made her way to the sitting room. 'Might as well be comfortable,' she said, settling onto the battered sofa.

Neville chose an overstuffed armchair covered by a worn tapestry rug. It looked pretty robust, but was so soft it almost swallowed Neville whole. He sank into it, his backside coming to rest only a few inches above the floor. The resulting posture was comfortable, but unnervingly low, and far less business like than he had been aiming for.

Fliss uncorked the wine. Rhian lurked in the doorway.

'Haven't you got some homework you should be doing, Rhi?' her mother asked.

Rhian scowled. 'Just tell me to bugger off, why don't you!'

'Rhian ...'

'Don't worry, I won't stay where I'm not wanted,' she said, slamming out of the room.

'Sorry,' Fliss handed Neville his drink, 'she's at that awkward age.'

'From what I've heard it starts when children are born and ends shortly after their parents enter senility.'

'That's about right. None of your own, then?'

'No,' he took a swig of his wine. 'This is really quite good.'

'Is it? I wouldn't know. I've a friend who's trying to educate my palate, but I'm afraid it's a lost cause. As long as it's got alcohol in it, I'm happy. Now, tell me what you found out about Withy Hill. You said there was something.'

'There was nothing enlightening on their website, but, well, the planning application ... it's been rushed through.'

'What, approved and granted and everything? Already?'

'Looks that way. And I didn't even get to pass an opinion.'

'And you do normally?' asked Fliss.

'Yes, of course, that is my job. The oddest thing about it is the speed it's all been done. Nothing happens quickly in planning, and yet this thing's whizzed through.'

'So who's being paid off?'

'Well it certainly isn't me,' Neville drained his glass. 'Not that people haven't tried.'

'Really? You were offered money to rubber stamp the thing?'

'Well, not money, but ... let's just say someone tried to persuade me to look favourably on the application.'

'And you didn't think that was odd at the time? You didn't do anything about it?' Fliss refilled his glass.

'I really didn't take it seriously, to be honest. I had other things to think about.'

'I hope you're going to take it seriously now. For heaven's sake, you saw the rat.'

'Don't remind me. I've had nightmares, you know.'

'You think I haven't? There is something very, very nasty going on up at that farm,' Fliss topped up her own glass. 'You have to see that now.'

'Yes, okay, I agree, but we still don't know what, exactly.'

'We know they're breeding monster rats. We know they're planning a proper laboratory. We're pretty sure they've bribed someone to get permission for the building.'

'The thing that baffles me,' said Neville, trying to adjust his position to something a little more appropriate, but sinking deeper into the man-eating chair, 'is what a five-legged rat has got to do with chicken farming. I mean, what in God's name are they going to do to the actual chickens?'

'It makes me very glad to be a vegetarian, I can tell you. I can't believe we were stupid enough to lose the rat in the woods.'

'I like the "we", you were the one in charge of exhibit A, as I remember it.'

'What does that matter? The point is it's out there somewhere. And what's going to happen when somebody notices it's missing?'

'I should imagine they'll worry that someone's going to let the cat out of the bag. Or should I say the rat out of the bag,' Neville allowed himself a little chuckle at his joke, but it was clear from Fliss's expression she didn't find it funny.

'It's all very well for you,' she said. 'I work up there. They may very well start to point the finger of suspicion in my direction.'

'Nobody saw you take it.'

'I hope not. But I told you I was nearly discovered by that bizarre chef of yours.'

'He is most definitely not my anything. I'm afraid he is not the man I thought he was, and frankly, after last Saturday's fiasco, if I never hear the name Claude Lambert again it will be too soon.'

'Well you may be hearing it quite a lot from now on,' Fliss warned him. 'It's obvious he knows all about these experiments, he was in that room, and it wasn't the first time he'd been in there. He already knew about the rats. He's in this thing up to his popping little eyeballs. More wine?'

Neville nodded and struggled to reach the offered bottle. From his inelegant, low-slung position, Fliss looked taller and slimmer than he remembered.

'What was he looking for, d'you think?' Neville asked as she poured. 'And why is he hanging around at the farm anyway?'

'I can't imagine. The Christians didn't tell me he'd be staying there while they were away, and he's been keeping a pretty low profile. That was the first I'd seen of him.'

'You didn't see what he took out of the cupboard?'

'A jar of something, I couldn't tell what.'

'I'm guessing coriander is unlikely. Perhaps it was medicine of some kind. He's obviously pretty ill.'

'That's one word for it,' said Fliss.

'Meaning?'

Fliss sat back on the sofa, shaking her head, and ran a hand through her long loose hair.

'Meaning I had a boyfriend once who looked like that, and a very expensive luxury he was too. When we split up he still had a habit that cost more per week than I live on for a month.'

'Drugs?'

'Well poor old Claude didn't get to look like that by eating all his posh nosh and then spending four hours a day on an exercise bike. Cocaine, I should imagine. That would explain the runny nose too. How I ever found that attractive ...'

Now it was Neville's turn to slump back even further into his seat.

'This gets worse. No wonder the man was so moody and unreliable,' A thought occurred to him, 'Your old boyfriend, he wasn't blue, by any chance?'

'No. That's new to me. I don't think I've ever met anyone such a peculiar colour,' she said.

'Oh yes you have,' Neville corrected her.

'I have?'

'Short fellow, twitchy, leggy, you might say. Houdini tendencies. Ring any bells?'

'My God, the rat! The rat was blue too.'

'Ergo, either our long-tailed chum had a cocaine habit, or ...'

'It's not cocaine. Claude's using something else. Something they give to the rats. Something to do with the experiments.'

'Poor sod must be even madder than we thought.'

'Wait a minute,' Fliss held up a hand, shaking her head again. 'This is getting too weird. Blue rats with five legs. Blue burnt-out chefs. What are they trying to make? Colour co-ordinated manic chickens? And why on earth would Claude take the stuff?'

'Presumably it has some attractive side effects. Did you happen to notice if any of those caged rats were sleeping? Or were they all busy re-arranging their little bits of furniture, or spinning round in their wheels and chatting to one another ceaselessly? Or partying, perhaps?' Neville took another drink.

'I'm glad you find this funny. I find it extremely scary,' Fliss told him.

'Sorry, you're right. Not funny.' He thought for a moment. 'There's another thing, who were those two heavies hanging around Claude's car on Saturday? And why did the sight of them make him bolt like that?'

'To know that I think you'd have to talk to Claude.'

'Is he still up at the farm?'

'I suppose so, I haven't been back since the rat-nap. Anyway, we can hardly just waltz up and ask him, can we?' Fliss pointed out.

Neville sighed, closed his eyes for a moment, and rubbed his temples wearily. The room was warm and quiet, the wine fairly strong, and the chair seductively comfy.

'You know,' he said, 'I really can't think about this any more at the moment. My head is starting to spin. What say we sleep on it? The Christians are still away, so surely nothing much is going to happen for a day or so.'

'Okay, but we have to come up with something,' Fliss said.

Neville clambered to his feet.

'Thanks for the wine,' he followed Fliss out of the sitting room, watching the way her red hair swung as she walked. At the front door he paused, another urgent matter having come into his head.

'Look, I'm going out for a bite to eat with my sister and her husband on Saturday night, nothing fancy, just up the road. I don't suppose you'd like to join us?'

Fliss turned and smiled, a lovely, big, warm smile.

'That's really sweet of you, Neville. But I'm afraid I'm busy on Saturday. Well, weekends in general. I have a friend who comes to stay ...' she trailed off.

'Oh, yes of course. Fine, forget about it.' Neville squeezed past her and hurried out. 'I'll call you if I have any brainwaves about Withy Hill,' he assured her, then headed home, wondering why he felt a strange mixture of happiness and disappointment.

CHAPTER FOURTEEN

To Rose's surprise, when Ryan returned home from work that Wednesday evening he was actually whistling. He even gave Baby his sunglasses to play with for a moment, as he slipped his jacket over the back of a kitchen chair.

'There you go, mate,' he said. 'Proper Pilots those are, none of your cheap rubbish. Mind you don't bend them, or it'll come out of your pocket money.'

'They're not really suitable ...' said Rose.

'Don't fuss, woman. He knows quality when he sees it. He's a chip off the old block.'

'You sound as if you're feeling better.' Rose put a mug of tea in front of Ryan. 'Did you have a good day at work?'

'I did indeed. Closed a blinder of a sale on a crap flat in Barnchester, thought we'd be stuck with the sodding thing forever. And yeah, I do feel better. At last, guts seem to have stopped giving me gip.'

'Oh, that's good.' Rose hovered next to Baby, keeping a keen eye on the sunglasses.

'In fact,' Ryan swigged at his tea, 'I'm feeling so much better I'm going to work late tomorrow night. Catch up on some stuff.'

Rose stiffened a little, her grip on Baby's highchair tightening.

'Tomorrow? That's Thursday, isn't it?'

'Generally is after Wednesday. Don't wait up.' He threw her a glance, and then paused, looking harder. 'You had your hair done?' he asked.

'Oh, yesterday.'

'You didn't say you were going into town. How much did that set me back?'

'Nothing, a friend did it for me.'

He gave a short laugh. 'Didn't know you had any friends. Hey! Watch the lenses, you little monster.' He snatched the sunglasses from Baby's over-enthusiastic grasp.

Baby responded by letting out an uncharacteristic wail of protest. Rose quickly calmed him by giving him her house keys to play with.

'I'll cook something nice for your tea, seeing as you're feeling better,' she said. 'How about spaghetti bolognese? With lots of herbs?'

'Sounds good to me,' he stood up, taking off his tie. 'I'm off to watch the footie. Give me a shout when grub's ready,' he said, heading for the lounge.

Rose heard the noise of the television and set about fetching the ingredients she needed – onions, mince, green pepper, tinned tomatoes, and herbs. Lots of herbs!

It was well past midnight when Ryan's stomach finally settled enough to allow him to drop into an exhausted sleep. He had eaten well, enjoyed his food. He had even said as much to Rose. But then, an hour or so later, the cramps and nausea had started again. It seemed he still hadn't completely shaken off his tummy bug. Rose had fetched glasses of water and Pepto Bismol and hot-water bottles, while Ryan had spent the evening dashing to the bathroom, then staggering back to the bed.

Once he and Baby were at last sleeping deeply and peacefully, Rose went back downstairs. Quietly she took the car keys from Ryan's jacket pocket, and then made her way into the garage. She stood for a moment, looking at the sleek, flashy car in front of her. Then she picked up the Haines manual and began searching purposefully through it.

Fliss waited until Rhian and Sam had gone back upstairs after supper before picking up the phone and settling herself on the window seat in the sitting room. It was still light, and the village looked its chocolate box best in the low summer sun. She dialled Daniel's home number, and was a little surprised to find him in.

'Hi, Babe. How's it going down there in darkest Dorset?'

'Fine, well, sort of,' she said.

'Oh? Something nasty in the woodshed?'

'Unfortunately, yes.'

'Hmm, tell me more.'

'I will,' she said, trying a firm, level tone. 'But only if you don't just make a joke of the whole thing.'

'Now, does that sound like me?'

'I mean it, Dan. This is serious.'

'Okay, you've got my attention.'

Fliss took a deep breath. 'You remember I told you I had my suspicions about Withy Hill, about what they were up to?'

'Yes, of course, I do have a marginally more long-term memory than a goldfish. They want to build a laboratory of some sort. You did mention it, once or twice.'

Fliss chose to ignore his sarcasm, and resisted rising to the bait. 'Well I've found out more. I've been talking to Neville, and he says ...'

'Neville?'

'Yes, Neville Meatcher, he works in the planning department of Barnchester Council. He says the plans have already been approved. We may even be too late to stop it. When we discussed it last night ...'

'Last night? Work late at the Council down there, do they?'

'What? No, he came round here.'

Daniel's tone grew sharp. 'Oh, I see, house calls. Better still.'

'This was not something he wanted to discuss in the office. Besides, he lives in the village, he didn't even need to get his bicycle out – it was easy for him to pop round.'

'I'm pleased to hear you're getting to know the neighbours at last.'

'Can I get to the point, or are you going to interrupt me every two seconds?' It was Fliss's turn to be sharp. Daniel didn't respond, so she pressed on. 'The thing is, it's really unusual for an application to go through that quickly. And it bypassed the normal channels. Someone's been bought.'

'You can't know that. Why would anyone go to so much trouble to get a chicken feed lab built?'

'It's not for chicken feed.' Fliss paused. 'I decided to have a look around at the farm. The boss is away at the moment. Anyway, I found this room, a locked room. They've already been doing experiments and stuff in there, but keeping it secret. I found something. Something, horrible, Dan. They've been messing about with rats – I found one with five legs.'

'Yeuch!'

'That's exactly what Neville said when I showed it to him.'

'You stole this freak and took it home?'

'No, no, of course not. We met in the woods at night. It seemed more sensible.'

'Meeting a strange man in a remote place after dark with a half-deformed rat, yeah, Babe, really sensible.'

'Look, never mind about that. The point is, we've got to do something. They can't be allowed to build the laboratory and do God knows what up there.'

'I'm sure your friend Nigel ...'

'Neville.'

'... Whatever, I'm sure he has a chum on the local rag. The provincial press must be starved of decent stories, I'm sure they'd run with this one. It clearly has legs.'

'Daniel! This is not funny.'

'Well I don't know what else you expect me to suggest. Doesn't Neville have any bright ideas? You could pop round for a cup of sugar – muscovado, of course – and pick his brains. Assuming he has any left, given where he works.'

'For heaven's sake, I had hoped you'd support me in this; that you'd actually pull your overpaid, over-qualified finger out and be of some help. But, oh no, you have to come over all adolescent and jealous ...'

'Jealous! Of Neville, the neighbourhood nerd? I don't think so.'

'Listen to yourself! Why can't you behave like a grown up for a change? Sometimes you're more of a teenager than Rhian.'

'Well excuse me for not being mature enough for your liking all of a sudden. Your new best friend isn't a few years older than us, by any chance?' Daniel wanted to know.

'What on earth has that got to do with anything? I can't believe you are more concerned about me talking to someone who happens to live in the village than ...'

'Talking to, meeting in woods, entertaining in your snug little home ...'

'Oh fine. Forget it, Daniel. Just forget the whole thing. You're obviously not interested. Sorry I even bothered to ask. I'll deal with the situation on my own.'

'But you're not on your own, are you – you've got Neville. Well, I'd hate to get in the way of burgeoning rural relations. Maybe I'll give the sticks a miss this weekend. Leave you to it.'

'Fine, you do that. Goodbye, Daniel.' Fliss clicked off the phone and sat seething, her hands shaking more than a little. She bit her lip to stop infuriating tears from emerging, but a noise behind her made her jump. She turned to see Rhian standing in the doorway, arms folded, mouth set in that determined line.

'Ah,' said Fliss, 'I take it you heard ...'

Rhian didn't move an inch.

'I want to know everything. Right now, all the details, particularly about the rat.' She yelled over her shoulder, 'Sam! Get down here! You're going to want to hear this.'

It took Fliss some time to tell all she knew to Rhian and Sam. Both girls were furious. Sam felt scandalised to think that such revolting activities had been going on right under her nose. Clearly her information sources were fallible after all. Rhian was shocked and mortified on behalf of the rats and chickens, and full of pique and indignation that her mother had tried to keep the whole business a secret from her.

'We didn't want to worry you,' Fliss tried to explain. 'Especially when we weren't sure what was going on.'

'Huh, it's typical of Daniel,' said Rhian. 'He pretends to treat me like an adult, but when it comes down to it he still thinks I'm a child.'

'No, actually, Daniel didn't know about the rat and the planning until just now. You heard me telling him.'

'So who is "we"?'

'Neville and me. You know he came to see me last night.'

Sam shook her head solemnly. 'He's in the enemy camp, Mrs Horton. You really shouldn't be fraternising with him.'

'He's not in any camp. Nor am I. And I wouldn't know how to fraternise. Anyway, it was your idea I speak to him in the first place.'

'To gain information,' Sam reminded her. 'There are clearly delineated boundaries in a case like this. It is important to observe them. Few people can be trusted with such sensitive evidence.'

'Maybe so, but I had to show Neville the rat to convince him there was something going on. Otherwise he would never have checked up on the planning application. We've only just met, for heaven's sake, why would he take my word for anything? Besides, he's okay. He doesn't approve of what's going on any more than you do.'

'Oh yeah?' Rhian was unconvinced. 'So what's he going to do about it, then?'

Fliss tried to sound positive, hoping to give the impression that everything was being dealt with. 'We're giving it some more thought – we need to come up with a sensible plan of action. No point rushing and making a mess of things.'

'Right,' said Rhian. 'Can't imagine that anorak having a crap without putting it in his diary first.'

'Rhian! You don't even know the man. Just for once could you give someone the benefit of the doubt? Would it kill you?'

'Well what's he waiting for? A real man would be doing something, not just thinking about it.'

'Rhian's right,' said Sam. 'This is clearly a situation demanding direct action.'

'Now hold on,' Fliss stood up, the better to make her point. 'Let's be absolutely clear about this. You are to do nothing, do you hear me? Nothing. This is important, and there are clearly some devious and single-minded people involved. I'm trusting you two to behave like adults here; I've told you everything.'

'Only because you had no choice,' Rhian pointed out.

'That's as may be, but you have to give me your word on this. Both of you, your word that you won't go charging off on your own doing something harebrained.'

'Harebrained!' Now Rhian stood up. 'Oh yes, you're really treating us like adults, I can see that.'

'You know what I mean. No graffiti on the chicken sheds. No chaining yourselves to the yard gate. In fact, no going anywhere near Withy Hill Farm. Do I make myself clear?'

The girls responded with a wilful silence.

'I promise I will tell you as soon as there is something for you to do. Some way you can help. In the meantime you keep what I have told you to yourselves. Sam, that means not telling your parents for now, I'm afraid. Neville and I are going to come up with something. Trust me, this is not something we are going to sit back and let happen. Okay?'

Still there was no response.

'Okay?' Fliss tried again.

There was another pause, and the girls looked at one another for a moment. Sam gave a nod, and Rhian turned back to her mother.

'Okay, you've got a week. If you haven't come up with something by then, we will. Deal?'

'Deal,' Fliss agreed, before slumping onto the sofa as the girls went back upstairs. She sat for a moment in the increasing gloom, exhausted by the hoop jumping she had to perform to communicate with Rhian, and flattened by her telephone conversation with Daniel. After a little more thought she picked up the phone again. She carried it out to the hall and searched through the local phone book, then dialled. The ringing tone sang away merrily for what seemed an unnecessarily long time, then Neville answered.

'Hi, it's me, Fliss.'

'Ah, afraid I haven't come up with a master plan yet,' Neville told her.

'No, don't panic, nor have I,' said Fliss. She took a steadying breath. 'Actually I was calling to ask if your offer of dinner of Saturday night was still open? It seems I won't be busy, after all.'

'Oh, I see. Yes, of course. I'm glad you can make it.' Neville sounded quite chipper all of a sudden. 'I did warn you my sister and her husband will be there too, didn't I? They're determined to go to the Farmer's Lodge on the Barnchester Road. Not exactly a menu to die for.'

'As long as it's not a menu to die of.'

'Fortunately they keep a surprisingly good cellar. Helps wash the scampi down. And it's close. We could walk, if you like.'

'Great. That'll give us a chance to discuss you-know-what. Rhian knows everything, so we're on borrowed time.'

'I'll call for you at seven on Saturday then,' said Neville.

After she had rung off Fliss sat for a while on the bottom stair, telephone in hand, and laughed when she realised she was worrying about what she was going to wear.

Neville puffed as he pedalled, finding the journey home longer than usual. He had been forced to stay late at the office, yet again, due to an apparently urgent pile of trivia arriving on his desk at 5:30. Sharon had assured him it all had to be done then and there – orders from above, it seemed. This was the third day running Neville had to work well beyond his normal hours, and he was beginning to think Mr Forbes was deliberately filling his time. Could he have got wind of Neville's investigations into Withy Hill? It was possible. His increased workload had certainly had the effect of hampering his attempts at thinking up some way of exposing Withy Hill. Some way that did not involve losing his job, preferably. But time was running out. Since Fliss's revelation of the night before that Rhian now knew about the rat, he was keenly aware they would have to come up with something soon. But what? There was no point going to the press without some sort of proof. At best they would be laughed at, and at worst his boss could dismiss him and sue for slander. It was obvious they needed evidence, something incontrovertible. However, the idea of what might be involved in getting such evidence brought Neville out in a cold sweat.

He kept his bike well into the side of the road, hearing a fast car approaching from behind. He still bore the scars of his encounter of a few weeks ago with the Withy Hill lorry, and was somewhat wary of the combination of narrow roads and speeding traffic. He wobbled slightly as the car flashed past; registering only as it disappeared that it was somehow familiar. He paused, foot on the floor, catching his breath, trying to focus his mind on a vague memory. Then it came to him where he had seen the blue Subaru before.

'Claude sodding Lambert! Now where's he going?' he wondered aloud. He heard the engine noise change as it rounded the bend. Instead of gearing down and revving up to climb the hill towards the village it slowed almost to a halt. Neville pedalled on and made the corner just in time to catch sight of the car turning left up a private drive. A For Sale sign sat on the gatepost, above a smaller one bearing the name *The Larches*. On impulse, Neville followed, taking care not to get close enough to be spotted.

The short drive led to a secluded and apparently empty house. Neville parked among the branches of a late-flowering rhododendron and watched. The car stopped to one side of the house and the driver got out. Neville was still some distance away, but even so he could clearly see that this was not Claude Lambert. He couldn't make out the passenger, who was still sitting in the car. Curious, Neville left his bike hidden in the bush and crept forward until he reached the remnant of an old holly hedge. He hunkered down behind it, squinting out from the dense cover of the glossy leaves. Now he recognised the driver as a man from the village – Ryan Behr. Neville had dealt with the young estate agent several years ago when he first rented his flat above the Post Office. Ryan was plainly furious about something, his voice raised sufficiently for every word to easily carry as far as Neville.

'Stupid, bastard, sodding thing!' he yelled, banging his fist on the roof of the car. 'What the fuck's wrong with it now!' He tore off his jacket, threw it onto the driver's seat, then bent down to try and peer underneath the vehicle.

The passenger door opened. Neville craned his neck to try and identify the person who was climbing out. It definitely wasn't Claude. Nor, if memory served, was it Ryan's rather plump, mousy wife, as far as Neville could see. The young woman was tall, slender, and expensively dressed. She had glossy blonde hair, held back off her face by a pair of sunglasses perched carefully on the top of her head, and a sharp, strident voice.

'There's no point losing your temper,' she told Ryan. 'I don't know why you're getting so upset anyway, I couldn't hear anything.'

'Then you must be sodding deaf,' Ryan shouted back from under the car.

'Oh, charming. Look, I didn't come all the way out here just so you could spend the whole time searching for a silly rattling noise in your precious car.'

'A clunk, not a rattle. It was a clunk. And it was coming from somewhere under here. It's just one thing after a bloody 'nother, for Christ's sake.'

'Can't you look for it later? I want to go inside. Where are the keys?'

'In my jacket. You go on, I'll be up in a minute.'

'Promises, promises.'

Neville watched as the woman checked through Ryan's pockets. He had no interest in the car or the couple now he knew Claude was not there, but he was sure he'd be seen if he tried to leave. What would they think if they found him lurking in the bushes apparently spying on them? He would have to wait a few more minutes, just until they'd gone into the house.

'I can't find them,' the woman spoke to Ryan's back as he grovelled beside the car shining a torch on its underbelly. 'Are you sure you brought them?' she asked.

'Of course I did.' Ryan straightened up with some obvious difficulty. 'Ow! Sod it!' he grimaced and leant heavily on the car.

'What on earth's the matter now?'

'My stomach, oow!'

'Again?' the woman's voice showed more than a hint of impatience. 'I thought you said you were better. You said you'd finally shaken off that bug.'

'I thought I had, but ... ahh ... it's more than sodding obvious I haven't, isn't it? Where are those keys? I need the bog.' He shook his jacket, then dived into the car and searched inside.

'I told you, they're not there. You must have left them in the office.'

'Bastard, sodding, keys!'

'Wonderful evening this is turning out to be,' complained the woman.

Ryan emerged from the car, bent double, clutching at his stomach and groaning loudly.

'I gotta get to the bog!'

'Well I don't know what you expect me to do about it. You're the one who forgot the keys.'

'Fuck!' shouted Ryan, before sprinting for the shrubbery.

Neville gasped as he realised Ryan was heading straight for him. He forced himself to burrow deeper into the holly bush. A hundred prickles stabbed at his hands and face. It took a considerable amount of willpower for him not to cry out. He froze, squashed into the damp earth, spikes pinning him down.

Ryan blundered into the undergrowth, tugging at his belt. Not more than a few yards from Neville's hiding place he dropped his trousers. There was a tortured moan, then the unmistakeable sounds of violent, explosive, and abundant diarrhoea.

Neville's jaw dropped in horror. He quickly shut it again as an acrid and repulsive stench reached his nostrils. He closed his eyes and tried to imagine he was somewhere, anywhere, else. The foul smell grew stronger. Ryan's moans continued for what seemed like days, accompanied by graphic sound effects. Neville clung to a holly bush root in an effort to stop himself bolting in search of clean air. Vomiting could only be moments away, for both Ryan and himself.

Then, mercifully, the noises stopped. With a deep sigh, Ryan hitched up his trousers and staggered back out to his car.

Neville pressed the back of his hand hard against his mouth and dared to open his eyes. Ryan was already behind the wheel of his car, the woman hurrying to the passenger's seat complaining all the while.   With much slamming of doors and revving of the engine the hapless couple sped away.

The moment they were out of sight Neville shot from his cover like a driven pheasant. He put as much distance as he could, as quickly as he could, between himself and the revolting scene of Ryan's evacuation. Gulping fresh air he retrieved his bicycle, and peddled, not a little unsteadily, in the direction of home.

The full midnight moon shone with a silver brilliance over the sylvan scene. Nettlecombe Hatchet slept. Beneath the shimmering lunar beams the village lay peaceful and quiet, a preternatural stillness stopping time. The landscape slumbered in the ageless night under softly strobing starlight, while below its turfy surface troglodyte creatures stretched and stirred and poked twitching snouts out into the warm air. Hedgehogs made prickly progress across the village green in search of snacks. Dozing ducks sat in impossible paper-clip shapes beside the pond. The water, dark and smooth as an oil slick, held its secrets of coins and wishes and the dunking of witches. In the bins behind the shop a twentieth century fox foraged for his fix of fast food past its sell-by date. In gardens and above doorways and up trellises and over arbours jasmine and honeysuckle released their heady scents to steal into the senses and intoxicate with ideas of sweetness and romance. Moved by the magic of the glimmering moonshine, a nightingale cast its own irresistible spell, all who heard it at once enchanted and beguiled.

At 3 Brook Terrace Fliss slept naked under the white cotton sheet, her red hair a Pre-Raphaelite dream on the pillow. The open window let the birdsong in to mingle with the curling smoke of the incense cone by her bed into a fragrant lullaby. In the next room Rhian snoozed, still wearing her headphones, serenaded by more modern sounds.

In Honeysuckle Cottage, Ryan snored and moaned in a sleep achieved only with large doses of kaolin and morphine. Rose slept happily on the single bed in Baby's room; her own foetal posture echoing that of her child's.

Upstairs in The Soldier's Arms, Pam lay large on her back in her inappropriately lacy bed, open-mouthed and rasping, her diminutive spouse beside her a mere bump under the tented sheets.

In the Old Vicarage a restless Cynthia wandered the room in her candlewick housecoat, cooling herself with a Spanish fan, trailing a favourite shawl, like a portly Miss Haversham, Hamlet shuffling in her wake.

In her tiny bed in her tiny flat only a few feet and a flimsy wall from the sherbet dips, Miss Siddons fidgeted and itched, and her dog curled himself into a brown and white croissant and farted at ten minute intervals.

Upstairs in his flat, Neville wrestled with dreams that began with a solitary, questioning mouse, and ended in a phantasmagoria of mutant creatures, their imploring eyes allowing him no escape. Driven from his bed by such nightmarish scenes he roamed his rooms in his boxers, finally coming to rest in a cool leather chair in the sitting room. He gazed out of the window at the softened shapes of the trees and their perfect moon shadows, listening to the rare birdsong, breathing in the pure, uncontaminated night air, and, as Cilla landed lightly on his lap, he fell at last into a weary, mercifully dreamless, sleep.

CHAPTER FIFTEEN

Rose was weeding in the back garden, with Baby sitting on a rug beside her, sunhat firmly in place, when Ryan did something so surprising that she dropped her fork. He came out into the garden carrying an enormous bunch of flowers. Ryan had never given Rose so much as a garage forecourt bunch of wilting crysanths, and yet here he was, approaching her bearing the most enormous and expensive bouquet she had ever seen. As he came closer, she could see from the black expression on his face that the flowers had absolutely nothing to do with him.

'Who the fuck is sending you flowers?' he demanded, all but throwing them at her.

Baby clapped his hands at the sight of so many fabulous colours. Rose gently picked up the bouquet and searched for the card.

'Oh, aren't they beautiful!' she said.

'Never mind that, who are they from? A man has a right to know who's sending his missus flashy bunches of flowers.' Ryan stood, hands on hips, attempting to look threatening, but clearly still suffering with stomach trouble. One hand slipped towards his tummy and he bent forward a little.

Rose read the card. *Congrats to you and Baby on a stunningly successful shoot. Warm kisses to your little star, Annabel.*

'Oh, they're from a friend,' she said.

'What friend?'

'Just someone I met through Baby, you know, mothers and babies and toddlers, that sort of thing.'

'Some other mother sending you flowers? I don't think so. Give me that,' he snatched the card from Rose's hand. There was a brief pause while he read the note. A puzzled frown crossed his face. 'Annabel? You turned lesbian on me, or what? And what's she on about, a "shoot" and "your little star" – what's all that about, for crying out loud?'

Rose looked at Baby, then back at the flowers, trying to avoid meeting Ryan's eye. At least the flowers weren't from Marco. Ryan would have gone mad if they really had been from a man. But did he actually believe she might have an admirer? Could he, when he thought so little of her himself? Rose tried to sound as matter of fact as she could.

'You know Baby won that competition, well, there was an agent, at the finals, and she saw him and liked him and ...'

'What sort of agent?'

'From a modelling agency, anyway, she thought Baby had potential, that's what she said. So she signed him. And now that he's on her books we get offered advertising work – pictures for magazines, or TV ads, that sort of thing. Baby's really very good at it. I think he enjoys all the attention. So, on Wednesday he had to be a bumblebee for a new range of baby food – Honey Pot Organics – it's for a TV advertisement. Annabel said she'd let us know when it's going to be on.'

Ryan held up both hands.

'Stop! Have you gone mad, woman? Agencies? TV? Bumblebees? Is it that post-natal depression thing?'

'No, really, it's all true. Annabel's the agent. She sent the flowers. You've read the note.' Rose stroked the silky petals of the tiger lilies and breathed in their perfume.

'You're telling me you and the kid have been off doing all this stuff? On your own? You? Without telling me?'

'I did tell you about the competition, remember? And we've only done the one advert so far. Besides, you're always so busy, and you haven't been well. I didn't want to bother you.'

Ryan sank painfully onto the rug next to Baby, rubbing his stomach.

'I can't believe you've been doing all this. You never do anything. You never go anywhere. You can't even drive.' A thought occurred to him, 'What about the money?   They must be paying you something, can't be all sodding vouchers for TV ads.'

'Oh, Annabel will sort all that out at the end of each month. She's setting up a special account for Baby.'

'Baby? What's the good of that? Can't see him signing cheques, somehow.'

'Well, no, I'll do that sort of thing for him.' Rose looked down at her pale, sweaty husband, and this time she met and held his gaze.

'You don't know anything about money,' he said. 'You haven't even got your own bank account. How do you think you're going to manage all that stuff?'

'I'll learn. For Baby!'

Ryan looked at his son as if he had never seen him before.

'How much money are we talking about, then?'

'He gets a one-off payment for the bumblebee ad of £800, then £12 every time it's shown on TV. Then there's more for the poster campaign, and they're even thinking of putting him on all the jars. He did look very sweet. Annabel said that would mean thousands, with all the extra photo shoots, and maybe other promotional work. And she says there's a baby clothes company who's really interested. And one of the top nappy companies wanted him, but I said no because he doesn't use disposable nappies. But he might do the bubble bath one. He likes Bertie's Bubbles. Annabel says there's lots more stuff coming up. She says he's going to be the first baby Supermodel. Such a clever boy, aren't you, Baby?' Rose turned her attention back to her little boy, passing him a giant daisy to play with and smiling at his delight.

'But,' Ryan struggled to take it all in. 'You didn't tell me,' he said in a small voice.

Rose looked at him again. He seemed so little and unfrightening sitting next to Baby.

'We didn't need to tell you,' she said. 'We managed on our own.'

Ryan looked up at her, squinting against the sun.

'But I could help,' he said. 'I could take care of the business side of things.'

'No thanks. No need.'

There was a long silence. Ryan clutched at his stomach and groaned.

'Tummy hurting again?' Rose asked. 'Are you sure you wouldn't like me to call the doctor?'

'No, no doctors. Besides,' he struggled to his feet. 'I haven't got time. I've got to have another look at the car. If I'm not up to going to work, at least I can try and find out what's up with the motor.'

'Oh! Another problem?'

'Yes, another sodding problem.'

Ryan turned for the house, then paused and looked back at Rose. 'Don't suppose you met any mechanics while you were off on your secret modelling assignments? No, not likely, all bloody arty farty types, nobody useful.'

Rose shrugged and shook her head. 'Just photographers, hairdressers, that sort of thing.'

'Typical of you. You're off enjoying yourself, having a good time, making friends. You don't care about me. Oh no, doesn't matter that your husband, the man who pays for everything and does all the work around here, doesn't matter that he's ill and suffering.'

'But, you won't go to the doctor ...'

'Doesn't matter that his car, the car he goes to work in, doesn't matter that it's falling to bits,' he took a few quick paces towards Rose so that he was standing in front of her, unnervingly close, his face flushed with pain and anger. 'You can't be bothered to help with something important like that!'

'I don't know anything about cars.'

'Wouldn't hurt you to find out, would it? Ask your posh friends to recommend a garage, tell us where they get their flash motors fixed. Would never occur to you to do something helpful like that, now, would it?'

Rose took a small step back, battling with the desire to pick up Baby and run for the house, but determined not to be pushed around anymore. She kept her voice as level as she could.

'I don't really talk to people about their cars,' she said. 'But, well, I did notice that famous chef, Claude Lambert, you've seen him on tele, he's got a car exactly like yours. Same colour, same spoiler thing on the back, everything.'

'And how, exactly, is that information of the slightest fucking use to me?' Sweat trickled down Ryan's temples as he spoke.

'I saw him up at Withy Hill. He was there for the fundraiser. I've seen his car since, going through the village. Perhaps he's still there. Maybe he's had the same problems as you. You could talk to him about it.'

Ryan drew back, frowning, considering the idea. Then his shoulders sagged a little, the tension seeming to go out of his body.

'Maybe I will,' he said. 'Maybe I just sodding well will.'

Rose stood, still holding the flowers, and watched him walk unsteadily back to the house. She waited until her pulse had returned to a more normal rhythm before scooping Baby up under her other arm.

'Come along, little one, let's put these pretty flowers in some water,' she said. 'Then I think we'll give that nice Doctor Richards a call again, just for another little chat.'

Fliss was running a brush through her hair when she glanced out the window and saw Neville approaching the front door. She picked up her velvet jacket as the doorbell rang, pausing only to shout up the stairs.

'I'm off now, Rhi, won't be late. Don't forget the quiche is in the oven.'

'Whatever!'

Fliss opened the door.

'Hi,' she said. 'You're nice and punctual.'

'It's a curse. Socially unacceptable, I know, but I can't help myself,' Neville said.

Fliss couldn't help noticing the state of Neville's face.

'Oh dear,' she said. 'I hope that's not catching.'

'What?'

'You have a nasty rash there.'

'Oh, actually it's not a rash. Don't worry, you're quite safe, unless you're given to snuggling up to holly bushes.'

She raised her eyebrows.

'Trust me, you don't want to know,' said Neville.

They left the terrace and headed for the stile on the other side of the road.

'This is the shortest route,' said Neville. 'We take this footpath across the meadow, then up the bank behind Withy Hill Farm, and cut through the woods. It'll bring us out onto the main road, in sight of the Farmer's Lodge.'

'It's a lovely evening for a walk. Just remind me not to get too drunk. Don't want to end up nose down in a cowpat on the way home.'

They walked in silence through the meadow and up the hill. Fliss followed Neville as he strode ahead, and was amused at the way he paused to offer her a hand over each stile.

'Look,' she said as they crested the hill. 'You get an unusual view of Withy Hill from here. I'd never even noticed that old barn in the field behind the chicken sheds.'

'Part of the original farm by the look of it, just full of straw now as far as I can tell.'

'I wonder if Claude is still staying there. I can't see his car. I hope he hasn't disappeared.'

'Oh?'

'Yes, don't you see? We've got to talk to him,' she said. 'I've been thinking about it. He knows what's going on, and he's clearly in a bad way. I think we should confront him, while he hasn't got Michael Christian to hide behind.'

'Well if he's gone, he's gone,' said Neville as they reached the woods.

Fliss looked around, peering into the gloom between the trees.

'I wonder what happened to that rat,' she said.

'Please, I don't want to be put off my dinner.'

'Doesn't it worry you?'

'Of course it does, but there's not a great deal we can do about it, is there? Look, let's have something to eat, get this family meal thing over with ...'

'Oh, I wasn't aware it was a "family meal thing".'

'... yes, well, I mean let's have dinner, then talk about Withy Hill afterwards. Sandra always rushes home to the twins. We can discuss it when they've gone. Okay?'

'I take it you've said nothing about it to your sister?'

'No. Sandra is well meaning, but would have more success keeping an elephant than a secret. Let's hope your daughter can be more discreet.'

'I didn't mean for her to find out. But maybe it's for the best.'

'Oh yes, taking a teenager into our confidence was a really good idea.'

Fliss fought her instinct to fly to her daughter's defence.

'Like you said, let's discuss it after dinner.'

The Farmer's Lodge was exactly what Fliss had expected. It might once have been a coaching inn, but had been stretched and added to in all directions to accommodate as many hungry mouths as possible. The beer garden boasted an enormous wooden climbing frame and a wishing well. The car park was already full. Inside all was chintz and pretend beams and horse brasses and sheaves of wheat and corn dollies in a perfect example of pseudo rustic décor.

'There they are,' Neville pointed to a window seat.

Fliss tried to forget that the last time they met she had been lying in the mud, tied to Neville by her hair, as Sandra and Brian had rescued them from beneath the marquee. It might be hard to shake off such a novel first impression.

'Hello!' Sandra waved cheerily. 'Thought we'd bag a good table before they all went. Goodness, Neville, have you fallen off your bike again?'

'Must we sit in the window?' Neville asked, ignoring her question.

'Best seat in the house,' Brian assured him. 'Always sit here if we get the chance. Now then, let's do this thing properly. Don't leave your lovely lady standing about.'

'Yes, Neville, where are your manners?' Sandra offered a hand. 'Lovely to see you again, Fliss. I was so pleased when Neville told us he was bringing you. Now, where would you like to sit? By the window? Or on the end? Personally,' she dropped her voice to a stage whisper, 'I like to be able to get out to the loo.'

'Window's fine for me,' said Fliss.

'Thank God for that,' said Neville. 'Can't stand sitting on display, makes me feel like a tailor's dummy.'

'Nonsense,' said Sandra, 'they'd be better dressed.'

'Right!' Brian rubbed his hands together. 'What's everybody drinking?'

'Ahh,' Neville brightened visibly. 'Let's have a squint at the wine list. Here we are. Hmm, not bad, amazingly.'

'I'd like red,' Sandra volunteered. 'What do you prefer, Fliss?'

She opened her mouth to speak, but Neville beat her too it.

'I expect that rather depends on what she's eating.'

'She hasn't decided yet,' said Brian.

'Who's "she" – the cat's mother?' hissed Sandra.

' "She" is a vegetarian,' said Fliss. 'So I just drink what I'm in the mood for.'

'Vegetarian, eh?' Brian smiled at Neville. 'That must play merry hell with your cooking frenzies. No red meat to mess about with.'

'I don't mess about.'

'Actually,' said Fliss. 'I don't eat white meat either, or fish. And Neville's never cooked for me.'

Both Brian and Sandra looked shocked.

'What?' Sandra stared at her brother. 'You've never even cooked the poor girl a meal? Really, Neville, it's the one thing you do well.'

'Thank you for those kind words, Sandra,' he hid behind the wine list. 'Can we get on with this? The Chilean Merlot looks okay, everyone happy with that?'

'Sounds good to me,' said Brian.

'You're driving,' Sandra reminded him.

'Yes. I know. I can have a glass or two with my meal.'

'As long as that's all it is. You know what you're like.'

'You make it sound as if I'm going to stick a straw in the bottle, for heaven's sake.'

'Here you are, Fliss,' Sandra handed her a menu. 'I can recommend the crispy potato skins for a starter. Oh, and the garlic mushrooms are very good. But they are very garlicky.'

'I'll watch out for that.'

Neville looked at the menu with ill-disguised horror.

'Good Lord,' he said. 'Can there be anywhere else on the planet that still considers fruit juice to be a starter? And chicken in a basket. We're in a culinary time warp.'

Fliss smiled. 'In London this place would be marketed as retro and booked up months ahead. Look, there's even Black Forest Gateaux for pud.'

'Ooh,' said Sandra, 'I can't resist that, can I Brian? Have it every time. Shouldn't, of course,' she patted her modest tummy. 'Have to watch the pounds.'

'Rubbish,' said Brian. 'You know I like a bit of flesh on a woman, something to get hold of.'

'Brian, really!'

Fliss put down her menu. 'Well, I'm sold on the garlic mushrooms, and then it's vegetable lasagne for me.'

Brian gave her an approving look. 'A woman who knows her own mind, I like that.'

'Just as well, seeing as you're married to my sister,' said Neville. 'Spoilt for choice, but I'll have the salmon. Whitebait to start, I think.'

Brian and Neville went to the bar to order and pay for the food, leaving Fliss at the mercy of Sandra's curiosity.

'Isn't this nice?' Sandra beamed. 'We don't often get a chance to meet Neville's friends. He's a very private sort of person. How did you meet?'

'Oh, we're neighbours, you know, small place.'

'Isn't that nice? And do you share Neville's interest in cooking?'

Fliss shrugged, 'I share his interest in eating.'

Sandra laughed. 'Ahh, that's nice, too,' she gazed over at the men fondly. 'He's a funny old stick, my brother, but he's really very ...'

'Nice?'

'... yes, he is. I'd love to have a boyfriend who could cook. Huh, catch Brian with a potato peeler! You must get Neville to do you one of his special meals. He's really very clever.'

'I'm sure he is, but you know, I wouldn't call him my boyfriend.'

'Oh I know, it seems silly at our age, doesn't it? Not that you are quite the same age as me and Neville, but you know what I mean. And partner sounds so, well, business-like, don't you think?'

'My daughter tells me I'm much too old to have a boyfriend, whatever you call him.'

'Oh? You've got children?'

'Just Rhian. She's 15 going on 42. And she hates me. Well, she hates everyone. I think she feels it's expected of her.'

'My boys are only seven,' Sandra rolled her eyes. 'I daren't think what it'll be like having twin teenagers in the house!' She paused and fiddled with the silk flowers on the table. 'I always thought Neville would make rather a good father. I know he might seem a bit serious, perhaps, but I think he'd do a good job. He'd be very fair, and very practical. Can you ever see yourself having any more?' she asked.

'Oh, I don't know. Thought I might just get a poodle next time I feel broody.'

Sandra's face registered complete bewilderment.

Fliss felt relieved to see Neville and Brian returning.

'Has she been giving you the third degree?' Neville asked.

'No,' said Fliss, 'she's been telling me all your darkest secrets.'

'That can't have taken long,' he said.

'Now, now, Nev,' Brian tapped his nose, 'we know there's more to you than meets the eye, eh? Safety in numbers, wouldn't you say? Cast your net wide ...'

'Brian!' Sandra was horrified.

'Don't worry,' he smirked in Fliss's direction. 'I'm sure Fliss is more than up to him. Tell me,' he leant across the table, 'is it true what they say about redheads?'

'That rather depends who they are and what they are saying.'

'Well, you won't hear any complaints from me,' Brian told her. 'I've always had a soft spot for women with red hair,' he paused for dramatic effect, 'as long as the collar and cuffs match, eh?' He laughed heartily at his own joke.

Sandra looked cross enough to give him a slap. Fliss glanced at Neville and noticed he was trying hard not to laugh.

'Ah!' Sandra saw salvation arriving in the shape of the wine. 'Here we are, mmm, looks lovely. Here you are, Fliss. Now, everybody got some? Let's drink a toast. To Fliss! Welcome to our little family.'

'To Fliss!' Brian raised his glass. 'God bless her and all who ...'

'Brian!' Sandra snapped.

Neville had stopped laughing and had his head in his hands.

Fliss leant over to whisper in his ear. 'Okay, I promise not to let on the only date we've been on so far was chaperoned by a rat, if you promise to tackle Claude about Withy Hill, deal?' She sat back and smiled at him, giving a very good imitation of someone entirely enthralled by her escort.

Neville mustered a humourless grin and clinked his glass against hers. 'Deal,' he said.

Two uncomfortable hours later, Neville helped Fliss over the stile from the main road onto the footpath. The pub had become unbearably busy, so, after Sandra and Brian had finally left for home, Neville had suggested they escape the noise and talk while they walk.

'Sorry about that,' he said. 'I did warn you about the food.'

'The food was fine, really. What was a little unnerving was the way Sandra was practically planning our wedding.'

'I know. She was just being sisterly, and bossy, and ridiculous.'

'Oh? Thanks very much. That's how little you think of me, is it?'

'No, I didn't mean ...' Neville struggled to explain.

'Relax,' said Fliss. 'I'm winding you up. Though if you'd told me I was supposed to be playing the part of your girlfriend I'd have been better prepared. Still, I think I did a pretty good job – though why you had to make such a thing up in the first place, I can't imagine.'

'Look, it's all really rather embarrassing. Can we just forget about it?'

'Sure. So long as you keep your part of the bargain. Look!' she pointed through the trees.

'What? Not that bloody rat again?'

'No. Look, there's someone down at Withy Hill Farm, by the French windows.'

'So? Loads of people work there. Someone doing an evening shift.'

'No, it has to be Claude. Look at him.'

Neville looked. The farm was some distance away, but he could clearly make out a person standing in the garden just to one side of the house. There was something unmistakeably rangy and scrawny about the figure, even at this distance. And the singular way in which he stood – slightly hunched, leaning forwards, as if about to topple. It was definitely Claude.

'Now's our chance,' Fliss told him.

'I was rather afraid of that,' said Neville.

'Come on.'

He followed her out of the woods and over a gate and along the hedge of the meadow behind the farmhouse.

'Now what?' he asked. 'We can hardly expect him to answer the front door, given the way he's been avoiding everybody lately.'

'You're right. And anyway, there's Eric and Vinnie to consider.'

'And they would be ...?

'Michael Christian's extremely unpleasant Dobermans. Or should that be Dobermen? Anyway, we don't want to meet them.'

'Ah.'

As if on cue a frenzied barking began inside the house.

'Oh well,' said Neville. 'Nice idea, but there it is. Best laid plans of mutant mice and men; let's get out of here before they find us.'

'No way, we're going to question Claude while he hasn't got Michael Christian to hide behind. This is the perfect opportunity.'

'Perfect, for me, rarely involves large dogs with sharp teeth.'

'Don't be such a wimp, Neville.'

'You have been spending too much time with my sister.'

'We can get in through the French windows – they lead into the small sitting room, which is probably where Claude is anyway. And the dogs aren't allowed in there.'

'And they are both sticklers for house rules, no doubt.'

They crept around the side of the house. The French windows were still open, light from inside falling onto the flagstone patio.

Neville was on the point of arguing once more for abandoning the whole idea, when Fliss grabbed his hand and pulled him into the house. The sitting room was cosy and comfortably furnished, with squishy sofas, expensive rugs, shapely table lamps and a large television. In an armchair, facing the TV and apparently deaf to both dogs and intruders, Claude Lambert sat, staring at the screen, eerily still.

For want of a better idea, Neville cleared his throat loudly. The effect was remarkable. Claude leapt up from his seat as if stung by a hornet. He turned to face them, clinging to a dangerously flimsy occasional table. His eyes were even more bulging and reddened than usual. He looked years older than before. His skin, even in the warm light of the little room, was unmissably blue.

'Who are you?' he demanded in his bizarre accent. 'What is it you want from me? Why do you come here?'

Neville stepped forward.

'You may remember me from the fundraising committee; name's Neville Meatcher.'

Claude stared harder, running a sweaty palm through his unwashed hair. 'Oh. Yes. You are the man with the bicycle,' he said at last.

'I suppose there are worse ways to be remembered,' said Neville. 'This is Fliss Horton. She lives in the village too.'

'What do you want? Mr Christian, he is gone away now.'

'We know that,' Fliss told him. 'It's you we want to talk to.'

'For what reason?' he asked, sniffing heavily.

'Look,' Neville flopped onto one of the inviting sofas. 'Do you mind if we sit down, now that we're here? No? Good. This may take some time.'

Fliss sat next to him. Claude looked as if he might bolt from the room at any moment. Neville took a breath and tried to calm the nervous chef.

'The thing is, we, that is Fliss and myself, have some ... concerns, about what is being planned, development-wise, up here at Withy Hill. It has come to our notice that certain projects are being undertaken which, while quite possibly legal, may not be entirely ethical. That is not to suppose, of course, that ...'

'Oh, for heaven's sake,' Fliss could stand it no longer. 'Claude, I've been in that locked room out there. I found one of the rats. I showed it to Neville. And the planning application has been rushed through. What do you know?'

Neville looked hard at Fliss. 'I was coming to all that,' he said.

Fliss returned his stare. 'This man's life expectancy is not good,' she told him.

Their attention was wrenched back to Claude by the sound of sobbing. They watched as he staggered to the other sofa and sank onto it, weeping loudly.

'I am a man who is ruined *completement*!' he wailed. 'All my years of travail, all that I have done, my books, my restaurant – all is for nothing!' He turned his face towards a silk cushion, sharp shoulder blades shaking beneath his shirt.

Neville and Fliss exchanged glances as the muffled sobs continued.

'Mr Lambert,' Neville tried, 'Claude, it might help if you talked about it, don't you think? Perhaps you would like to tell us ... everything?'

There was no answer, save for the continued crying.

'This is hopeless,' Neville said to Fliss.

'You've met him before, he almost knows you,' she pointed out. 'Win his confidence. Comfort him, or something.'

'Me? Why me? You're a woman.'

'What's that got to do with it? He's hardly in a fit state for seduction. Go on!' Fliss pushed him firmly off the sofa.

Neville sat gingerly next to Claude. He reached out and lightly squeezed the snivelling man's arm.

'Now then,' he said, 'I'm sure it's not as bad as all that.'

Claude's reaction was to turn and throw himself, weeping all the more, onto Neville's shoulder.

'I am finished!' he howled, tears splashing onto Neville's jacket.

Neville looked beseechingly at Fliss, who merely shrugged. He looked desperately round the room.

'Brandy,' he said at last. 'See if you can muster up three large ones, Fliss.'

Twenty minutes later a considerably calmer Frenchman sat at a respectable distance from Neville, explaining the what, the how, and the why of his situation.

'You have to understand me,' he said in a voice still choked with emotion. 'The pressures of a famous life, they are great. You have to do so much, to be so much for so many people. And so, I began to need help. And I found that help,' he swallowed more brandy. 'Oh my God, what poison! You think the drug she is your friend, that she will set you free ...'

'Cocaine?' asked Fliss.

'Yes, very good, very expensive cocaine. Soon I could not pay for what I needed. Soon I owed money to the devil who sold the stuff to me. Now I owe him more than ever I can give back,' Claude started to tremble. 'And now he sends his heavy men to find me. Oh my God, if they find me ...' he shook his head.

'Ah,' said Neville. 'Those will be the two well-dressed gentlemen I saw on the day of the fundraiser. Checking out your car, I seem to remember.'

'You saw them too? Yes, they look for me, and they find my car. Now I have to hide her in the woods, or they will see I am here still.'

Neville was confused.

'But they obviously know you're connected with this place. Did they know about the partnership with Withy Hill?'

'Yes, I have told their filthy boss that when the partnership is agreed and launched I will be able to pay him.

I have been promised the money from Michael Christian. It is for this reason I agree to the partnership.'

'I thought it was odd, you associating yourself with a place like this,' said Neville. 'I know it's not battery chickens, but it's hardly organic produce either, is it?'

Fliss shook her head.

'Not to mention the experiments,' she said.

'I knew nothing of these!' Claude protested. 'When I said yes to the partnership I knew nothing of the experiments, of the laboratory, of what it is they want to do to the chickens. I would never have agreed. Never! But now,' he sniffed again, rubbing at his eyes, 'now I have no choice.'

'You always have a choice,' Neville told him. 'You could go to the police, tell them about the villains.'

Claude looked at him as if he were an idiot. 'To the police it is I who am the villain, do you not see? And, there is more. Not just the money. Withy Hill helps me now that I can no longer afford to buy cocaine. There is a *medicament*, something they use in their experiments, and this substance, it has effects to the side. It was seen in the rats. Effects very like amphetamines, perhaps a little like cocaine, also.'

'The powder you took from the locked room,' said Fliss. 'That was some of this drug?'

'Bah! Yes, but I do not have the key. And the idiot who keeps the room while Michael is away, he locks me out, so I must beg for what I need.'

Neville picked up the brandy bottle from the coffee table and topped up all three glasses.

'Strikes me,' he said, 'your Mr Christian could make more money flogging this drug than doing anything with chickens. The man clearly has no morals, so what's to stop him?'

'Look at me!' said Claude. 'Do you think I have this colour from your weak English sun? No, the drug, she is called Blustaine. You can look at me and see why.'

'Yes, I take your point.'

'But what about the chickens?' Fliss wanted to know. 'You still haven't told us what the point of those terrible experiments is.'

Claude sighed, his enfeebled shoulders sagging even further than usual.

'The most important part of the chicken, for making money, this is the legs. Many people grow the bigger chickens for the bigger legs. Here, they will do more. They will grow the chickens with four legs.'

'Oh my God,' said Fliss, downing the rest of her drink.

'That's completely disgusting,' said Neville. 'And what is more, the British public would never swallow it. I mean, stomach it. Put up with it, for pity's sake.'

'Who would see these chickens?' Claude stared into his glass. 'They would be in the chicken houses. The workers, they would be paid plenty of money to keep shut their mouths. It can work.'

'We have to stop them,' said Fliss. 'And you have to help us.'

'But I cannot! I am emasculated! I can only wait until Michael gives the money to the dealer, and then hope to escape with my life, back to France. It is all I can do. If I attempt anything different ...' he made a graphic gesture indicating his throat being slit.

He cried a little more and then slouched down into the chair and closed his eyes.

Neville and Fliss left the broken chef sleeping fitfully on the sofa and headed back to the village. As they walked away from the farm Neville examined the soggy state of his shoulder.

'Why do so many people see fit to use me as a handkerchief?' he wondered.

'Rhian might tell you it's because of your squareness,' said Fliss.

'A comment worthy of a teenager.'

'Actually, I think she'd be wrong.'

'You mean after such an original and stimulating evening, you have come to realise what an exciting and wholly unsquare life I lead.'

He fell into step beside her as they crossed the meadows, a slightly waning moon still strong enough to light their way.

'I think it's a front,' said Fliss. 'All this uptightness and being so proper and stuffy about everything.'

'Flatterer!'

'I believe, deep down, you're like me.'

Neville stopped and looked at Fliss, with her colourful velvet clothes, her Indian jewellery, her fabulous long hair, and her overall impression of health and serenity.

'How so?' he asked.

She smiled at him.

'You care,' she said. 'You don't really want to, but you can't stop yourself. It concerns you deeply, what's going on up at the farm. And the rat – you said you had nightmares, and I believe you. You and me, we want to get on with our own quiet little lives, but we can't just look the other way and do nothing.'

'Are you sure you've got the right person?'

'Oh, you won't bother about the small stuff, but things that really matter – you have a conscience. You have to act.'

'No, you're definitely confusing me with someone else. Che Guevara, perhaps. Or Bob Geldof, easily done.' He began to walk on again.

Fliss trotted after him.

'Don't be embarrassed. Are you so unused to being paid a compliment?'

'Is that what you were doing?' He gave her his hand as she climbed the stile. 'I thought you were trying to talk me into doing something probably dangerous, almost certainly illegal, and not a little ridiculous.'

When they reached the front door of 3 Brook Terrace, Neville watched as she put her key in the lock. Considerable amounts of alcohol, followed by mild fright and adventure, rounded off with gentle exercise all had a mellowing effect on him. He could have gone on watching Fliss for a very long time.

'Sleep on it all,' Fliss told him. 'Tomorrow we've got to decide what we're going to do. And then do it. Okay?'

'I still think you've got the wrong man,' he said. 'But, well, thank you, for tonight.'

'Pleasure.'

'Don't exaggerate. I saw you force down that slice of Blackforest Gateaux.'

'Your sister is a hard woman to say no to.'

She stepped inside, then changed her mind, leant forwards, and planted a whisper of a kiss on Neville's cheek. 'I hope I am, too,' she said, before shutting the door.

Neville stood on the doorstep for a full minute, enjoying the warm fuzziness of the moment, then turned and headed back to his little flat.

CHAPTER SIXTEEN

Neville sat in his pyjamas and gazed out of his kitchen window as he waited for his coffee to brew. He had slept badly. His every instinct told him not to get involved in the whole sorry Withy Hill affair and that way, just maybe, he might hold onto his job. But what of his integrity? His self-respect? The village? And Fliss? Especially Fliss! He poured his coffee and dropped in a necessarily heavy dose of sugar crystals. Cilla sprang onto his lap, purring.

'It's all right for you,' he told her. 'Your life couldn't be simpler. Mine suddenly seems ridiculously complicated.' He stirred aimlessly, the teaspoon tinkling hypnotically against the fine china. The fumes from the cup reached his nostrils. He sipped slowly. At last, he made a decision. Pushing Cilla off he went to the phone and dialled Fliss's number. The line was busy. He hung up, drank more coffee, and tried again, still busy.

'Sod it,' he said to Cilla. 'Why is it all women spend hours on the phone?'

He picked up his cup and headed for the shower. Twenty minutes later he dialled Fliss's number once more, still engaged.

'Oh for heaven's sake,' he paced the kitchen for a few moments, then looked at the clock. It was nearly ten thirty. 'I can't stand this,' he said to the now sleeping cat. 'I need fresh air to clear my head.'

He took a notepad from beside the telephone and wrote quickly.

I think you might have got the right man after all, mad as it seems. You have a point about us being alike, and about things that matter. We mustn't lose any more time. Meet me at the old barn behind Withy Hill Farm tonight. Ten o'clock. Bring a torch.

He signed the note, folded it, and stuffed it in the pocket of his tracksuit top. Once outside he was on the point of swinging his leg over his bicycle when he was knocked off his feet. As he lay face down on the pavement it was the smell that gave his assailant away.

'Hamlet! For pity's sake, get off me, you wretched hound!'

Hamlet's lack of response suggested deafness had been added to his list of ailments. Neville struggled in vain to escape from the dog's embrace. For once he was glad to hear Cynthia's voice.

'Ah, Neville! How lovely to see you.'

'Good morning, Cynthia. Oof!' he gasped as Hamlet shifted his weight the better to lick Neville's ears.

'Such a splendid day, I thought I'd take Hamlet out for a little walk. The fresh air and sunshine is so helpful for his poor skin, and the vet told me gentle exercise will help combat the effects of arthritis,' said Cynthia.

'Fascinating information, I'm sure, but right now my main concern is being able to breathe. Do you think you could see your way to getting him off me?'

'Oh, of course, how silly of me. Hamlet, come along, let Neville get up now. He doesn't want to play any more.'

Neville scrambled to his feet, brushing gravel from his clothes. He picked up his bike from where it had fallen. He glanced at Cynthia and noticed she looked older, paler, and altogether sadder than usual.

'So,' he said. 'How have you been?'

She smiled at him weakly.

'Oh, one battles on. Though, I have missed seeing you. You know how I enjoyed working with you on NHEC, and now ...'

'Yes, I'm sorry. I have been very busy,' he said uncomfortably.

Cynthia nodded. 'I understand,' she said quietly.

Neville was finding this new meek Cynthia a little worrying.

'Actually,' he went on. 'I had planned to call in on my way past the Vicarage this morning. Just to see how you were.'

'Oh? How kind,' she brightened visibly.

'Yes, so bumping into you, or rather Hamlet bumping into me, has saved me a detour.' Neville's concern for Cynthia didn't extend as far as actually spending any time with her if he could avoid it.

'Oh, do say you'll still come. For coffee, perhaps?' she pleaded.

'Well,' he looked at his watch and shook his head. 'As a matter of fact I really am running behind schedule.'

'On a Sunday?'

'I'm expected at my sister's for lunch,' he did his best to sound convincing.

'But it's barely ten thirty!'

'Ah yes, but I'm the one cooking lunch,' he explained, stepping onto his bicycle. 'You take care now. We'll meet again soon.' He managed a wave as he pedalled off in entirely the opposite direction to the one he had planned, his note still undelivered. Somehow being seen by Cynthia posting missives through Fliss's door did not strike him as a good idea.

'A bientôt!' Cynthia called after him.

Neville peddled for two invigorating, mind-clearing hours, and returned home re-energised. He took another shower, ate a light lunch of *salade nicoise*, then dialled Fliss's number again. This time she answered.

'Ah-ha,' she said. 'I was hoping it might be you.'

'It would have been me considerably earlier if you hadn't been chattering on the phone endlessly.'

'Not me, that's Rhian – tying up the telephone for hours at a time is in every teenager's job description.'

'Oh, yes. I see.'

'Anyway, I'm all ears now. Tell me what you've come up with.'

'It still amazes me that I seem to have been appointed Commander-in-Chief of this business,' he said.

'If the cap fits ...'

'Alright, you don't have to persuade me any further, my mind is already made up.'

'You have a plan?'

'Of sorts, more a vague notion and an over-optimistic belief that things will just happen in the necessary way.'

'Sorry?'

'Look, just meet me up at the old barn behind Withy Hill Farm tonight. We'll take it from there.'

'What time?'

'What time does it get dark?'

'About nine thirty, I think,' said Fliss.

'Nine-thirty it is, then. And bring a torch. And a bag of some sort. And anything that might be useful for breaking a lock.'

'Sounds exciting.'

'Frankly, I could use a little less excitement in my Sunday evening,' Neville said. 'A relaxing hour or two with my feet up listening to something sublime and drinking a large glass of Claret sounds far more attractive.'

'You know you can't relax until we've sorted this horror story,' Fliss pointed out. 'Tell you what, we get this mission out of the way, I'll supply the wine, and you can show me what sort of music you consider sublime. I'll even throw in a free crystal healing session to calm you down. Deal?'

'You're very keen on making deals, Fliss.'

'I come up with good ones, though, don't I?'

Neville had to admit that she did.

The twilight air was warm and still as Fliss waited impatiently behind the barn. She was early, and she was pretty sure Neville would be on time, but even so she couldn't stop herself checking her watch every minute. The small stream beside the barn trickled sweetly but provided an unwelcome supply of hungry midges. By the time Neville appeared Fliss was scratching her head.

'Don't suppose you brought any mozzie repellent with you?' she asked.

He frowned at her. 'I have a torch, a shoebox, some parcel tape, and a pair of pliers. *Deet* I do not have.'

'Pliers? Are we going to pull somebody's teeth out?'

'Forgive me for not possessing a regulation burglar's toolbox. I thought they might prove useful. What did you come up with?'

Fliss pulled things from her backpack and laid them out on the grass.

'A torch, a jemmy, a hammer, a rechargeable screwdriver, a Swiss army knife, a can of pepper spray, oh, and these,' she dangled an impressive bunch of keys under his nose. 'Had them years. Can't remember what doors they fitted, or even what house.'

'Funny, I hadn't got you down as someone with squirrelling tendencies. Still, we may just strike lucky with these. Not so sure about the pepper spray,' he peered at the small can in the gloom.

'If nothing else we could use it on the dogs,' said Fliss.

'How does that sort of behaviour fit with the fluffy vegetarian side of you, I wonder?'

'Better than being bitten. So, what now?'

'We have to get into that locked room and steal another rat, or something equally hideous. And something on paper, if we can find anything.'

'How about some of Claude's magic powder, too?'

'Why not? Right, stuff that lot back in your bag. We can stay more or less out of sight of the house if we head round the back of the big chicken sheds.'

They crept away from the barn and made for the main part of the farm. Vinnie and Eric could be heard barking inside the house. Fliss slipped the pepper spray into her pocket, just in case. They had nearly reached their destination when Neville signalled frantically for her to keep still. He pointed towards the side of the house. Two large, dark figures were trying doors and windows.

'Real burglars?' Fliss hissed at Neville.

'No, I've seen those two before. They're the hoods looking for Claude. Come on, let's get on with this.'

They hurried round the last shed and scuttled over to the small laboratory. Neville crouched at the door, while Fliss handed him different things to try on the lock.

'Nothing's budging it,' he said after a while. 'Let's try those keys of yours,' he held out a hand.

Fliss dug in her bag.

'Oh shit! They're not here.'

'What?'

'We must have left them up at the old barn.'

'We?'

'I'll go back for them,' she stood up.

'No, wait,' Neville pulled her back down. 'You stay here, I'll go. My knees are seizing up sitting like this. Keep in the shadows.' He looked at her for a moment. 'Got your pepper spray?'

She held it up.

'Good. Don't hesitate to use it. I'll be as quick as I can.'

Fliss watched him go. The place felt eerily silent all of a sudden. Even the dogs had stopped barking. The reason for this quickly became obvious – they had been let out. Horrified, Fliss watched as the dogs trotted purposefully about, sniffing with expert and infallible noses. It could only be a matter of minutes before they found her. She made the decision to move. Slowly she raised herself to a half-standing position, then scampered along the side of the building and made for the safety of the chicken sheds. The huge galvanised door was unlocked. She opened it a little, wincing at the sharp squeak it made, then slipped inside and shut it again. Perhaps the strong pong of several hundred hens would mask her own scent. She went over to one of the small windows and scanned the yard. The dogs were still there. There was nothing else for it, she would just have to stay put until they moved off, or, better still, went back inside the house.

Up at the old barn Neville searched for the keys. After a fruitless minute on his hands and knees he risked switching on his torch, keeping the beam low. The last thing he wanted to do was attract the attention of the scary-looking men who were after Claude. Suddenly, there was a rustling noise from inside the barn. Neville held his breath. He heard the noise again - more rustling, then, unbelievably, humming. He lifted his head. The sound was flat, unmelodic, and grating, but just recognisable as Carmen's *Amour.* Slowly he stood up and peeked through one of the arrow-slit windows. A sight far more terrifying than any muscle-bound henchman greeted his eyes. Amongst a gap in the straw bales two large rugs were laid out, the area illuminated by a number of tea-lights. In the centre of the space danced Cynthia, clad only in the most see-through of negligees which revealed the exact size and quality of her every curve. In his haste to escape the nightmare vision, Neville's foot found the bunch of keys. The jangling was loud enough to reach Cynthia.

'Hello?' she called out. 'Neville, *Mon cher,* is that you?'

Neville grabbed the keys and was about to flee when Cynthia threw open a small door and stepped out in front of him.

'Here you are!' she cried upon seeing him. 'I knew you wouldn't keep me waiting long.'

'Cynthia ...?'

'Of course, it should have been little me exercising my lady's prerogative and making you wait, but I wanted to get things ready. I so want everything to be perfect,' she said as she took his hands and led him into the barn.

'Cynthia, what's going on? The candles ...'

'Oh I know you asked me to bring a torch in your *billet doux*, but candles are so much more romantic, don't you think? And give a more flattering light.' She laughed lightly. 'We women of a certain age have to consider these things. But, oh, just to know that you want me! It makes me feel as though I am the most beautiful woman alive.'

She spun away from him, executing some surprisingly light steps, which had the effect of making her short, floaty garment lift to expose pasty buttocks. Neville forced himself to speak.

'Cynthia, what are you doing here?'

'Forgive me,' she giggled. 'Just *une petite* dance for joy. Come, step into my cosy little nest,' she beckoned.

Neville narrowed his eyes, trying to make sense of it all. Then it came to him – the note. Bumping into Cynthia outside his flat had prevented him from delivering it to Fliss, and he had telephoned her instead, never giving the note another thought. It must have fallen out of his pocket when Hamlet knocked him over. And Cynthia found it, and assumed it was meant for her. He remembered telling her he was on his way to call in at the Vicarage.

'Cynthia, that note, the things I wrote, you have to understand ...'

'Oh but I do, my darling boy, I do. Such beautiful words, "the right man". You were right about us being alike. And I understand your need to write to me first, to break the ice, as it were. It takes courage to reveal one's feelings, and you found a way. Of course you were reticent, it cannot be easy to realise that your true one is a more mature woman. And people can be so cruel.'

She suddenly rushed to him, stopping close enough for him to be staring down at her generous cleavage. Although the night was warm, Neville was all too aware that Cynthia's nipples were registering their excitement, protruding through the flimsy fabric that covered them and looking as hard and as huge as Scania wheel-nuts.

She threw her arms around his neck and pressed her head against his chest. Neville reeled from the impact of both the woman herself and her powerful perfume. He noticed not a single mosquito dared come near her.

'Wait!' he said, 'I've forgotten something.' He pulled her hands from his neck and attempted to hold her at arm's length. 'I have to nip back to my flat.'

'Now? Is it so important?' she asked.

'Oh yes. Definitely,' he tried hard to sound convincing. 'Just like you, I want everything to be perfect. You understand, don't you?'

'Of course, my sweet,' she stepped back from him and lay down, draping herself over one of the rugs, gazing up at him with dreamy eyes. 'I will wait for you,' she told him.

'Great, back soon,' said Neville as he fled, shaking from his head the image of a semi-naked Cynthia gazing at him with a come-hither expression.

In the garage of Honeysuckle Cottage, Ryan lay beneath his car cursing, while Rose looked on.

'Nothing!' he snapped. 'Not a single sodding sign of what's wrong with the bastard thing!' He crawled out and struggled to his feet, leaning heavily on the car. His clothes were covered in oil and large patches of sweat spread out from his armpits and down his back.

'Can't you take it back to the garage?' Rose asked.

'What for? For Christ's sake! They're all fucking useless, all of them. They can't fix it, so they just stick together and pretend there's nothing wrong. One of them even told me I was imaging things,' he wiped his brow with his sleeve. 'Can you believe it? What do they think I am, some sort of nutter?'

'Are you coming in for supper?'

'I can't sodding eat, woman! My guts are on fire, and so is my arse. Anyway, I'm not stopping until I sort this pile of crap out!' He kicked the wheel of the Subaru.

'Oh dear,' said Rose.

There was a silence broken only by Ryan's uneven breathing and the hum of the fluorescent light.

'I'm not going to let it beat me,' he said through clenched teeth. 'I'll show those idiots. Imagining it, for crying out loud.' He picked up the manual and began turning pages angrily.

Rose gave a start as she saw a small piece of paper flutter from the book. It was one of her little drawings – the ones she had made to help her work on the car. She had been so careful, destroying all the evidence, but there it was, a small piece of paper lying on the floor next to Ryan's foot. She stepped forward so that she could cover it with her own fluffy slipper. She forced herself to put her hand on his arm. Ryan looked up, surprised.

'It's only an idea,' said Rose quietly, 'but you could go up to Withy Hill and ask that chef. You remember? He's got the same sort of car. He might be able to help.'

Ryan rubbed the back of his neck with a grubby hand.

'It could be worth a try,' he said, eyes wide at the thought of a solution. 'Maybe that frog cook's had his fixed. If he'd talk to me – might think he's too high and mighty to help a nobody. That's what they're like, those celebrities. We put them where they are, but do they thank us? Do they hell! Well this one's gonna do something for the little man for a change. The man in the sodding street. The one who earns his living from hard graft, not poncing about on tele chopping up bloody garlic.' He wiped his hands on his trousers and climbed into the car. 'Well don't just stand there, open the doors, will you?'

He revved up the engine as Rose hurried to do as she was told. She watched the dirty, sweaty, dishevelled, desperate man her husband had become as he drove past her and roared off up the hill towards the farm. She picked up the small paper with her drawing and went into the kitchen. At the telephone, she pressed one of the memory dial buttons.

'Hello? Ah, sorry to bother you on a Sunday night, Doctor, but it's my husband ... yes, the same sort of things we talked about before. Only this time he's worse. The thing is, he's gone off in the car, driving much too fast, and he's really not well at all. To be honest with you, I am very worried about his state of mind. Yes, that's right ... he's still convinced he can hear things in the car. And now he thinks people are ganging up against him. What? Oh, he said he was going up to Withy Hill Farm. He seems to think someone up there has exactly the same car. I know, it is a bit unlikely, isn't it? And anyway, what will they think? Him turning up all upset and ill at this time of night? And he does have such a temper ... Oh. I see. Well, of course, if you think that's best. They won't hurt him, will they? Oh yes, I'd feel much better about it if I knew you were going to be there too. He might listen to you. Thank you, Doctor. Goodbye.' She put down the receiver and sat looking at the phone for a moment or two. Then she went to the cupboard and removed the jar of special herbs, consigning them to the bin, before switching off the light and heading for bed.

Back in the chicken shed, Fliss was on the point of opening the door when she heard footsteps. She dived behind a row of chicken coops, keeping as low and as still as she could, silently cursing for not positioning herself with a view of the door. She heard the sharp squeak of the sliding metal, and two flashlight beams strobed over the chickens. The door closed again, removing the option of a quick dash for freedom. Fliss waited. She couldn't tell how many people had entered the building, but it was definitely more than one. Were they looking for her? She stiffened as the footsteps drew closer. One of them was walking directly towards her hiding place. In seconds, she would be trodden on. Heart pounding,

Fliss waited until the last possible moment, then uttered her best frightening scream, leapt to her feet, and gave the intruder a face-full of pepper spray.

'Out of my way!' Fliss shouted as she squirted. 'Let me go!'

'Argh!' The figure in front of her clutched at his eyes and staggered back.

His dropped torch shone up from the floor, illuminating his face. The stricken man had a ski mask on, but clearly the spray had temporarily blinded him. Fliss gave him a hefty shove as she went past, breaking into a run, as the man's accomplices turned their lights on her.

A shrill cry caused Fliss to stop mid flight. 'Mum!'

She turned, shielding her eyes against the beam in her face. 'Rhian!' Fliss squinted into the darkness. 'Rhian, what in God's name are you doing here?'

Rhian was dressed all in black with a ski mask of her own. A smaller figure stood beside her. Fliss pulled herself together.

'Well, I assume that's Sam with you, but who on earth ...?' She turned to the man still kneeling on the floor.

He wrenched off his mask, rubbing at his eyes.

'Daniel!' Fliss hurried over to him. 'Oh my God, Dan, are you all right? I'm so sorry.'

Daniel lay on the floor still too busy gasping and cursing to answer.

Fliss looked up at her daughter, a mixture of anger and anxiety making her voice sharp.

'Right, young lady, you've got some explaining to do.'

'I've got some explaining! I like that! What about you? I don't remember you telling me you were going out to spend the night in a chicken shed.'

'Never mind that now. What do you think you are doing? And as for you, Dan. The minute you've recovered sufficiently I'm going to murder you. What were you thinking of, bringing the girls up here on some mad escapade?'

'He was helping us,' Rhian told her.

'Helping you do what, exactly?'

'Rescue the chickens, of course.'

'Have you gone completely bonkers?' Fliss asked. 'There are over three thousand birds on this farm. What were you planning to do, keep them in your bedroom?'

Sam stepped out of the shadows.

'Obviously, Mrs Horton,' she mumbled through her ill-fitting mask, 'this was to be a symbolic action. We would liberate a token number of fowl, to make our point.'

'Which is?'

'Look, Mum, we warned you. We said we would take matters into our own hands if you and your new boyfriend didn't stop going on cosy dates and do something. You might be able to sit by while animals are being tortured, but we couldn't.'

'Our aim,' Sam explained, 'was to go to the press with the rescued birds, and give them the information about the use of the horrific and entirely unethical genetic engineering in pursuit of commercial gain that is taking place on this farm.'

'Oh, brilliant, girls. You really think anyone is going to believe a single word coming from two teenage chicken rustlers? Where's your proof? There's nothing wrong with these chickens.'

The girls were quiet for a minute, contemplating the blinking birds around them.

Daniel struggled to his feet. 'Before you have a go at me,' he said to Fliss, 'I did this for you, you know.'

'Me?'

He shrugged. 'Things haven't been so good between us lately, Babe. I wanted to do something to show you I care.'

'Oh, and you thought assisting my daughter in a bit of breaking and entering would win me round? That makes perfect sense.'

'We needed someone with a car,' Rhian said. 'I phoned Daniel. I asked him to drive us up here. I told him you'd been going out with that Neville bloke. I said he'd have to do something dramatic to impress you.'

Daniel put a hand on Fliss's shoulder.

'It seemed like a good idea at the time,' he said. 'I really thought I was losing you, and I knew how much this stuff mattered to you. Sorry if I made a balls-up of things.'

Fliss shook her head and sighed.

'This is not the time or place for a discussion. We've got to get out of here. Neville must be back from the barn by now. He'll be wondering what's happened to me.'

'Neville?' asked Dan, dropping his hand.

'I said we'd do something, and we are, right now. It just might work, too, if you lot haven't blown it.'

'Listen!' said Sam. 'I can hear a car.'

They hurried to the small windows and looked out.

'That's Ryan whatsisname,' said Fliss. 'The creepy little estate agent. What's he doing here?'

They watched as he parked his car and then started hammering on the front door.

'Oh well,' said Fliss, 'at least he'll be a distraction for Eric and Vinnie. Come on, let's get out of here.'

Rhian stood firm.

'Not without some chickens,' she said.

Even in the gloom, Fliss could see the determined expression on Rhian's face. She knew that look.

'Okay,' she said. 'Just get a couple, and be quick. I've got to see a man about a rat.'

When Neville returned to the lab and found Fliss gone he was at a loss to know what to do next. He stood for a moment, mouth open, looking around, hissing her name into the shadows, but there was no sign of her.

'Bugger!' he said through gritted teeth, then knelt down and started trying keys in the lock. There were dozens that looked possible. He glanced over his shoulder more than once, reacting to a sound or movement that wasn't there. He worked systematically through the keys, taking care not to muddle them and so end up having to try duds a second time.   He had just selected one that looked a particularly suitable shape when a small noise behind him caused his stomach to lurch. The sound grew subtly stronger. Slowly, very, very slowly, Neville turned his head. Standing behind him, piggy eyes glinting in the moonlight, were two of the most viscous-looking dogs he had ever seen. Their growling grew louder and harsher. Both dogs pulled back their lips to expose, even in the darkness, fine and ruthless teeth. Neville swallowed hard, and turned carefully back to his task, holding the key with trembling hands. He had almost succeeded in getting it in the lock when the note of the growling changed to something altogether wilder and even more menacing. In his fear Neville dropped the bunch of keys. The jangling of metal on tarmac spooked the dogs into action. Neville screamed and threw his arms over his head as they charged. The first one leapt at him. Neville screamed again, bracing himself for impact. It never came. From somewhere in the shadows a gigantic dark shape hurtled through the air, connecting with the leaping Doberman, knocking it yelping to the ground. The second dog's growls turned to frantic barks. Neville peered up from his cowering position to see Hamlet, tail wagging madly, throw his full weight behind a charge at the barking dog. The leaner, lighter creature was no match for the size and sheer blundering bravado of the Great Dane. The old dog snarled and spluttered and wheezed as he tossed one dog into the air, then turned and barged at the other, flattening it. The guard-dogs had met their match, and they knew it. Tails tucked down, ears flat, they ran, with Hamlet lumbering relentlessly after them baying and farting as he went – the granddaddy of all hellhounds. Neville watched them disappear up across the meadow and towards the woods. He remembered to breathe again, gulped air and picked up the keys with hands shaking unmanageably. He found the hopeful key again and this time succeeded in getting it in the lock. It worked. He fell through the door and slammed it shut behind him, his heart still thumping out a syncopated beat.

Once inside he focused on the task in hand, switching on his torch and rustling through papers and files on the desk, in search of something, anything, incriminating and useful. There was nothing. He tried the desk and filing cabinet drawers. All locked, as was the metal cupboard.

'Bugger,' he said again. 'Now, where did Fliss say the critters were kept?' He walked to the far corner of the room and saw some small cages on a bench. As he leant nervously over the first one, the door burst open behind him.

Neville shone his torch at the interloper. 'Claude! What the hell are you doing in here?'

The beleaguered chef looked even more wrecked and distressed than usual. 'I saw you go in here,' he said, turning wild and staring eyes on Neville. 'You have to help me. I must hide. Those men are here for me once again. If they find me, I don't know .... And there is a madman running around shouting about cars. It is not safe for me. I will stay in here.'

'Oh alright, for pity's sake, sit down before you fall down. And keep quiet, my nerves are in shreds already.'

'But, you have the keys?' Claude wanted to know, 'I can go into the cupboard.'

Neville frowned at him.

'For heaven's sake, man, you'll never fit in there.'

'No, the Blustaine, she is in this cupboard. Please, give me the key.'

'Here,' Neville threw him the bunch. 'Good luck to you. And if you do open it, half of whatever you find is mine, okay?'

Neville left Claude to his mission and stooped over cages once more. Small shapes scuttled away from the torchlight.

He spotted a likely looking, multi-limbed, blue-tinged rat sitting in a corner.

'Okay, my little malformed friend, you are about to become a celebrity.'

He lowered his hand towards the creature, at which point the door flung open again. Both Neville and the rat jumped as four figures piled into the little room, slamming the door behind them. Claude screamed. Neville flattened himself against the wall and dazzled the newcomers with his torch.

'Fliss!'

'For heaven's sake, Neville, point that thing somewhere else,' she told him, squinting into the light.

'What happened to you?' he asked. 'And who the hell are this lot?'

'Rhian and Sam and Daniel, there isn't time to explain. What's he doing here?' she pointed to the crumpled chef by the cupboard.

Neville looked at him. 'Nothing useful,' he said and stared at Fliss's companions, two of whom were still wearing ski masks. The man looked red-eyed and weepy. He noticed the two girls were holding bulging pillowcases. 'What's in there?' he asked suspiciously as the bulges wriggled a little.

'We are liberating these chickens,' Rhian explained.

'Right,' Neville nodded. 'I bet they're really enjoying their newfound freedom.'

'These birds,' said the smaller girl in a muffled voice, 'are symbolic. They will go out and speak for the others.'

'Oh good, talking birds now. Just what the world needs.'

'So, Nev,' Daniel stepped forwards, putting his arm around Fliss's shoulders. 'How's your master plan going?'

Neville straightened up a little in front of the younger man, irritated by his proprietorial manner with Fliss.

'It would go better if half the world didn't keep butting in,' he said. 'Now for pity's sake everyone sit down and keep quiet. Believe it or not, there are still some people left out there who we do not want in here.'

There was a deal of shuffling about and bad-tempered muttering as everyone fought for a space. Neville made a third attempt at nabbing a rodent, and had actually got his hand on the thing when Claude let out another scream.

'Sod it! What now?' cried Neville, watching his prey scamper into a loo roll.

'There! *Mon dieu!* A phantom!' gasped Claude, pointing a trembling finger out of the window.

The others, Neville included, rushed to look. What they saw was undeniably terrifying. The old barn was on fire, flames feeding on the dry straw and leaping thirty feet into the air. Running from the building, negligee floating up to leave every detail of her body exposed to all who dared look, Cynthia tore across the field, arms held high. Backlit as she was so dramatically by the inferno, her diaphanous garment blurring her silhouette, she did indeed resemble some ghostly apparition.

'Cynthia!' Fliss was the first to find her voice. 'What on earth is she doing here?'

'Blimey,' Daniel laughed. 'You have a pretty weird breed of arsonist down here in Hicksville.'

'I think,' said Neville. 'You'll find the real culprit is behind her.' He nodded in the direction of a gloomy shape lumbering after the shrieking woman. 'I can't imagine candles, straw, and Hamlet would be a very safe mix.'

Fliss picked up the phone.

'What are you doing?' Daniel asked.

'Calling the fire brigade, what do you think?'

'Whoa, hold on, Babe,' he took the receiver from her. 'Firemen mean cops, and I'm not about to get a criminal record here.'

Neville took the phone from him and handed it back to Fliss.

'Fliss is right,' he said. 'That fire is already out of control. It could easily spread to the sheds.'

'Look,' said Daniel, snatching back the receiver. 'I get done for something like breaking and entering and I lose my job, it's as simple as that, company policy. I'm not gonna get sacked for the sake of a few scrawny hens.'

'Oh?' Fliss glared at him. 'I thought you were doing this for my sake?'

'I didn't know something this heavy was going to go on.'

'You should have thought about that,' she snapped, 'before you decided to encourage two teenagers to do something illegal!'

'Your precious daughter doesn't need any kind of encouragement!'

Neville took the phone again.

'Do you think you two could have your domestic argument some other time? Preferably after we have called the emergency services and before we are all roasted alive in here.'

'*Alors!*' wailed Claude, sinking to the floor. 'Then this is how the life of this miserable chef will end. How pertinent – to be baked *comme une pomme du terre!*'

'If someone doesn't shut him up soon,' said Neville, 'he won't live long enough to be cooked. Now, Fliss, make that call. Daniel, you're as big a waste of space as Claude is. If you no longer wish to be involved, I suggest you act as your instinct dictates and run away. You won't be missed. I am going to catch that sodding rat before something else happens.'

Daniel hesitated. Fliss looked at him hard, then shook her head and started dialling. Muttering curses, Daniel fled.

'Lightweight bastard!' Rhian called after him.

Neville tapped the side of the cage gently.

'Come along, now, time to go, Ratty.'

Fliss finished her call. As she hung up the sound of an approaching siren filled the room.

'Blimey,' she said. 'That was quick.'

Rhian and Sam moved to the front window.

'It's not a fire engine,' said Rhian. 'It's an ambulance, and there are two big men running away from the house. Where did they come from?'

'Don't let them find me!' begged Claude.

Neville left the cage and peered out of the window. 'Ah yes, looks like your friends, Claude. They seem to have taken fright at the siren. But who called an ambulance, I wonder?'

Fliss pointed to the side of the house. 'There's Ryan again. Look, the paramedics are after him. They've got someone with them.'

'Dr Richards,' said Neville. 'Is it me, or has the world gone stark staring mad on a Sunday evening?'

As they watched, a number of small, feathery shapes made their way onto the scene.

'The chickens!' cried Rhian. 'Someone didn't shut the shed door properly. I bet it was Daniel, the creep.'

'The fire must have woken them up,' said Fliss. 'Oh my God, they're everywhere.'

Just as it seemed impossible for things to become any more chaotic, there was a dazzling flash, which illuminated the night sky and, for a fraction of a second, floodlit the entire farm. This was instantly followed by an eardrum bursting bang, accompanied by yet more flames.

Everyone in the room instinctively flattened themselves on the floor, hands over their heads. As the noise subsided, Neville climbed cautiously to his feet and peered out the window. What had once been a smart, sleek, shiny Subaru Impreza was now a tangle of metal and smouldering rubber, billowing black smoke.

Fliss stood beside Neville. 'Good grief,' she said, 'they've blown up Ryan's car.'

'What for?' asked Rhian.

'Presumably,' said Neville, 'because they thought it belonged to Claude.'

Somewhere behind them the Frenchman began to weep.

Neville ignored him, and watched as Ryan screamed and shook his fists at the heavens, standing over the remains of his car. The paramedics and the doctor took hold of him and frogmarched him to the ambulance. He swore an increasingly obscene stream of curses and abuse until the doors of the vehicle shut behind him and he was taken away. The ambulance had to pause in the gateway to let in two enormous fire tenders.

By now chickens were running and flying in every direction. A handful of unfortunate ones had been caught in the blast, and now their feathers rained silently down on the farmyard.

Neville gave up his vigil at the window, strode purposefully to the cage, picked up the now familiar rat and carried it back to Fliss. He opened her backpack and snuggled the rodent down inside before buckling it up securely.

Fliss smiled up at him, and put her hand on his.

'You know, Neville, I am seriously impressed by the scale of this plan of yours,' she said.

Neville smiled back and gave her hand a brief squeeze.

'Team work,' he told her. 'Oh look, new arrivals.' He pointed towards the road.

A large, expensive car had arrived. It stopped in the gateway and two stunned figures climbed slowly out to stand and stare at the carnage and madness in front of them. Mr and Mrs Michael Christian had come home.

Nearly two weeks after the events at Withy Hill, Fliss stood outside the front door of the Old Vicarage, bracing herself for a greeting from Hamlet. As she waited she looked at Cynthia's free-range garden. It had subtly altered since her last visit. What had been blossoming abundance seemed now to have spilled over into chaotic wilderness. The relentless heat and ferocious thunder storms had first frazzled and then smashed the flowers. The weight of water had dragged down boughs and flattened shrubs, so that everything looked beyond the point of recovery. It was as if the glorious garden party of early summer had collapsed into an August hangover.

At last Fliss heard footsteps and Hamlet's rasping bark. She prepared herself for his welcome. What she was not prepared for, however, was the sight of Eric and Vinnie standing shoulder to muscly shoulder in Cynthia's hall.

'Come in, Fliss, do come in,' Cynthia beckoned. 'Don't mind them. Move over, boys, make a little room for our visitor.'

'But, what are they doing here?' Fliss nervously edged past the dogs, not taking her eyes of them for a minute. Hamlet slurped at her hand, clearly delighted to see her again.

'When the Christians moved back to London they didn't need guard dogs any more, so I took them in, poor things.' Cynthia fondled their ears as she spoke. 'They're pussy cats really. All they needed was a little love, wasn't it my darlings, yes it was,' she cooed.

Fliss watched in amazement as the dogs wagged their tails wildly and gazed up at their new mistress with open adoration.

'So good of you to come,' Cynthia pushed the animals to one side and ushered Fliss towards the kitchen. 'I hope you didn't mind my writing, but I felt I must talk to you. Here we are, please, make yourself comfortable. I've made a pot of Earl Grey.'

Fliss sat on the only empty chair as Cynthia tossed a pile of newspapers onto the floor to make space for herself.

'You're looking very well, Cynthia,' said Fliss, and meant it. She had been half expecting to find the woman a wreck, having been heartbroken, rejected, humiliated, and very nearly burned alive. Instead Cynthia seemed positively chipper.

'My dear, I feel wonderful. And it's all thanks to you. You and poor darling Neville, of course. Shortbread?'

Fliss shook her head. 'Me? I don't see ...'

'I have had an epiphany, Fliss. A moment of revelation and clarity that has changed my life forever. Sugar?'

Fliss shook her head again, and took the cup Cynthia handed her.

Cynthia sat back in her chair, which made a worrying crack, and fixed Fliss with an intense stare.

'I have looked death in the face,' she told her. 'I have glimpsed my own end. One cannot go through such an experience and come out unchanged.'

'No, I suppose not.' Fliss shifted her foot as Hamlet tried to sit on it. Eric and Vinnie lay on either side of Cynthia's chair, still as sphinxes.

'Even as I fled the flames I knew my life would never be the same again.' She cast her eyes down for a moment, stirring her tea. 'Sometimes it takes something momentous to shake a person out of a ... a certain state.' She glanced up at Fliss, then back down to her tea, and took a noisy sip. 'I realise now that I was in the grip of an obsession. *Un amour faux.* Heaven knows how long I would have gone on making a complete fool of myself had not the Grim Reaper himself brought me to my senses. And Neville,' she closed her eyes briefly, 'the innocent object of my fixation, what must he have thought of me?'

'Oh, I'm sure he understood,' said Fliss.

'Yes, I believe he did. It is a measure of the man that he suffered my unwanted attentions for so long. And that now he has forgiven me.' She leant forward, grasping Fliss's hand. 'I have written to him, explaining how I was not myself, how depression, borne of delayed grief for my late husband, had affected my judgement, and indeed my perception of the world.' She paused for a moment, turning her gaze to a photograph on the mantelpiece above the Aga. The handsome, ruddy face of Edmund Danby could just be made out through the dust.

Fliss drank her tea, shifting slightly in her seat as Hamlet sought to scratch his back on the arm of her chair.

'Well, of course, I'm glad you're feeling better,' Fliss said. 'But I don't see why you're thanking me.'

'You were an example to me. You showed me what can, indeed what must be done. It is not enough to think, or to talk, one must act.'

Fliss shook her head. 'No, sorry Cynthia, I still don't understand.'

Cynthia leant forwards once more. 'When I had recovered from the shock of the fire, and when I regained my senses, I thought about what you were doing up at Withy Hill. Of why you were there. Of what you were prepared to risk in the name of what is right and honest and decent. You took action, my dear, without regard to your own safety. You have set the bench mark by which we must all be measured.'

'I have?'

'I saw then how small and selfish my life had become. Oh I busied myself with things for the village – little, unimportant, unnecessary things.'

'Oh, surely not.'

'It's true. I can see it now. Most of the causes in which I involved myself in the name of Nettlecombe Hatchet were nothing more than distractions to fill my empty life, and for my own self-aggrandisement. But you, you were doing something worthwhile, something that mattered.'

'I wasn't on my own, you know. It was really down to Neville.'

'Please,' Cynthia held up a hand. 'There is no need for false modesty. Of course dear Neville was an enormous support to you. But I see a woman's hand here, a strong, courageous woman.'

'I really think you're making too much of my part in all this,' said Fliss.

'Enough. Not another word. I will not hear you belittle your achievements. Look what you brought about. That appalling place, those dreadful experiments, exposed! And the whole enterprise closed down.' Cynthia sat back in her chair with a sigh. 'So, you see, it is your example which has spurred me on, which has helped me to see that I too can make a difference.'

'Good for you, Cynthia. What are you going to do?'

'It came to me in the woods on that terrible night. There I stood, shivering in my negligee, watching the inferno that had so nearly claimed my life. Then that fearful explosion, and those poor, poor chickens – I was in a state of shock, of course, completely bewildered and unable to move. At that moment I felt a warmth against my tiny frozen hand,' Cynthia's eyes brimmed with tears. 'It was Hamlet,' she said in a small voice. 'My dear, faithful hound, standing by me in my darkest hour.'

Fliss opened her mouth to point out that it was Hamlet who had started the fire, but decided against it. Hamlet wheezed and shook his head in a very un-heroic fashion, his loose jowls sending out a heavy shower of drool.

'I wanted you to be the first to hear my plans,' Cynthia went on. 'I have decided to put all my energies into animal welfare. More specifically, into the welfare of farm animals, who are often so cruelly abused, and whose suffering goes unheard. Not any more! In me they have found their champion.' She beamed at Fliss. 'Tell me your thoughts.'

'Well, I'm really impressed, Cynthia. You've been through so much, and you've come out of it all fighting. I'm sure you'll make a fantastic campaigner.'

Fliss was amazed to see a little pinkness glowing beneath Cynthia's generous layer of powder. It had never occurred to her that such a woman was capable of blushing.

'I'm so glad you think so. Your approval matters a great deal to me. If you agree, I shall run any plans for action past you in the initial stages.'

'Actually,' said Fliss. 'I think there's someone you ought to meet. Have you got a piece of paper?' She wrote down Sam's name and telephone number. 'I think you'll find this young lady a very good ally. And you won't be able to stop my daughter being involved.'

'Oh, really? Marvellous! And I'm going to take in farm dogs, too. The ones too old to work who need a loving home for their sunset years. Silly for just little me to live in this great big house. Why don't you stay for supper, then we can talk some more?'

Fliss drained her cup and shook her head.

'That's a kind offer, Cynthia, but I'm afraid I can't. I'm busy tonight.' She allowed herself a small smile. 'I've got a date.'

By 7:30 that evening Neville was in a dither. He stared at the shirts hanging in his wardrobe, waiting for the right one to present itself. None did. There were shirts suitable for work, and shirts suitable for dinner in smart restaurants, and shirts suitable for being at home and doing nothing in particular. Apart from cycling (which was in another cupboard altogether), Neville didn't do anything else. Now, however, the need had arisen for shirt suitable for seduction, and his collection had been found wanting. The sound of his front door buzzer forced him to make a choice. He shrugged on something pale blue and harmless and hurried downstairs, buttoning as he went.

'Hi,' he said as he opened the door, doing his best to sound relaxed.

'Hi, Neville, sorry to be so punctual. I've never managed to be fashionably late for anything,' Fliss told him.

'An affliction we share. Please, come in. Ah, what have we here?'

'Well, I hope it's a bottle of delicious, sophisticated, and very drinkable white wine. But as I chose it for the colourful label, it could be anything. I no longer have a visiting wine expert. It says "dry", so I'm expecting something between vinegar and battery acid.'

'Mmmm, can't wait,' he waved her up the stairs. 'Mine's the penthouse apartment,' he told her.

'Very rare in Nettlecombe Hatchet, I should imagine. Oh, hello, I didn't know you had a cat.'

'That's Cilla. If you're very lucky she won't sing. I'll just put this in some ice.' Neville busied himself with the wine, stealing surreptitious glances at Fliss when he could. She looked particularly lovely. She was wearing her hair loose, and it gleamed as the early evening sun fell on it. Her dress was cotton and flowing in subtle shades of peach and cream. It fell loosely about her fine, lithe body, touching a curve here and a hollow there. She smelled divine – a mixture of patchouli and bergamot – and on her slender bare arms were dozens of thin silver bracelets.

Fliss turned and smiled at Neville. He realised he was staring at her. Embarrassed he rattled the bottle in the ice bucket.

'So,' he asked, 'liberated any more beleaguered creatures recently?'

'Oh, not in the last few days. You?'

Neville shook his head.

'Far too busy studying Situations Vacant in the *Barnchester Echo*.'

'I can't believe you lost your job over what we did at Withy Hill. It really doesn't seem fair.'

'I managed to jump before I was pushed. Decided "career change" looks so much better on one's CV than "Kicked out for exposing his boss as bribable". Actually, I was glad of the excuse to leave. I fear my soul was beginning to rot.'

'What will you do now?'

'Who knows? For the moment I'm enjoying being unemployed. Feels quite decadent, though I suppose it won't be once my savings run out.'

'I must say,' Fliss looked around the kitchen. 'I expected this place to be all creative mess and activity. Your cooking has been hyped up so much, I was looking forward to a real performance, but there's not a saucepan bubbling, nothing sizzling, not a sniff of supper. Have you sent out for takeaway?'

'Ah, well, we're not actually eating in here. All will be revealed.' Neville made an elaborate bow and opened the door to the sitting room. 'Would Madam like to walk this way?'

Fliss stepped past him.

'Wow! Neville, this is beautiful!'

Neville had been busy. The little room had been transformed into a flower filled English country garden. The furniture had been pushed back and was all but hidden behind armfuls of greenery. Bowls of roses, vases of honeysuckle and lilies, baskets of meandering nasturtiums, and pails of delphiniums crowded together in a random display. Trailing ivy dangled from pictures and lamp shades. Clematis festooned the open windows, through which soft sunshine fell, illuminating the picnic rug in the centre of the room.

'I don't have a garden,' Neville explained, his voice unusually halting. 'But I thought you might like this.'

He stood awkwardly in the doorway, waiting for her response.

'I love it. It's fantastic. Where did you get all these fabulous flowers?' she asked wandering from one bloom to the next.

'Oh, hospitals, graveyards ...'

She smiled at him. 'You went to so much trouble, for me?'

'Of course I was banking on you not being a hay fever sufferer. Could have been disastrous, there must be a lethal pollen count in here right now.'

'It smells heavenly.'

'I turned the heating on. I know it's the middle of summer and our mothers would be sucking air through their teeth in horror, but I thought it would make it feel more like a summer's day in here. And the flowers would smell better.'

'Nothing to do with encouraging me to take some clothes off then?'

'Thought never entered my head.'

They stood in silence for a moment. When Neville could hold Fliss's gaze no longer he hurried over to the CD player.

'Now, sit yourself down on that rug before everything wilts. Sublime music you were promised, and sublime music you shall have.'

'This was definitely one of my better deals,' said Fliss, arranging herself comfortably on the floor. 'Even if we were nearly eaten by dogs, burned alive, blown up, and arrested.'

'I thought you enjoyed all that.'

'I'm enjoying this more. Ooh, asparagus, and champagne!'

'We can still drink your wine if you like.'

'No chance. This looks much more interesting.'

There was a short pause and a buzz as Neville set the CD going. Fliss looked at Neville and raised her eyebrows. He grinned back. A few seconds more of anticipation, and then the unmistakeable opening notes of *The Birdies Song*.

Fliss sat visibly shocked. Neville closed his eyes in apparent rapture, and then opened them again, laughing as he switched the dreadful noise off.

'Sorry,' he said, 'couldn't resist.'

'As I'm hoping that didn't come out of your own collection I suppose you must have had to hunt it down.'

'I didn't have to look far, as a matter of fact.'

'Sandra?'

'Sandra.'

Neville made a second selection and adjusted the volume. The mellow, melodious sound of Otis Reading's *Sitting on the Dock of a Bay* lilted around the room.

'Well?' asked Neville.

Fliss nodded. 'Completely sublime.'

Neville lowered himself onto the picnic rug, knees cracking like rifle shots.

'Good grief, Neville, you'll have to let me try and do something about those legs of yours.'

'What had you in mind?' he asked, expertly uncorking the champagne.

'A Crystal Healing session of course.'

'Ah yes, that should be ... interesting.'

Fliss laughed. 'Somehow I don't see you as a devotee of alternative medicine.'

'I'm ready to be convinced. Do your worst – after we've eaten.' He handed her a linen napkin. 'Dig in.'

They dined on tender young asparagus, dripping with melted butter, mopped up by bread Neville had baked earlier in the day. Neville found himself unable to take his eyes of Fliss, even as butter dribbled down her chin. He admired her ability to seem so at ease, so natural, so herself. As time went by and champagne went down he began to lose some of his initial awkwardness. After they had washed their fingers in water with lemon slices, Neville uncovered an enormous bowl of strawberries.

'Oh,' said Fliss, 'those look particularly good.'

'Everything in this room is local and organic, I assure you. Now, the secret of the truly blissful strawberry lies in how you eat it,' he said, and produced a large, wooden pepper mill.

'Pepper?' Fliss looked dubious.

'I'll show you.' Neville ground half a dozen twists of pepper over the strawberries, then picked up a prime specimen. He dipped it in the dish of lightly whipped cream, then topped it off with a tiny mint leaf.

'Close your eyes,' he told Fliss. He leant forward and popped the berry into her open mouth.

She ate slowly, wearing a slight frown. Gradually a smile of delight lit up her face.

'That,' she said, opening her eyes to find Neville's face very close to her own, 'is the most exquisite thing I have ever tasted.'

Neville smiled and gently dabbed away a speck of cream from the corner of her mouth.

'And you,' he said, 'are the most exquisite woman I have ever met.'

Then he leaned forward and kissed her, and Otis sang, and the birds outside the window sang, and somewhere in it all Neville's own, happy heart sang, too.

Rose sat on the wooden bench on the village green, the bright summer sun warming her bare shoulders, and watched Baby as he toddled about on strong little legs. He had grown so quickly; it was hard to see the infant in him any more. He had learnt to walk on his first birthday, and was now quite steady on his busy feet. Rose glanced down at the envelope in her hands. She still wrote to Ryan every month, just to keep him informed of his son's progress. He never wrote back, of course, but then he never had liked writing letters. She ran a finger idly over the address – *Woodleigh Nursing Home, Toller Porcorem, Dorset.* The last time she had visited him had been nearly four months ago now. He had seemed settled, but the nurses didn't think further visits a good idea. Better not to confuse him.

'Duck! Duck, Mummy!' shouted Baby, pointing at the birds waddling by.

'Yes, sweetheart, duck. Clever boy!'

A Range Rover drove past carefully and beeped its horn. Rose waved back at the friendly new family who had moved into Withy Hill Farm. Ryan would have been so annoyed about missing the chance to handle the sale. Just as well he didn't know about it.

Rose looked over at the Post Office and saw Miss Siddons locking the door behind her last customer of the day. She had recovered well from the shingles, but didn't go out much, especially after her Jack Russell failed to wake up one morning.

A large figure came to stand by the bench, casting a cool shadow over Rose. She looked up and smiled.

Marco handed her one of the three ice creams he had bought.

'Strawberry for you, my lovely; and chocolate for the little one.' He bent down and helped Baby take hold of the cone. 'There you go, *bach*,' he said, sitting down beside Rose.

'Look,' she pointed to the short row of houses on the far side of the green. 'The new restaurant is opening tonight.'

As they watched, a small van bearing the same words as the sign over the restaurant, *The Leggy Rat*, drew up outside. Fliss climbed out and opened the back doors. Neville emerged from the restaurant, and together they carried in boxes of all shapes and sizes.

'Do they serve our sort of food, do you think?' asked Marco, licking vanilla ice cream off the back of his hand.

'I shouldn't think so; it's all vegetarian. Nice that it's organic, though. And it does look very pretty inside. They've done so much to it since your last visit. Me and Baby had a little peep through the window yesterday.'

'Well then, *cariad,* I shall take you there for a meal. In the daytime, is it? So Baby can come too.'

'Oh yes, he loves his vegetables.'

They sat for some time in the lowering sun, enjoying their ice creams, and watching the gentle business of the village going on around them. At last Rose decided it was time for Baby's bath, so they fed the last of their cornets to the ducks, and set off for Honeysuckle Cottage.

***

Acknowledgements

I'm grateful to George Green at Lancaster University for his invaluable feedback and support, as well as the input of my fellow students on the MA course. Thanks, also, to Jennie Tierney for applying her sharp eye to the manuscript. I feel so lucky to have been a part of the Hookline Novel Competition, and would like to thank the book group members for their comments and their votes! And to the Dorset villages that inspired this book, thank you.

About the Author

After publication of her non-fiction and short stories,
PJ Davy enrolled at Lancaster University and gained an MA
in Creative Writing in 2004. In 2007 she was shortlisted in
the Crème de la Crime search for new writers. Her first
comic novel, *Nutters*, was published in 2009, and shortlisted
for the Mind Book Award in 2010. She also writes historical
fantasies as Paula Brackston - her first novel, *Book of
Shadows*, was published in February 2009, her latest, *Lamp
Black, Wolf Grey* came out in March 2010.

Paula spent four years working part-time as a script reader
and was recently selected as one of the BBC's New Welsh
Writers. She runs creative writing classes and workshops,
and is a Visiting Lecturer for the University of Wales,
Newport.
She is currently working on her fifth novel, and a screenplay.

Paula was born in Dorset and has happy childhood memories
of the villages and landscape. A life-long connection with the
place is what inspired the setting for *Village Fate*. She now
lives in Wales, half way up a Brecon Beacon, with her
partner and their two children.

Other Hookline Books chosen for publication by book groups:

The China Bird by Bryony Doran

A young art student sees beauty in Edward's twisted spine, and begs him to sit for her. Dubious but flattered, Edward sheds his clothing and emerges from years of apathy. This tale of secrecy, love and eventual understanding explores our perceptions of beauty.

The Half-Slave by Trevor Bloom

The year is 476 AD – the Roman Empire is disintegrating and northern tribes are moving south. As rivalry among them grows, one young man is caught between the people who raised him and the leader who offers him freedom – at a price! He must summon all his resources and his courage to discover where his loyalties lie.

A Young Woman's Guide to Carrying On by Jilly Wosskow

After a row with her mother, Kathryn collects her belongings and slams the door for the final time. It's 1974 and the beginning of a new life – but how much can Kathryn really leave behind?
She takes a live-in job as a waitress at a country house, working alongside the outrageous Dee-Dee. Both 17, and both with their own tragic past, they learn how to bag a bloke, get through testing times and even how to get on the property ladder.

Lightning Source UK Ltd.
Milton Keynes UK
13 December 2010
164313UK00001B/8/P